I've travelled the world twice over,
Met the famous: saints and sinners,
Poets and artists, kings and queens,
Old stars and hopeful beginners,
I've been where no-one's been before,
Learned secrets from writers and cooks
All with one library ticket
To the wonderful world of books.

# 10,000 DAYS

At a rough estimate, the world holds enough oil to fuel mankind for 10,000 days. Not surprisingly, with so much at stake the Western nations, strangled by rising OPEC prices, decide they must control some of that oil themselves. But already the Middle-Eastern countries have mined their oilfields against invasion, and it is necessary for the Western powers to treat carefully. So, in Washington and London plans are made for the invasion of Iran, and at the same time for certain diversionary incidents to draw the Russians off the scent.

# KENNETH ROYCE

# 10,000 DAYS

*Complete and Unabridged*

# ULVERSCROFT
*Leicester*

First printed 1981

First Large Print Edition
published August 1984
by arrangement with
Hodder and Stoughton, London
and
McGraw Hill Book Company, New York

British Library CIP Data

Royce, Kenneth
 10,000 days—Large print ed.
 (Ulverscroft large print series:
  adventure suspense)
 I. Title
 823'.914[F]     PR6068.098

 ISBN 0-7089-1175-7

# FOR STELLA

Published by
F. A. Thorpe (Publishing) Ltd.
Anstey, Leicestershire
Printed and Bound in Great Britain by
T. J. Press (Padstow) Ltd., Padstow, Cornwall

# Acknowledgement

I should like to thank Dr. Don Greenaway for his help and advice on oil pipe lines.

KR

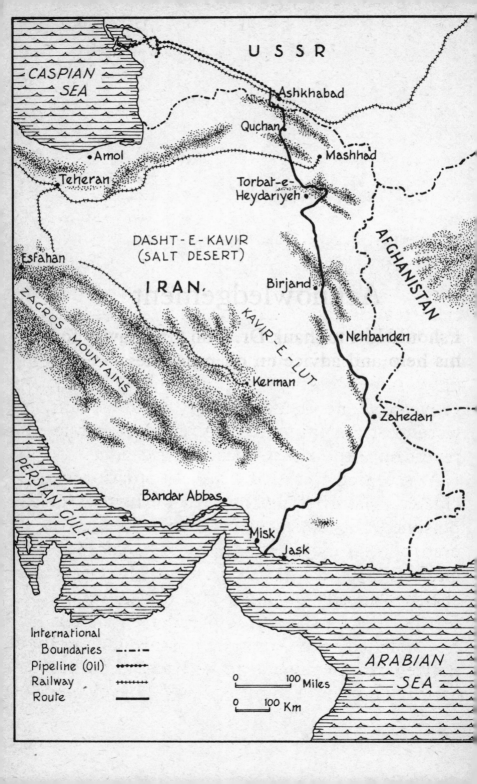

# Prologue

THE heat was blistering, the hot air shimmering over the sand. The flat horizon wavered like the edge of a calm sea caught by an early morning sun. It was difficult to know why the small group of Arab sheiks faced the emptiness instead of the ugly steel complex behind them. They viewed a scene unchanged for centuries, and were perhaps thinking that the land could revert once the last drop of oil had gone.

A scorpion scuttled from a small rock cluster. Disturbed by the sheiks it halted, its poisoned tail looped over its squat body, its crab pincers extended almost to a complete circle as they groped like antennas. One of the sheiks glanced down. He did not move his feet nor did he show concern. For a moment he watched the stationary scorpion and noticed the movement on its back; a mother carrying dozens of minute young. One by one

1

they should eventually drop off to go their own way. But it was not to be. The sheik drew a curved knife from a silver scabbard. The movement attracted his colleagues, and they watched with mild interest as he bent over the scorpion, the end of his kaffiyeh falling forward, to touch the insect's back almost delicately with the point of the knife. The tail stabbed down at the intruder who was worrying its young, and it impaled itself with its sting to die from its own poison. Conscience was satisfied; the arachnid had killed itself.

Dispassionately, the sheiks watched the insect's slow death throes. One of them, with care, placed his sandalled foot on the writhing scorpion and ground it into the sand. His act was motivated by a degree of compassion, for the young would not survive without the mother. The act symbolised what they had all been thinking. He said, "And so it will be when the first American soldier sets foot on Arab soil. The West will destroy itself, to die slowly and painfully of its folly."

As the group turned to face the untidy sea of oil derricks, Ibrahim Kawar concealed his thoughts very carefully. He was from Libya.

Security chiefs from other Arab states were also present to witness the completion of the mining of the wells, a precaution started some years before. It would be fatal for him if the others had the slightest inkling of what he was thinking. If the Americans landed, as had been rumoured following the latest crippling increase in oil prices, they would not find oil but a massive desert of fire.

Kawar allowed his gaze to linger on the emptiness behind the derricks, reflecting briefly on the leader of his own country, Colonel Rachid, and of the Colonel's best friend Nabih Haddad, shortly to go to London for specialist surgery. And he was deeply afraid. It was July 1984.

# 1

THE hospital was in Bloomsbury. The cost of staying there was prohibitive but the treatment was the best. The wealthy of the world came to it for neurology and neurosurgery. Among them, Arabs.

Britain's connections with the Middle East went back a long way: many wealthy Arabs had been educated in Britain. A bitterness had crept in, however. In certain quarters payments were long overdue, and lack of funds could hardly be an excuse. Representations had been made to the Libyan Embassy in London, for instance; but still a good many bills remained unpaid. Claims of overcharging were levelled yet the basic charges were known in advance, and in other countries would have been considerably higher.

The friction between Libya, in particular, and the British hospitals did not diminish the number of Libyan patients. The hospitals, by common consent and for economic need, decided to demand part-payment in advance.

5

Justifiable as this might be, the effect was to strain relations further.

It therefore came as a great surprise to hospital secretaries to receive a directive from the Health Minister that in future such patients should be received unconditionally. The sop was the promise that the Government would underwrite all unpaid bills for Arab private patients if, after nine months, they had not been met. The delay for settlement was a long one, but was at least guaranteed. Given the usual delays caused by bureaucracy this could mean a year before settlement: still better than having no payment at all.

These letters of instruction were sent to the secretaries by registered mail and marked MOST PRIVATE AND CONFIDENTIAL. There were two conditions attached to the promise. The press should not be informed in any circumstances and any leakage would be penalised by immediate annulment of the guarantee. The arrangement was to remain strictly between the Health Minister and the individual hospital secretaries.

As a result of this, the relatively few hospitals concerned removed their demand for partial pre-payment and the Libyans gleefully accepted this as a sign of weakness. Oil was the most powerful weapon of the day. Without it the world would not survive. It was true that Britain had her own, but that was an over-simplification. Her oil was light and she still needed heavy oil. Also, what happened to her friends affected her. At least that was how it was seen and that was how the Libyans, aided by an egomania derived from the strength of their position, were encouraged to see it.

The Bloomsbury hospital was called the Royal Cross, and the history of the Cross, decreed Royal by the third of the Georges, lay somewhere in its archives. Nabih Haddad was admitted as a private patient on 15th July. His bed had been booked some weeks ahead.

He was wheeled in on a trolley, put to bed, and was seen by Professor Murton two hours later. Previous medical reports had already been studied. It was certain that Nabih Haddad would need neurosurgery at the comparatively young age of forty-six. In Libya he was high up the tree of power and a fanatical Moslem. He was a close personal friend of Colonel Ali Rachid, the Libyan President, and had been since childhood.

Later that same day, Haddad had a visit

7

from Sir Maurice Higgs. The round-faced chief of external intelligence smiled benignly, introduced himself, and pulled up a chair. "I'm told the pain has been relieved or I wouldn't have worried you. You realise, of course, that in Professor Murton you have one of the finest specialists in the world. You could not be in better hands."

Dark eyes swivelled to Higgs. There was no humour in them, no expression at all, not even fear which could have been understood. "What do you want?" The English was clipped.

"To see that you have what you need. To protect you."

Resentment showed as the dark lashes flickered.

"I have all I need and all the protection I want."

"I'm aware of your personal bodyguard outside, Mr. Haddad. I know of the others who work shifts with him. But there are many entrances to this ward. Too many for one man to guard."

"I am not in danger. The bodyguard is standard practice, no more. Your own ministers have more need of them."

Higgs did not reply at once. He well understood what Haddad meant. Terrorist groups were befriended by Libya, many trained there. Haddad had nothing to fear from them; they were his protectors by the very nature of their worldwide reputation for violence.

"Nevertheless, it's my job to see that you come to no harm. You wouldn't want me to neglect my duties while you are here."

"Provided it does not amount to intrusion."

"So you don't think you're in danger."

The double-edged question got through to Haddad. He was lying flat, his head turned towards Higgs. Uncertainty at last tinged his expression. "Are you talking of the operation?"

"No, Mr. Haddad. I've already told you that you're in the best of hands. The Metropolitan Police have received a threat against you. Someone wants to kill you."

The lashes blinked. "A crank. Why would someone want to kill me?"

"Most such threats are from cranks. This one seems to know a very great deal about you, though. We are forced to take it seriously."

The dark lips curled. "No Arab would

want to kill me. We are the friends of all Arabs."

"Is that why you always carry a gun? Why should it be an Arab, Mr. Haddad? The Israelis don't forget you harbour their enemies. We think this is a 'white' threat. It's difficult to judge from a letter but that's the view of a very high ranking police officer who is extremely experienced in this sort of thing."

"A letter? You have it?"

Higgs pulled an envelope from his pocket. "Can you read comfortably?" He pulled the letter out and straightened it.

Long bony fingers reached up and took the letter but Haddad's gaze was still suspiciously on Higgs. He held the letter well away, the sinews on the back of his hands stretching the brown skin. The letter was typed, single spaced and quite long. Haddad read it slowly. At last his hand dropped to the bed, the letter still between his fingers.

"This information could have come from many sources: newspapers, magazines."

"Not in this country. That's a brief resumé of your domestic and political life. Cranks invariably respond spontaneously. Their motives are as varied as their threats. I must tell you that I have not personally come across a threat from a crank who has done so much homework about his subject."

Haddad raised the letter again and re-read it. He shook his head slowly as if his headache had returned. "Why should he want to kill me?"

"It may be personal or political. You would have more experience than I about political killing. The reason doesn't matter." Higgs reached for the letter, ignoring the burning anger in the glaring eyes as a result of his pointed remark. "I believe this should be taken seriously. I intend to provide you with extra bodyguards."

"I can arrange for more of our own people."

"Neither the police nor the hospital authority would permit it. There is already strong resentment that an armed foreigner stands outside the ward every day. We've turned enough blind eyes for you already, Mr. Haddad." Higgs's words were more aggressive than his manner of delivery; his tone was quite friendly.

"I must speak to our Ambassador. We will see whose bodyguards I will have."

"That is your prerogative, sir. The telephone is by your elbow and I'm sure you know the number. You agree, however, that guards are necessary?"

Haddad lay back staring at the ceiling. His gaze switched briefly to Higgs but, learning nothing there, he switched it back.

Higgs said smoothly, "I understand your dilemma; I really do. But one factor above all presses home the danger as no other does. It must have also occurred to you." He waved the letter. "This person—or persons—knew you were coming here, yet you only arrived today. How many people were told?"

Haddad thought it over. He realised that quite a few people knew. "It must be someone here in the hospital."

"Possibly." Higgs wouldn't bite. "If you're right we had better get some men up here quickly." His tone changed. "Mr. Haddad, I really do have your safety at heart. Our separate political convictions have nothing to do with it. Even if you won't accept that, on purely materialistic grounds, I don't want anything to happen to you while you're here. If it does then I, and others, will be in deep trouble. Politically it would do none of us any good. For that reason alone

you must trust me and accept my judgement.
I will protect you. Believe me."

Jennie Palmer took off the blond wig and
shook out her close-cropped auburn hair. She
put the wig on a papier-mâché dummy.
"Let's get married," she said.

Ray Wilson looked up from the armchair,
lowered the letter he had been reading.
"Eighty-seven," he replied with a grin. One
long leg was hooked over the chair arm.

Jennie raised a brow and started to empty
her bag of shopping. "Eighty-seven what?"

"Eighty-seven times you've asked me."

She showed no surprise. She examined a
packet of vegetable rice and said, "The price
is up again." She looked over at him, smiled.
"You've been counting?"

"Ever since I bought that calculator. I must
have missed a lot before that."

"You should be flattered."

"I am. But it won't make any difference.
I've told you: divorce left a nasty taste. I'm no
good at marriage."

"But I might be."

"There you go," he said easily.

They had lived together for over five years
and they no longer argued about marriage. It

was rarely mentioned these days but sometimes she would chide him when he least expected it.

Then she said, "What are you doing here anyway? You should be working."

He rose slowly, not using his hands, and he stretched. He stood just under six feet and looked fit, though his stomach was plumping just a little. His face was open, his eyes wide and humorous. He owned a small garage and took part in motor rallies when he could, Jennie sometimes going with him. He waved a letter at her. "Got an appointment. Some character wants to discuss hiring a fleet of cars."

"That's nice," she said, studying her shopping bill. "For someone to come to you with business."

"Very odd, love. We're small fry. We don't have a fleet of cars although we could get one with backing."

Her expression changed as she caught the inflection in his voice. Her heart beat increased. It was a very long time since she had felt like this and suddenly she wanted to be sick. She looked at him again but he was reading the letter once more. "Let me see it." She held out her hand and realised that she had involuntarily screwed up the shopping account.

He passed the letter over. Her hand was shaking as she read it and she steadied herself to read it a second time. It was quite innocuous and was from the Hadfield Combine, signed by a T. A. Richards. So why was she so fearful.

"You look as if you've seen a ghost," he said. "What's upset you? It's only a business letter."

"Is it?" She handed it back. "Then why do you think it odd?"

"I told you. But that doesn't make it sinister. It's not from Fairfax, and anyway, he's retired." Fairfax had been the codeword for Sir Stuart Halliman.

"Why should you mention that? Is that how your mind is working?" She slowly continued to unpack the shopping.

He crossed to put an arm around her shoulders. "No. But it's how yours is. It's written all over you. It's crazy after so long."

"Perhaps it's because it is so long. I've seen the restlessness in you." She glanced up. "You've been marvellous, Ray. I know there have been times when it hasn't been easy." And then casually, "I suppose you'll go."

15

"What else can I do? Business is business."

"I suppose so." She had recovered a little. She kissed him lightly on the cheek. "I'm sorry. Someone must have stepped over my grave. Be careful, though. Don't believe everything you're told."

He playfully slapped her behind. But he was as concerned as she. The letter *was* odd. It reminded him of the past and it had clearly struck the same cord with Jennie.

Ray Wilson searched the name board. Sixth floor. He moved to the elevator block. Good carpeting, aluminium and glass doors, uniformed attendants. Plush, he thought. It was second nature for him to record detail like this and by the time he reached the sixth floor he could still have recounted the colour scheme of the entrance hall and how many people had been waiting for the elevators. As he stepped out, he didn't ask the attendant the way; he preferred to find it himself.

The higher floors in office blocks invariably lost out in quality and decor; this one did not, it was quality all the way. Had it become seedy he might have left. He followed the gold-coloured arrows and the office numbers, found the engraved brass plate. He

16

rang the bell and heard the whirr of the electric release as the door unlocked.

He entered an empty, well-carpeted room with two desks, one of which had a covered typewriter. A wild-life calendar was pinned to one wall. He walked between the desks. The name on the inner door plate was T. A. Richards. This time he knocked.

"Who is it?"

Wilson was startled. The voice box was just above the door. He saw no microphone to talk back into.

"Wilson," he replied softly to test it.

The door released and he helped push it back. As he entered it closed automatically behind him as the first one had. Green, top-quality carpet. Rubbishy, modern desk, all sapele and chrome. The tubby character behind the desk should be in a bank manager's office refusing loans with the same soft smile and handshake he now offered. Wilson returned the handshake and penetrated the spectacles to see the grey eyes behind them; they watered slightly but they were steady, well camouflaged by the crinkles around them.

"Do sit down, Mr. Wilson."

There was only one choice near the desk.

Another chair was over by the wall next to a bank of filing cabinets. The top of the desk looked as if it had not been used. There was a blotting pad but no signs of pens or paper; no calendar, no filing trays. It's some sort of con, Wilson reflected as he sat; he'd met these mild-mannered, soft-voiced characters before.

"What do you think?" asked Higgs.

Wilson produced the letter. "It doesn't say too much, does it?"

Higgs smiled again, this time genuinely. "Not the letter, that's rubbish. Of what you see? You've been soaking me up like blotting paper."

Wilson grinned. "And you've been doing it like a sponge."

"You haven't answered me."

"I didn't think I was supposed to. Behind the jolly flab, I think you're a hard bastard. But, let's face it, I don't know you. So the letter's rubbish? I thought it might be."

"But you still came."

"You never know. What's your game, with your electrically operated doors?"

"It saves staff. Government cut-back."

"Aah!" Wilson was uneasy. Old memories stirred.

"Sir Stuart Halliman suggested I contact you."

"Why? Are you looking for a mug?"

It was too discerning. Higgs probed carefully. "That's not how he sees you. He has the very highest opinion of you."

"It didn't stop him taking me for a mug."

"A mug would be of use to me, Mr. Wilson."

"Have you taken his place, then?"

"I'm with a different department. We liaised a lot. I wondered if you'd be interested in doing a job for me."

Wilson crossed his legs easily. The relaxed attitude meant exactly the opposite. He felt as Jennie had felt at the apartment; she had always been more perceptive about the preludes. "You're Mr. Richards, then?"

Higgs felt himself on the defensive, recalled what he had learned of this man. It was difficult. "No. I'm Sir Maurice Higgs." Wilson would find out anyway.

"What sort of job?"

"Initially as bodyguard to an Arab."

It was so unexpected that Wilson burst into laughter. "I'm not a 'minder'. Cars but no muscle."

"Not *that* sort of bodyguard. You'd be armed."

"I've never used a shooter." Wilson rose. "You've got it all wrong, cocker. You've been misinformed."

"I don't think so. I've seen your army report."

"That was a long time ago and for a reason."

"This is for a reason."

Wilson moved towards the door with a shake of the head. "It's not my scene, guv. You've made a mistake."

"I can give you a reason that might change your mind."

Wilson reached the door. "I doubt it," he said good-naturedly.

"Fifty thousand reasons. Tax free."

"That's inflation for you." Wilson hesitated. "You've just scared the life out of me. That number of reasons don't come for looking after an Arab."

"That's part of it. Do you want to hear the rest?"

Curiosity wouldn't let Wilson walk away; he'd been trapped by it before. He thumbed at the door. "I suppose it's locked anyway?"

20

Higgs nodded. "Listening costs nothing. Have I your trust?"

Wilson returned slowly to the chair. "To keep my mouth shut?"

"Yes. That includes from Jennie Palmer."

Wilson shrugged. "She's no fool; she saw through the letter."

"No detail, not even the barest suggestion. You tell her what you like but no truth."

"I'll listen. That's all. Okay, you have my word."

Higgs held out his hand and Wilson took it. An old-fashioned bond, but Higgs knew that many of Wilson's values were old-fashioned.

Higgs said, "Before I explain I'd like to say this. I've done my homework on you. You'd expect me to. You're doing well but you're living up to it. Sir Stuart thinks the world of Jennie Palmer and always thought she was too good for you." There was a twinkle in Higgs's eye.

"She is. She's the only one who doesn't believe it."

"If you get run over tomorrow she's on her own. I believe you've made a will in her favour which is sensible, but what does it leave her? Your garage trades well but depends almost wholly on yourself. Wouldn't it be nice to have a real legacy for her? Something for life. Something you don't have to worry about?"

"Are you expecting me to curl up?"

Higgs smiled easily. "I'm prompting you about something that must frequently have entered your mind. She hasn't the protection of marriage, not even a widow's pension."

Wilson sighed. This bastard knew how to play on his weaknesses. "Let's hear it," he said. "But no guarantees." Yet he knew he wanted to listen. He always would. It had been too long.

Doug Shearer was suspicious from the start; there were many reasons. He had been deputy head of the Company's London office for several years during which time the head had been changed twice and there were rumours of yet another change. No rumours ever included plans for him. Second-in-command it seemed was to be as far as he would go. What made it worse was his wife's early acceptance that he had reached his limitations. She had always been full of ambition for both herself and him. When she believed that he could progress no further, she left him. That had been two years ago.

Shearer had arrived in London full of hope and with a good field record. London had been promotion, the beginning of the real climb up. Yet eight years later he was on the same rung.

He believed the root lay with his original London chief, Carlin. From the outset they had not got on. This was largely due to Carlin's feeling insecure in his job. He hadn't been ready for it and he had always seen Shearer as a threat. Shearer knew his job and did not take fools gladly. Carlin was a bad choice; seniority was no guarantee of the best man for the job. Snide reports went back to Langley about Shearer and the seed was sewn over a lot of ground.

When Carlin was eventually replaced his successor had read the reports on Shearer and others at the London station. Sutter had no hang-ups about Shearer breathing down his neck and soon found him to be highly efficient. He used that efficiency to lean upon and it wasn't until Shearer had gone on a prolonged and overdue vacation that he realised just how heavily he relied upon him. Reports back on Shearer were no longer snide but guardedly complimentary. Sutter didn't want any promotional posting for Shearer. If

Shearer went his ability might show through his absence. Shearer was too valuable as number two. Why rock the boat?

Joseph Marshall had carefully scanned the personnel reports from London. As Director of the Central Intelligence Agency, in collusion with his British counterpart Sir Maurice Higgs, head of D.I.6., he preferred not to use a home based operative. Which was why he had flown to London the previous day. By using someone far from home better scope for excuse was presented. That wasn't the sole reason, of course. Secrecy was easier to maintain away from one's own colleagues and headquarters.

The choice had not been easy. It was of no use picking someone because he would not be particularly missed although that was a big factor. The man had to be highly capable. Relative failures had to be weeded out. Shearer appeared to be one but Marshall was shrewd, adept at reading between the lines.

They met for dinner at the Connaught. Marshall had telephoned Shearer direct. That was unheard of. The Connaught is a venue of the wealthy. That the Company Director, a man of some very considerable power with the ear of the President readily available to him, should invite Shearer there alone was a matter for conjecture.

They shook hands and sat at the reserved table at the rear of the restaurant; not the best position except for observing, and for maximum privacy. Marshall ordered drinks and they'd seen the menu, so he came to the point. "I've been bringing myself up to date on a few things. You've been over here some time, Doug."

"Eight years." If Marshall had been bringing himself up to date he would already know that. Shearer's firm face was uncompromising, his mouth tight with a corner twist of the lips. He was well built, had kept himself fit. He'd had a hair cut that day which gave the grey-flecked head a severity that matched the non-committal eyes.

Marshall smiled. "You look as if you'd like to hit me, sitting there like that." He raised his glass. "Someone out of an old gangster movie. You forgotten how to smile?"

"Have you got something for me to smile about?"

Marshall was prepared for the insolence; Shearer was nobody's toady and had been a field man of considerable courage. He grinned. "Have I upset you in some way?"

Shearer relaxed. He held up a hand in peace. "I'm sorry. That was uncalled for."

"You feel you've been badly treated here?"

"I *have* been badly treated here."

"I've read the reports from way back. You think you've been used?"

"Not used on the one hand and over-used on the other. I guess that's a fair comment even if it comes out sour."

Marshall said carefully, "Not all appointments are the right ones. That's the way it goes. Carlin was out of depth and Sutter was talented but lazy. Reading between the lines it would seem that you did the clearing up for them. Why didn't you complain?"

"I did. It didn't get me anywhere. Maybe my timing was bad."

"I'll see if I can put it right."

"Here in London?"

"No. I'd have to do some adjusting to make it look right and that would be too complicated."

"That figures." Shearer had shown no surprise. Nothing had changed.

"You think I'd give you a sideways shift?"

"I'm wondering why you're dealing with me at all. I'm a long way from your throne."

Marshall smiled, leaned back as the waiter

26

brought his paté. "I won't insult your intelligence with bullshit. I need a man for a certain job. An extremely important one. My analysis of the U.K. staff points to you."

"Why."

"Why not? You've done it all in your time. If the last few years have been stagnation then let's put it right."

"Why you, sir? You don't deal with minions."

"I'm dealing with it because I should. What I say to you is to stay between you and me. The button might get pressed if it doesn't."

Shearer showed his first real interest. "You're not kidding?"

"I've never been so serious. How're the prawns?"

Shearer took his hands from the finger bowl, wiped his fingers on the napkin. "Is this a field job?"

"Not at first. Later."

"I'm too old for it."

Marshall looked up, toast halfway to his mouth. "Balls."

Shearer smiled involuntarily; it felt good. "I'm not used to that sort of language. What do I do?"

"Initially? Bodyguard to an Arab."

"Shit. I left that work behind when I left the secret service. Years ago."

"I know. But you've had the training for it. Don't be misled. There's a reason."

Shearer was silent. He cracked the shells and ate reflectively. He was clearly not happy.

"You won't be paid out of London any more. There'll be a direct credit to your London bank from the U.S." Marshall wiped his lips. "Double what you're getting now. I'd call that promotion, wouldn't you? Plus bonus."

Shearer pushed his plate an inch or two. He sat back looking at Marshall closely. "So it's dangerous?"

Marshall held his gaze. "Not at first. There is a part that could be but it's as important to me that you survive it as it will be to you. There's something beyond that stage. Doug, I can't afford for you not to come through."

"No suicide mission?"

"Absolutely not."

The waiter took their plates. When he'd gone Shearer asked, "Are you telling me or asking me?"

"I need your cooperation, not blind obedience. You decide. I can't tell you too much at this stage." This was the gamble, had he said too much or not enough?

"On my own?"

"There's a limey who'll operate with you. Sir Maurice Higgs has picked him out personally. I understand he'll take a short course for bodyguards. He's green in that area. It might be an idea if you went with him. It would be a refresher for you and you could give him a few personal tips."

"Do I know him?" Shearer didn't like the idea; he preferred to work alone.

"I doubt it. I don't know who it is myself yet but I trust Maurice Higgs." Marshall paused. "You'll have to resign from the service. No scandal. You have reason. No one will be surprised."

Shearer looked at Marshall searchingly. "To make sure nothing blows back on you?"

"Right." Marshall waited until the waiter had gone again. "Yes or no?" A straight question.

Higgs switched the lights on. He crossed to the heavy velvet drapes and pulled them across. "I must get a cord fixed to do that job

29

for me." He'd said the same thing for years. He returned to his chair and picked up his glass of whiskey. "Cheers."

"What is it you want to know, Sir Maurice?" The doctor was smiling slightly over his glass, his shrewd eyes on Higgs. The few times he had been to Higgs's house the conversation had invariably been unusual and stimulating, sometimes bizarre.

"I need some more of your advice. Between these four walls, you understand, Peter."

"I've taken the oath. I don't need reminding."

"With respect, this time you do. Believe me. These four walls and us."

The doctor shrugged. "Of course. Without your warning it would have been the same."

"I know. You wouldn't be here if I had doubts of that, but this is rather special." He smiled a benign apology. "To what extent can a person be influenced to do something against their nature?"

"Do what, for instance?"

"To murder someone one loves. I understand that under hypnosis the subject will not act out of character."

"That's an over-simplification. It needs explaining."

"Obviously it's chancy. I want a guarantee. These drugs the Russians use on their dissidents, for instance. How good are they? How effective?"

"You're now talking of a personality change."

"But could one of them be conditioned to kill someone?"

"Only the Russians can answer that. Let's get it straight; you want a programmed killing?"

"I asked if it could be done."

"I need notice of the question. I will have to raise it with a specialist in the field."

Higgs said icily, "Be damned careful how you do that."

The doctor nodded with a smile. "It's easier between two medics than between you and me. It's a highly specialized field."

"Could it be done surgically? An operation on the brain?"

The doctor froze. Lowering his drink he looked across the room but Higgs still appeared the same, chubby face bland, legs stretched. "You're not serious?"

"These four walls, Peter."

"Christ, I can't answer that."

"You must. Even a device in the head.

31

Something tiny but that can be used to make a man perform a specific task on a signal. Think along those lines as well as the other." Higgs paused. "I haven't gone mad nor become inhuman. I'm trying to prevent a global war. That should aid your conscience."

The doctor could only stare. He said carefully, "There is a drug. V.269. They started to use it late last year with startlingly quick results."

"Tell me about it."

"I can't believe you don't already know."

"Then remind me."

"Named after Professor Vonersky of the Serbsky Institute. Some of the reports were horrific but they've got it more under control. They buried their mistakes and the poor devils who survived them probably wished they had not. If they can think at all."

The Serbsky Institute needed no explaining to Higgs. Professor Serbsky had founded it but officially it was called the Central Scientific Research Institute for Legal Psychiatry. Run by the K.G.B., many of the doctors wore K.G.B. uniforms with the light blue epaulettes. Even Professor Lunts, who had preceded Vonersky as head, had been known to arrive at work in a K.G.B. uniform.

"Can we get some?"

"I've no doubt we have some. But I must check. And on its present standard of efficiency." The doctor finished his drink and rose but Higgs motioned him down.

"We'll need a man to administer."

"You won't get one for what you want."

"For what I'm prepared to offer I'll get one all right. If you're suggesting doctors are all saints, I refer you to the insurance companies. Come off it, Peter. Get off your dignity. Tax free." Higgs leaned back. "What's your opinion of Professor Murton?"

"As a surgeon or for what you want?"

"I know he's a brilliant surgeon."

"You must ask him yourself. He wouldn't do anything of this kind."

"How do you know? He's a strong government supporter. A patriot; he's waved the flag abroad for us often enough."

"This isn't flag-waving. And he's got all the money he needs."

"Few people can say that with certainty. I understand his wife is a great spender. In Canada at present. Lovely woman, though."

The doctor was looking at Higgs as if he'd just met a stranger. "Any approach to

Murton must come from you. I wouldn't get away with it."

"Of course. Do your best, and quickly, Peter. We have at most three weeks."

The doctor rose shakily. "Three weeks? Well, that should be no trouble at all, should it? An eternity." He walked to the door, a bewildered and troubled man. When he opened it Higgs called out, a last soft warning.

"These four walls, Peter."

# 2

THEY disliked each other on sight. The easy-going Wilson was put off by the tough, uncompromising attitude of Shearer. Although he wouldn't say so, Shearer knew of Wilson; the Cockney had made a fool of two of Shearer's men a few years ago. It was one of the things he considered Carlin had held against him during his reign.

They flew to Milan and from there were taken by car to north of Riva at the top of Lake Garda. Wilson, very much a Londoner, felt out of place and lonely beside the taciturn Shearer. After their initial, suspicious handshake, they spoke little during the whole journey.

What reduced their uneasy alliance to an acceptable level was the beautiful scenery of the southern Dolomites. The weather held and the mountain trees were a myriad of colours backed by the evergreen firs. The air was crisp and clear and had a slightly intoxicating effect on them. If they could not appreciate each other, here was magnificence they could lose themselves in.

The training school was bounded by close wire fencing and fitted with an alarm system. Large and numerous signs warned, KEEP OUT, PRIVATE, in Italian and English. It could be said to be over-caution, for the place was completely isolated in a fold of the lower hills. The last two miles were rough track and Shearer wondered how they coped in the snows.

The school was run by an Englishman named Hunter. An ex-intelligence man himself, almost all his pupils had been previously highly trained in specialist military or intelligence units. The company was private and supplied bodyguards to those who needed them. These days there were plenty of prominent figures under constant threat.

They trained hard. From the beginning it was clear that they were a few years older than the others on the course. It became equally clear that they were already expert, if a little rusty, at most items on the curriculum. The full course was much longer than the two weeks they had been allowed so Hunter drove them hard. From the six a.m. run round the goat tracks to the final evening shooting practice, they had little respite. They went to bed with aching muscles and no inclination to talk.

Hunter quickly noticed how they needled each other and used it to good effect. As the first rule of bodyguarding is to get between the assassin's bullet and the client, he made them fire in the direction of each other daily. Each of them in turn had to stand between two wooden man-sized targets which touched them on either side, while one of them fired at the targets. They willed each other to show fear and cut their shots fine. The only re-action either showed was to eject a stream of jibes at each other.

Both were at one time familiar with the use of explosives. Fuses had changed a little; so had technique, but it was easy for them to update. Wilson had field experience as a war-rant officer in the Commandos. But Shearer, too, had served in the field in a variety of ways.

They lost surplus weight, toned up, became sharper, and continued to try to score over each other. It was difficult to know why they resented each other so much. Perhaps both felt the course a waste of time. Perhaps they detected in each other a doubt as to why they were being used. Why them? There must be available men already trained to the limit; why bring back old boys? Experience was beginning to make them suspicious.

When they looked at each other, particularly during the early days of the course when the strain was most obvious, they each perceived doubt. It was almost like looking at their own reflections and not caring for the uneasy image that stared back.

Higgs had gone to immense trouble to ensure that his movements weren't noticed. He had used men and cars in teams to cut off his tail. They finally met at Professor Murton's terraced house off Harley Street. The appointment was late because the Professor's duties had kept him at the hospital. The surgeon was tired and hungry by the time he walked into his study where Higgs was already waiting.

"Sorry to keep you, Sir Maurice. Understaffed as usual. And my wife's away."

"Then I'll be brief as I can."

They hadn't met before and shook hands before facing each other across the fireplace. Higgs felt uncomfortable.

"Before I explain it's important you know

why I'm about to ask of you something you would normally abhor. Times are not normal. Without being overdramatic, the West could be in danger of economic collapse which would mean Russia stepping in to collect the pieces. This is all about oil and survival. Friends within the oil group have done their best for us, but they are losing ground rapidly. God knows it's already bad enough. We're sliding back. The pressures to share our own oil will be tremendous and eventually impossible to resist. And ours is a mere drop in the ocean compared with the rest."

Higgs watched Murton; the surgeon had fatigue lines round his eyes but he was listening.

"This is war, Professor. Not the usual form but far more effective than guns and bombs in the final analysis. Like any other war, casualties are inevitable. It's from a position of war that I want to talk to you. It's important that you accept that premise, because there are very few options open to us and they are all distasteful. One must all the time keep in mind the alternatives and their effect on hundreds of millions of people. What I'm about to ask you is a minute price compared with the rest. Please bear it in mind."

Higgs watched for reaction in Murton as he continued but he saw none. The Professor met his gaze squarely; it was Higgs who felt discomfort. Higgs explained carefully. When he'd finished he felt exhausted and sat back, waiting with some dread for a reply to his bizarre request. Somewhere it had gone wrong. He had checked Murton's political background, of course, and had found nothing to alarm him. Yet now he was uneasy.

At last Murton stirred. "You've been doing some homework."

"Naturally. You may have better ideas."

"Let's see if I've got it right. I'll use laymen terms so that there can be no excuse of misunderstanding. You offer two alternatives. One, while I operate on Mr. Haddad to remove a small tumour, I insert a minuscule electronic device into his cranium, which will respond to outside signals directing him to take certain actions. How would I do that, Sir Maurice, without the rest of the theatre team seeing?"

"They wouldn't know what it was. It's very small."

"I see." Murton's voice was very even, his tone controlled. "Otherwise, after the operation, by using new hypnotic drugs, we make him completely malleable with the added use of a sonic device placed under his pillow to transmit instructions as he lies there. You finish with a changed personality and a partial automaton who will respond on a code. By so doing I destroy not one man, my patient, but two. Have I got it right, Sir Maurice?"

Higgs was warned by the tone. "You see it like that. I see the millions you help."

"But not one of these millions is being asked to do what I am."

"Very many would without hesitation. Given your skills and opportunity there would be a queue to kill Colonel Rachid."

"Then find one among them, Sir Maurice. This is not for me. I'm being as polite as I can be. My natural inclination is to throw you out."

Higgs felt better now he knew the position. "I understand. Perhaps I'd feel the same. But I have to solve the problem. And whether you like it or not you're reliant on people like me to preserve our standards. I just thought you might want to help do the same. I believed you might care what will happen to the others. I was wrong. I'm sorry."

"I'm a surgeon, not a butcher. Some Nazis were hanged for less."

Higgs rose. "The analogy is unfitting. We're out to save whole nations not destroy them. You insist on seeing this with the tunnel vision of your own part. Haddad would destroy you without compunction simply for what you stand for, if he could. Once you had saved him, of course."

"Get out, Sir Maurice. I'm about to lose my temper."

"Would you sleep on it?"

"How can I sleep at all? Please leave."

"All right. You do realise that this is in confidence." Higgs could see the extent of the Professor's anger.

"I feel under no obligation to you, Sir Maurice. I am appalled. You've made a request; I've declined it. Good night."

"I must insist on your discretion. Too much is at stake."

"You can insist on nothing from me. I'm under no obligation to you."

"Do you feel an obligation to the rest of the nation, then? Please, don't utter a word of this to anyone, I beg you."

42

"I'm not likely to go shouting it around. I'm too ashamed. You've asked me to turn one patient into a cabbage and murder another." Murton gathered himself, fiddled with his cuffs. "I'd have been less appalled had you asked me to kill Rachid myself. Given the opportunity I might have obliged. But you're asking me to betray everything I stand for. I won't. That's not pompous, it's the way I feel. I must think what best to do. This sort of shameful thing should be stopped. In England of all places."

Higgs ignored the naïvety. Gently he asked, "You won't reconsider?"

"Get out of my house before I'm sick."

Higgs picked up his hat and moved slowly to the door. "Thank you for your time. I'm sorry you feel this way. Deeply sorry." He took a last look at Murton, who had turned sideways to him. He caught a glimpse of the uncompromising face in the mirror over the fireplace. He was about to make a last appeal but refrained. No one could doubt the genuine anger of the Professor. What would happen when that anger passed? He wouldn't change his mind, but how would he react? Higgs decided he could not take the risk.

"I'm sorry it finished like this," he said. "So very sorry. Goodbye."

Higgs let himself out and the Professor made no move to help him. There was a housekeeper somewhere but at this late hour, presumably in bed. Higgs closed the front door but pushed the catch before descending the steps to his car. He paused, took off his hat very deliberately and wiped his brow. He then entered the car and sat for some moments holding the wheel. Removing his hat he laid it on the seat beside him. He was strained and depleted. This was only the beginning, he reflected: the first of the betrayals. He made no attempt to justify it—quite simply it had to be done—but it filled him with a sadness and a sense of his own inadequacy not to find another solution. There was no other solution.

When Higgs had gone two men stirred in another car across the street. They had been watching Higgs's every move down the steps and into his car. They saw him remove his hat and wipe his brow. The signal was clear. They took out guns and attached silencers to them, putting the guns into topcoat pockets.

They said nothing but waited five patient minutes before climbing out.

Choosing their moment they crossed the street silently, mounted the steps to Professor Murton's house and waited under the portico behind the huge pillars. With a gloved hand one of them pushed lightly on the front door and it swung back an inch.

They went into the hall, closed the door behind them, leaving the catch down. As they moved across the hall, guns in hands, a woman came to the head of the stairs above them. At first they didn't see her. One man caught sight of her just in time. He swung his gun up and fired as she was about to scream.

The shot made little noise but the terrible thumps as the dressing-gowned figure crashed down the stairs could not be missed. Her grey head hit the bottom balustrade and rested on the first stair. Her body reached grotesquely up the stairs, her feet now bare. Somewhere her slippers had fallen off. She was dead before she had started to fall.

The noise brought the Professor rushing from his study and he was shot dead by a bullet from each man. He crashed onto his knees and slowly toppled sideways.

With professional callousness the two men

made certain that both victims were dead. Satisfied, they pocketed their guns, walked back to the front door and released the catch. Outside they used the shadow of the portico before crossing the road to their car. Inside they removed the silencers and returned the guns to their holsters.

"I wonder why he had to go?" asked the driver as he pulled away.

His colleague made no attempt to answer. He might not have heard.

# 3

THE murders were too late to reach the national dailies. Enquiries did not start until the Professor failed to turn up at the hospital. But the news did reach the early afternoon editions of the London "evening". With a copy under his arm Higgs visited Haddad at the hospital.

Higgs had to identify himself to the bodyguards before he could enter the ward. Haddad's head had been shaved preparatory to the operation scheduled for the next day. Higgs came straight to the point. "I have bad news for you. Professor Murton was murdered with his housekeeper some time last night."

Haddad was shaken. His concern was for himself. "What will happen now? Who will operate?"

"That's the least of your problems. I'm told there will be a replacement for Murton, every bit as good."

Relief touched the dark eyes. "Why would someone murder the Professor?"

"You can't see why? Because they can't get at you, Mr. Haddad. They see this as another way of killing you."

"But if someone else can operate . . . ?"

"These people are clearly professionals. We didn't expect an attack on the Professor. They might try to get at the next neuro-surgeon but he will be guarded night and day." Higgs produced another letter. "The police received it this morning. They've only just released it to me. You can handle it quite freely; they've lifted what they need from it."

When Haddad finished reading he was thoughtful and worried.

Higgs continued softly. "Whether you like it or not your friend Colonel Rachid has made a lot of enemies in the West. If they can't get at him they might shock him by getting at you. I think you should travel back under another name with two of my best men on a commercial airliner."

Haddad was reading the letter again.

Higgs went on. "Take as many of your own men as you want. I'll arrange the seats. And be sure to wear your gun. I want you to get back safely."

"Oh, yes. I am sure you do." It was said

sarcastically but Haddad was confused. He did not want Higgs's bodyguards but the callous killing of the Professor and his house-keeper, about which he now read from the newssheet Higgs handed to him, undermined his attitude. He did not want Higgs's men to go back with him; but he would decide after the operation.

As he read about the murders he was convinced, without admitting it to Higgs, that the extra bodyguards had probably saved his life. Murton had taken what was really meant for him.

Higgs followed up again patiently. "Until you get back to Tripoli your safety is my problem. You don't have to like it or agree with it. I cannot be dissuaded from doing what I consider to be right. I don't think I've been wrong so far."

Higgs left the newspaper with its bannered question of why a famous surgeon should be killed. It was important to leave the thought, but he collected the letter.

Haddad said, "Are you near to knowing who is doing this?"

"We haven't got anywhere with it so far. It could be a new group. I've no doubt they too are fighting for some ideal, although you may wonder how you are caught up in it. Scotland Yard's forensic department are working on detail from the letter but it's a long, tedious business. Meanwhile we act sensibly."

"I would like my gun returned to me now."

"Here? In this ward? The hospital authorities wouldn't allow it."

"It's *my* life at stake, not theirs."

"It could be theirs if you fired inadvertently. I can't agree, Mr. Haddad, but I will see that it's returned as soon as practicable."

Higgs ignored the malicious stare as he walked to the door. He had almost achieved his objective: Haddad now believed himself to be in real danger. He hesitated by the door, then came back into the room thoughtfully. "You must forgive this question, but I really am puzzled by the amount of accurate information the two letters have supplied. I believe you are, too. Please don't misunderstand me, but could it be possible that you've upset Colonel Rachid in some way?"

"What do you mean?" Haddad was rigid.

"I don't know what I mean. Could your personal bodyguard be passing on information, for instance?"

"That's preposterous. What of your own bodyguards? The hospital staff?"

"We've already checked the staff. Few are actually involved with you. Our bodyguards weren't assigned at the time of the first letter. They're not *my* men. They're from a private, non-political company. Many Arabs use their services both in this country and out."

Higgs moved towards the door again. "I've no grounds for saying what I did. But I'm puzzled. It simply occurred to me that the root of your problem might be nearer to your own shores than ours. Tell me, did you choose your personal bodyguards or were they assigned to you?"

"They're totally loyal and would give their lives for me. Your implication is unsavoury."

"Yes, of course. I'm groping, Mr. Haddad. I'm sure you're right. Good day." The seed was sown.

"Did you have to kill him?"

Higgs raised a brow at Marshall. "That's a strange question coming from you. What would you have done?"

"The same as you. You're right, it was a damn fool question. You got another guy lined up?"

"Yes. Cash incentive. I don't think he needs it, though. He has an almost pathological hatred of Rachid. He was in a plane that was held by Palestinians for several days in the baking desert some time ago. He's never forgotten it; the conditions were appalling. Libya sheltered the hijackers later. He's the complete opposite of poor Murton; politically fervent and highly biased. We're lucky."

"Is the operation dangerous?"

"I gather all the brain jobs have their problems but this is comparatively uncomplicated. The tumour is relatively small and it's benign. I'm left with the feeling that our new surgeon would relish finishing off Haddad while he has him but perhaps I go too far."

"So they'll keep him drugged while this machine pumps instructions into his head until he's programmed."

"An over-simplification but, yes, that's about it. Once they're satisfied the operation has been a success. The use of the drugs must be carefully monitored. To overdo them could be fatal. The Russians found that out."

"Won't the charge nurses, you call them sisters, won't they be suspicious?"

"The drugs will be injected by the surgeon himself."

"You make it sound easy, Maurice."

"Joe, I hope to God it *is* that easy. So much is at stake; so much can go wrong. The whole business is a crazy gamble. Just one slip. One word. It makes me shudder. Murton was too close a thing. He might even have telephoned someone during the few minutes after I left and . . ." He shook his head slowly. "It can happen. Something like that at any time. We'd be crucified. The world would explode."

"I know." Then, "We're in touch with the Saudis. It's simmering nicely there. It will have to be convincing."

"Every bit of it. Can it all pull together?"

Marshall spread his hands. "I'm not sleeping well either."

Ibrahim Kawar lowered his head to the ground in supplication, his hands outstretched, his knees for some reason sore on the prayer mat. A devout Moslem—and who could survive in the Libyan hierarchy if he was not?—he had been praying all his life and his knees had never ached before. At forty-

53

eight he couldn't claim it to be old age.

The minareted mosque was one of the smaller ones outside Tripoli and as on all Fridays, it was full. A sea of arched backs covered the mosaic floor from which marble pillars rose to form Arabian arches. The sun reflected from the sand on to the white marble just inside, casting long shadows over the backs of the faithful.

For once Kawar's mind was not on Allah, although he would certainly need his help. After prayer he moved with the rest towards the huge doors and slipped his feet into his shoes. Outside he blinked against the brilliant sunlight. He put on dark glasses and walked slowly as the crowd gradually dispersed.

Kawar was in European dress but wore a kaffiyeh, the end flapping on his shoulder. It wasn't clear until he neared his Cadillac that another man was with him. Boulrouk always seemed to walk a pace behind yet he wasn't one of Kawar's bodyguards, who were slightly spread out.

Ibrahim Kawar was Colonel Rachid's security chief. In such a small population his job wasn't too difficult but he kept his ear very close to the ground. There had always been rumours of plots against Rachid. It was not everyone who wanted a religious fanatic as a leader.

Kawar climbed into the air-conditioned car and Boulrouk joined him on the back seat. Neither spoke, although there was a partition between themselves and the driver. Another car pulled out behind them and fell back to the statutory distance.

They drove towards the low sprawl of Tripoli, mirage-like in the distant heat haze. For an oil-rich country, Libya appeared to have little to offer the visitor. These were the thoughts of a foreigner yet Kawar had entertained them a great deal over the past two years.

A strange tension developed between the two men. Kawar hoped it wouldn't reach the driver. The strain was not caused by enmity, for they were the oldest of friends. One could go further; each was the only man the other would trust. To share controversial confidences was risky business in present-day Libya.

The strain was caused by the enforced silence between them. It was unnatural that they should not speak. Both were aware of it—aware, too, that the driver might find it odd between two friends, yet somehow they were unable to break the lull. They became imprisoned by their own fears. When they attempted conversation it sounded so false that they lapsed again into silence.

Kawar instructed the driver to stop on the outer fringes of Tripoli. He climbed out with Boulrouk. To the driver he said, "Go back to my office. Leave the car in the garage. I won't need you again until this evening."

When the driver hesitated Kawar smiled, "Don't worry. The walk won't kill us. There is something we must see."

But it wasn't so simple. The security car pulled up behind them and dropped two men off to follow them on foot. Kawar found himself a captive of his own security system. To change it was to invite speculation. He could not dismiss the men but he could ensure they remained out of earshot.

They walked side by side, used to the perpetual day-time heat but less used to the exercise. Riches did not encourage the use of limbs. The security car drew ahead and dropped another man in front of them; he cleared the way, ensuring that they would be unmolested by the natives of these poorer parts.

"Are you sure you can trust him?"

Kawar knew that Boulrouk meant the driver. "I picked him myself. But what difference can it make? We are under the scrutiny of my own men."

"Any sudden change of pattern can be misrepresented."

Kawar smiled, feeling better now they had left the restriction of the car. "I don't have a pattern. In my job that would be disastrous. Never develop too many habits. Don't make yourself predictable. But I do understand what you mean. And you are right to be so careful. A wrong foot now . . ."

"Have you news?"

"They killed the surgeon who was to operate on Haddad."

Boulrouk covered his alarm quickly. "Why?'"

"I don't know. They have another surgeon."

"Will it work?"

"Who knows? It won't affect us if it doesn't, except that we will have to start all over again. Rachid is mad. Everyone knows it and pretends it's not so. We have been brought into disrepute. Once the oil has gone this country will be nothing again unless we re-establish bonds with the West. And get back on a friendly basis with Egypt. The change will have to be gradual."

"Why preach to the converted? Are you ready to step in?"

"Of course. With your help. You say you have the army and the air force. I hope you're right. I don't see how you can be so sure, bearing in mind how careful you must be in sounding out."

Boulrouk grimaced. "I'm not so blatant. Nobody but you and I know there's a plot. And if it doesn't work nobody will ever find out. As security chief you would surely be informed had word escaped in some way."

"Unless there's someone cleverer than I. As long as no one shares this knowledge but you and I we are reasonably safe. Our lives are in each others' hands."

They travelled first class back from Milan. Such little touches of extra comfort should have pleased them. It did not. Neither spoke to the other about it but each, in his separate way, was uneasy.

Both Wilson and Shearer knew something lay beyond the bodyguarding. Neither man was a fool, each had accepted it for his own reason.

Another cause for doubt was their inability or unwillingness to trust one another. They made a strange team, and somehow each developed the idea, probably arising from their moments of friction, that the other man was watching. Having separate bosses did not help, and different nationalities was no aid; nor were their respective backgrounds and motives. At least uneasiness with each other took their minds off, to some extent, what they might really be needed for.

They had been allocated adjoining seats and it would have been churlish of them to sit apart; yet proximity increased their discomfort. They conversed in short bursts because they felt they must, but neither was good at small talk and neither was a hypocrite, a fact they had yet to find out about each other.

Higgs had sent a chauffeur-driven car to meet them and they were driven directly from London Airport to a house in Surrey. Shearer knew of its existence but had never been there before. Wilson didn't know of it. They were well looked after but neither could miss the roaming armed guards in the grounds. Nor the dogs. By unspoken consent they walked outside before darkness fell. Both located the odd television scanner; neither remarked on it.

Higgs and Marshall arrived that evening and they all met in the top security room. Seeing these two men together, adding the fact that they had arrived specifically to see Wilson and himself, raised fears in Shearer. It had to be of absolutely top importance for this to happen. In his experience it was unique, and he had qualms.

Wilson did not know Marshall, but it was easy to guess his nationality from his accent and the obvious familiarity between him and Higgs was a pointer to position. Wilson, too, found this suspect. For the first time fifty thousand pounds appeared trivial.

Higgs poured drinks. Neither Wilson nor Shearer smoked and it was left to Higgs with his pipe and Marshall with his cigar to foul the air. Higgs eventually said, in his quiet way, "There's a patient called Haddad at the Royal Cross Hospital. We want you to fly back with him, when he's better."

"Where?"

"To Libya."

"But why? They've their own men."

"There have been threats against him. While he's on my patch I really can't afford anything to happen to him. He's a bloody nuisance, but I'd be happier seeing him all the way back. Have a couple of days sight-seeing; then come home."

Higgs noted the suspicion of the two men. He continued, "When you arrive in Tripoli, the moment you set foot on Libyan soil, I want you to deliver a message to Haddad." Higgs turned to Wilson. "As soon as he's off the plane ask him if he has any further instructions for you. Those precise words. He's an awkward man and I don't want any kind of misunderstanding."

"Have you any further instructions for us." Wilson felt foolish and suspicious.

Observing this Marshall said easily, "They call you 'Ray'? Well, look, Ray, and you too, Doug. We won't insult your intelligence. It must be obvious to you that the message is coded. Get it absolutely right. The poor guy's been operated on in the head. He's not going to be all that fit and it might be difficult for him to grasp any deviation from what's been agreed with him. He'll need a long spell of convalescence. Just make it easy for him. Okay? The moment he steps foot on Libyan soil. It could be the only chance you'll get."

"Have you any further instructions for us."

"Word perfect. Don't change a syllable."

"Let's have another drink," said Higgs mildly. "Tomorrow you start your duties. We've arranged rooms at a hotel near the hospital. Not palatial but handy. You'll fit in with the general bodyguard roster."

Higgs raised his glass. "Tedious, gentlemen. But believe us, extremely important. We wouldn't have selected you if it were not." It was not entirely flattery. He glanced owlishly at Wilson. "I'd like your word that you'll stay away from Jennie Palmer."

"Can't I telephone her?"

"You can do it from here. The calls are recorded."

"Thanks for the trust."

"Young ladies in love can be persistent. Cheers."

He lay on his back, head swathed in bandages. The brown skin had sallowed. As Wilson sat on the chair by the window he could see the eyes moving under the thin lids as if he were dreaming. The body was still and the effect was disquieting. Wilson didn't like the look of Haddad. How could he be flown to Tripoli like that?

They had arranged for one man to be inside

the ward and the other seated outside. The job was boring in the extreme.

It was now a week since Haddad had been operated on, and, so far as Wilson knew, he'd been unconscious for all that time. At half past ten a nurse came in with the surgeon, a tall, fair-haired, craggy man named Medlip. All hospital staff who in any way had contact with Haddad now wore identity cards with a photograph pinned to their clothes.

A screen was pulled between Wilson and the patient so Wilson looked out of the window. At one time he peered through a crack in the screen and saw Medlip make an injection into Haddad's arm and then raise an eyelid to shine a small torch into the pupil. The pulse was taken. The screen was pulled back and Medlip left with the nurse, who returned later with a trolley. A drip feed was already fixed to Haddad. She pulled the screen again.

"You don't want to watch me wash him, do you?" She smiled professionally at Wilson.

"No, love. You wouldn't normally have a screen in a private ward, would you?"

"No. But then we wouldn't normally have bodyguards in it either."

"Has he been unconscious all the time?"

"Partly. Partly comatose."

"Anything I can do? Give you a hand?"

"No, thank you."

"His pillows look as if they could do with patting up." He was chatting her up, filling in time.

She gave him an old-fashioned look. "You do your job, I'll do mine. He's had a very delicate head operation. We're not allowed to touch the pillows or touch his head. Only Mr. Medlip may do that."

"You surprise me. I thought you lot were trained to deal with these situations."

She did not bite. Very sweetly, she said, "Never be surprised by the orders of a consultant surgeon, for verily, he is God."

Wilson grinned, left her alone to do her chores and returned to the window. He looked down into the street and idly started to count the number of different coloured car roofs. Why had he got an uneasy feeling again? He had been used before to his detriment and he now had the same qualms.

He looked back towards the screen. It was a little while before the nurse left with her trolley, and she did so without glancing at him. I must be losing my touch, he thought.

But it was Haddad that really held his thoughts.

Stepping nearer to the bed he studied the Arab's position; flat on his back with the head turned sideways. Had it been placed like that or simply inclined that way of its own accord? Earlier Haddad had been facing the ceiling.

He looked towards the door the other side of which sat Shearer. Moving in front of the folded screen he stood beside the bed, still facing the door. Haddad's head turned away from him. He slipped his flat hand under the pillow and gradually eased it forward.

He moved his hand a fraction at a time, keeping an eye on the door and the position of Haddad's head. When he reached the point where he could feel the weight of the head he almost withdrew his hand. He stayed still for a few seconds, then groped very slowly. His fingers touched something and he stopped.

# 4

THERE was movement outside the door. Footsteps passed, but he kept his nerve and explored with his fingertips. A hard casing of some sort. Very shallow. He wouldn't go beyond the first edge. He did not think he could do it without disturbing the head and that he was reluctant to do. He withdrew his hand slowly, careful to avoid the drip as he moved away from the bed to return thoughtfully to his chair.

Later, as Wilson and Shearer crossed to their hotel in another square nearby, Wilson said, "There's something I want to tell you. If we can stop diving down each other's throats for a few minutes I think you should hear what I have to say."

"Okay. Tell me over lunch."

It was another half-hour before they met up at their corner table. After they'd ordered but before the first course arrived Wilson told Shearer what had happened in the ward.

Shearer's first reaction was to be appalled by what Wilson had done. He was about to remonstrate when he saw Wilson's face. The Cockney was holding both hands up as if in surrender as he said, "I didn't have to tell you. I'm sharing it. All right?"

Shearer lost steam, annoyed with himself that he'd been so ready to go for the other man. Was his edginess due to his own disquiet? *"But what made you do it?"*

"Last night when Medlip came in alone I peeped through the screen and saw him fiddle under the pillow."

"It could be part of the treatment."

"Under the bloody pillow?"

"Whatever it is must have a purpose."

"Right."

"What are you trying to say?"

"I'd like to get it out from under his head and have a look."

"You might kill him."

The waitress came and they kept silent.

"You seriously think this concerns us?" Shearer asked after she'd gone.

Wilson shrugged. "Maybe I'm an idiot. And maybe that's why I was asked to do this job."

"I've had odd jobs to do along the line. Some have seemed suspect. Yet looking back later they've made sense. Not always success-ful, but identifiable."

"I don't think you're as satisfied as you make out."

Shearer stopped chewing and lowered his fork. He stared at Wilson for a while and neither man dropped his gaze. "I'll level with you. I wasn't happy as things stood. I needed a change."

"Would you have taken this job other-wise?"

"Who can tell? I don't know. Maybe not."

"There's something about it that stinks."

Shearer was holding himself in. Suddenly he relaxed. "I agree."

They ate slowly without saying another word for some time. Eventually Shearer said, "There's damn all we can do about it."

"I'm not in quite the same position as you. I haven't the same blind obligations."

"You either do it or not."

"Do you get the feeling that at this stage it's better not to say no?"

Shearer did not reply. He glanced up quickly, then continued eating at half pace.

"Whichever one of us is on duty when the nurse or the surgeon comes in, he keeps an eye on what goes on behind the screen. Is that reasonable?" Wilson kept his voice low.

"If it can be done."

"It can be done."

"What of the other bodyguards? How do they fit in?"

"You're better trained to answer that. I don't think you're really asking."

"Okay. They are what they seem to be. They're not staying here. We're the only two to be plucked from the tree, as far as I can see."

Wilson sat back satisfied. *"So you have been thinking about it."*

The Libyan Ambassador called briefly during the afternoon. He did not sit down but glanced coldly at Shearer, who was now inside the room and who had drawn his gun as a reflex action on seeing a strange face. Once identity had been confirmed the Ambassador spent a minute or two simply looking down at his compatriot. There was nothing else he could do. When he'd gone Shearer sat down again.

Shearer had chatted to both the nurses on duty when periodically they entered the room and one of them brought him tea. In their company he lost his hostility and his face could ease into lazy humour. He was satisfied that if anything odd was happening they knew nothing about it.

It was just before he was due to be relieved at six in the evening that Medlip called. He was wearing a lounge suit and looked as if he were about to go home. His identity tag was on his lapel. After a cursory glance at Shearer he said, "D'you mind helping me with the screen?"

Shearer pulled it across. A helping hand was one thing, expectancy another. He felt irritated, and stood by the screen as Medlip went round it. He moved his chair to give the impression he was near it, then stepped forward to peer through the crack.

Medlip was leaning over Haddad with his back to him. It was difficult for Shearer to see properly. The surgeon had slightly moved the drip to get at Haddad.

Shearer saw Haddad's head rise slowly off the pillow as Medlip carefully lifted it. More clearly he saw a hand go under the pillow. There appeared to be something in it when it withdrew, but Medlip's back was obscuring almost all his movements. The hand returned under the pillow, withdrew and Haddad's head

70

was gently lowered. Medlip bent lower. Shearer saw the pale flash of a torch and assumed the surgeon was examining Haddad's eyes again. As Medlip straightened, Shearer moved back and was seated when Medlip appeared; he let Medlip fold back the screen himself. All he was sure of then was that Medlip's hands were empty.

Three days later Haddad's eyes opened and stared blankly. The lids continually fluttered as if he couldn't keep awake. This happened before Wilson and Shearer came on duty, so that when they were told they were already prepared for it. Haddad was now in a constant comatose state. At one time Wilson hurried over to the bed when he saw the Arab's lips move as if he were speaking, but when he bent over he heard nothing and eventually went back to his chair.

The routine was the same over the following week. Each evening Medlip would slip in on his own without a surgical coat to give Haddad a last look and to lift his head and ferret under the pillow.

Then one evening it did not happen. That was the day Haddad became fully conscious. The routine was the same; so was the injection. But the evening visit by Medlip required no screen. He passed a few words with Haddad who replied weakly and who seemed bemused, his words sometimes difficult to find.

From that point the physiotherapist took over, another pretty face, another identity tag. Shearer tried to date her but it began to look as if the nurses had been warned off the whole bodyguard team.

It seemed that Haddad had pulled through. He was allowed to walk in the corridor, at first with help, then with a stick. Finally, when unaided, he had a relapse. The original routine was followed for a few more days. The evening visit of Medlip entailed the use of the screen again.

At dinner that evening Wilson said, "They must have turned him. Why would he need a message in Libya? Haddad's no friend of ours."

"You don't ask that sort of question."

"I'm going to have a closer look."

"Where?"

"Under the pillow."

"Don't be a fool. He's had a relapse."

"I'll take the chance."

That evening, well before Medlip was due to call, Wilson made his search. With heart in mouth he slipped his hand under Haddad's head as Medlip had seemed to do and raised the head from the pillow. Shearer had promised to kick the door if anyone approached. Groping under the pillow produced nothing. Whatever had been there had gone. He lowered the head carefully and Haddad started mumbling. Wilson listened but it was meaningless.

Disappointed, Wilson returned to the window and wondered if he had felt anything there in the first place. Medlip called. No screen. A brief examination which he had no objection to Wilson watching.

Off duty Wilson said to Shearer, "I'll lay you ten to one that Haddad is conscious by morning." He was right. From that point Haddad never looked back. He was weak, of course, and had lost weight his frame could ill-afford to lose; but he slowly regained strength.

The top strata of people was small and often too close. In a country with an area of over six hundred and seventy-nine thousand square miles and a population of about three million, private movements could easily be noticed. The amount of space was no protection. It was easier for Rachid to keep a watch on those around him than it would be in a more densely populated community. Which was why Kawar and Boulrouk occasionally met at prayer.

"Our London Ambassador has informed Rachid that Nabih is due home in a few days. The operation was successful."

"A pity. With Haddad back, Rachid has a powerful extra arm."

"Rachid has decided to meet him at the airport. I can't see why, but he insists."

"They've always been close, Ibrahim. What exactly are we waiting for?"

"A sign."

"From Allah?" Boulrouk was serious.

"It will come. Secrecy helps us. What we don't know we cannot confide. The British Ambassador gave an indication at last night's diplomatic round. I don't think he knows either, but he's expecting something. We must be ready. Keep a strong nerve."

"Will you go to the airport with Rachid?"

"I will have to. Be by his side. London has asked for a Libyan plane as decoy."

"Decoy?"

"There have been threats against Nabih. So London advises us."

74

Boulrouk was genuinely puzzled. "Who would want to kill Haddad in London?" Suddenly he smiled at his own question.

Wilson and Shearer were taken in a limousine with darkened windows for a final briefing in Surrey. Higgs did this alone. It put their role of bodyguards in a ridiculous light.

Higgs said brusquely, "I'm sorry about the blacked-out car. I simply don't want anyone knowing who's here." He seemed edgy and reticent as if holding too much back and he added nothing to his previous instructions. But he wanted to be absolutely satisfied that they had not forgotten the code phrase and the timing of its delivery. He laid such stress on it that it worried them.

"When you return," said Higgs, "I want you to meet someone. It's important, so don't stay on longer than a couple of days. You may prefer to come straight back."

"You mean, *you'd* prefer us to. You're making sure we earn our money."

Higgs smiled awkwardly. "You've earned nothing yet. You're being paid for sitting on your backsides." He had tried to sound humorous but he was masking too much and succeeded only in revealing his underlying strain. The unusual disappearance of his bland, easy-going manner, left the others uneasy.

Similar techniques were used for getting Haddad to London Airport. Two bodyguards took a decoy down in a closed car: he wore a turban and with a police escort boarded a Libyan plane. No big fuss was made but the departure was visible to interested eyes. The decoy was a Libyan who was returning anyway and the deception had been made with the aid of the London Ambassador.

Meanwhile, Wilson and Shearer had pushed Haddad on a wheelchair, blanketed, head covered in a wide brimmed hat, eyes hidden by large dark glasses, down the long ramp to the first class section of a British Airways plane before the other passengers were allowed to embark.

Once on the plane, Haddad handed the hat to the smiling stewardess. He loosened the flap of his kaffiyeh so that it fell to his shoulders; beneath it he now wore a lightweight dressing which would be removed as the hair grew. He was still in a slightly bemused state but well able to walk down the aisle unaided to his seat.

The Arab demanded that Wilson and Shearer stay near to him. He seemed to have a pathological fear of losing them, a condition that had satisfied Higgs immensely: he could only pray that the rest would work out as well.

Haddad took the starboard window seat and Shearer sat on the outside next to him. Wilson took the outer seat across the aisle from them. Piped music filtered through the cabin.

Wilson reflected that it was all so unreal. The painstaking plans for Haddad's safety, his and Shearer's isolated part in it all, Higgs, Marshall—everything. There must be more to it than guarding a man against threat.

Wilson had never carried a gun in a shoulder holster before. Even now, after weeks of wearing it, it was still discomfort. He looked across the aisle at Shearer.

Wilson now knew Shearer to be a sensitive person. It crept out rarely but it was there beneath the layers of disillusion. They hadn't become close. Neither could claim anything of real friendship with the other. But they had a slightly better understanding and appreciation than at the outset. They caught each other's glance and exchanged the briefest of spontaneous smiles. Shearer's thoughts were clearly similar.

The other passengers were boarding. The two escorts took notice of those who passed by. Wilson had to stand up to let a man take the window seat. As he stood he saw Haddad's own personal bodyguard sitting behind his master. Whatever number a bodyguard team comprised, this man always went with Haddad. They did not know his name; they called him Abdul. As Wilson sat down again he could not miss the Arab's burning resentment. The Arab had been deprived of status.

As the passengers finished fiddling in the lockers and finally were seated the engines started one by one and Wilson felt disquiet. He tried to think of warmth, sun and blue skies, palm trees and wide dusty streets filled with Cadillacs and Rolls-Royces, exotic dishes and sensuous dancers. But it wouldn't work. As the aircraft taxied forward all he could produce was a vision of hungry, lean-flanked desert dogs and the irritating bite of desert fleas, of street smells and children begging like old men. Had the oil done anything for them?

The big plane rotated, broke cloud and

roared above its rolling blanket. The weather did not clear until they were well south of Milan, and Italy lay far below like a scarred brown foot. By then they had all eaten and were mainly dozing. Haddad had taken prescribed pills with his meal and was now fast asleep with a pillow behind his head. Shearer was reading a newspaper and Wilson had given up trying to pick out likely patches for emergency landings from an aisle position. Every time he moved his left arm the damned gun got in the way. That was another thing: there must have been some high-powered wrangling to get authority for them to be carried on a British aircraft.

The slow descent started well out over the Mediterranean. The skies had remained clear for the larger part of the journey and the sea from this height was unrippled, apart from smears of froth where the odd ship was seen. They approached Tripoli with the haze fuzzing the hills inland and behind the hills the emptiness of sand and rock.

Before landing the chief steward had brought back a message for Haddad that a reception party would meet him. He would be the first to disembark.

The aircraft landed, the engines roared in

reverse thrust and finally trundled towards the low airport buildings. The usual announcement had been made for everyone to keep their seats. The chief steward gave a nod and Shearer eased into the aisle, then Haddad and Wilson followed him. Abdul came behind Wilson.

There was a slight delay over the mobile steps but at last they mounted the platform in a blaze of sunlight. They screwed their eyes against the glare. Instinctively, now, Wilson and Shearer stepped forward to shield Haddad. Below them a half-circle of cars had parked some fifty feet away and by them stood a group of Arabs, most standing behind and to one side of a small party of three. Of the three both Wilson and Shearer recognised with surprise that one was the country's ruler. Colonel Ali Rachid, dictator, active and successful enemy of the West, fervent Moslem, harbourer of terrorists, had come in person to greet his old friend Nabih Haddad.

Shearer went down the steps first, wondering what his reaction would be if anyone tried a shot at Haddad here, on Libyan soil. He suddenly felt notably out of place. Abdul should have led the way down. Haddad came next, holding on to the rail as he descended slowly. Wilson came last with Abdul.

Rachid was smiling broadly, his bodyguards just behind him. Heading the other group was Ibrahim Kawar, the security chief, with more men. The chauffeur already had the car door opened.

Shearer set foot in Libya, uneasy and suddenly afraid. Haddad followed, Shearer turning to help him down the last step. Wilson was one step behind and he moved up beside Haddad. Colonel Rachid stepped forward, both arms held wide in welcome.

"Nabih! Nabih, my dear friend."

Haddad moved forward slowly. Wilson, observing that he had only seconds before the two men embraced, skipped forward and asked carefully, "Have you any further instructions for us?"

Haddad paused, his expression clouded, then said quite clearly, "No, your job is done." He stumbled slightly, quickly recovered, his eyes glazed as if within him there was sudden torment.

Wilson stood aside, Shearer drew back, Haddad appeared to place his hand over his heart as Rachid approached to clasp him with uninhibited affection. Everyone was smiling except Wilson and Shearer who now felt totally superfluous. Over Rachid's shoulder Haddad's face appeared, his eyes now opaque and staring. There was the sound of a shot, partly muffled by the proximity of the two bodies, then Rachid fell to his knees, head back, eyes rolling upwards. He fell sideways almost in slow motion. Haddad swayed, smoking gun trailing in one hand. His eyes regained expression; disbelief, love, horror. His lips moved then he let out a terrible wail and fell to his knees, head back, gaze upward. He began to sob silently, quite still, his face screwed tight with a terrible anguish.

The only movement was in the vacillating shards of sunlight reflecting off the aircraft. Everyone had frozen in position. Rachid's personal bodyguards did not know what to do, how to react. Wilson and Shearer suddenly found their role reversed. They had to protect Haddad but he was now the assassin. Their impulse was to get back on the aircraft quickly but reasoning told them to remain still. Haddad himself still had the gun in his hand, but was clearly unaware of it. He was trapped by his own nightmare. Rachid did not move. The breeze caught the end of his kaffiyeh and tugged at it like a lazy flag.

It was Kawar, the security chief, who reacted first. He was stunned by the unexpected murder of his leader. He'd been unprepared for something so sudden but his mind was racing, computing the possibilities and knowing that whatever he did had better be right. He looked at the wreck that was now Haddad whose blank gaze was drifting slowly to the heap that had once been his friend, unable to grasp his own madness. There would never be a better opportunity to establish his own power. With a great roar of "Murderer," an accusation full of passion, Kawar drew his own gun, levelled it and emptied it into the luckless Haddad. Rachid's bodyguards belatedly did the same but Haddad was already dead before they fired their first shot.

From that point it was all shouts and turmoil. Kawar's mind was still working furiously. He needed to show some action in defence of his "beloved leader". He pointed to Wilson and Shearer and screamed, "Arrest those men. Disarm them." Abdul, standing behind them, having just been stunned by the violent death of his master, was the first to move forward. Without prompting Wilson's and Shearer's hands rose above their heads.

# 5

RACHID'S death was a sensation. The Colonel had probably made more impact than any other leader commanding so small a population. Rachid had made himself felt, usually to the fury and frustration of the Western bloc.

Television screens were the first to project the assassination, but by midday the next day the whole world was engulfed by the event. Speculation was rife. Could Haddad's brain operation have affected him in some way? Why would he kill his best friend? There was no way of finding out; he was dead. And news about the fate of Shearer and Wilson was vague: no names were issued.

Higgs flew out to Washington amidst mixed waves of relief and horror. The whole Islamic world was in mourning and in uproar. Among some there was secret relief too. Joe Marshall met Higgs at Dulles Airport and they drove together to an apartment Marshall sometimes used.

"It didn't go quite as planned," said Higgs.

"I had no idea the dear Colonel was going to the airport."

"I didn't know either. You forced Kawar to play it so close to the chest that you couldn't warn him what might happen." Marshall smiled. "You have a Cockney saying, 'He used his loaf'. He did, didn't he?"

"By killing Haddad? Indeed. What's cropped up while I was flying?"

Marshall continued to look satisfied. "Kawar has taken over as temporary head of government. With the power of his security forces, the secret ears he has to the ground, few would try to buck him. If things are going right for us out there Boulrouk will have tranquillised the armed forces. It could work, Maurice."

"It's certainly encouraging."

"What about Wilson and Shearer?"

"They'll have to take their chances. Kawar's in a difficult position."

The jail stank. Wilson sat in the corner opposite the squatting Shearer. "One night and I feel as though I've been rotting here all my life. We've got to get out."

Shearer raised his head. "And then what? Escape across the desert?"

85

Wilson struck the air. They had been badly roughed up on their way to prison. The Libyan Master had been destroyed. As his Islamic support could not inflict pain on the assassin, handy Westerners would do fine.

Nobody visited them. They had been hurled into a small cell with a bucket and two mats. The atmosphere was suffocating. Someone had ordered that they be kept apart from the other prisoners. That night they received no food or water. In the morning poor coffee and stale bread were thrust at them, and at lunch time a watery soup and more bread were pushed through the flap in the bars. As hungry as they were they touched none of it. With repetitive monotony they demanded to see the American and United Kingdom consuls but their jailers did not speak English. The two men were left alone.

They dared not discuss what was on their minds. They had searched for listening bugs. There was little scope to hide them. The brick walls were chipped and crumbling and filthy. Graffiti covered them. Although the cell was small the ceiling was lofty. There was no window, and as they had been bundled down stone steps they assumed they were below ground level. In spite of their negative search they were not willing to take the risk of being overheard.

Instead they talked round it. It would be unnatural and a pointer to their guilt if they did not discuss it at all. So they comforted each other by expressing their complete horror which was not far from the truth. But their horror was many-sided. They now knew the importance of the question Wilson had delivered; he had pulled a trigger. Haddad had been programmed to react to it. If Rachid had not come to the airport the assassination would not have happened in their presence and they would never have known the truth. It was knowledge neither wanted.

They had their jackets off and shirts undone. It was stifling with no movement of air. The night, on the other hand, had been so cold they had shivered just as they now sweated through the day. Common peril had built up between them a silent method of communication that bordered on the tele- pathic. They knew what to avoid in conversa- tion, they knew what they could dwell upon. They were sent for almost twenty-four hours after Rachid's death. As they passed other prisoners they were spat upon and screamed at. Tin plates were banged on steel bars. The word had got round: somehow they were responsible for the tragic death. The rough-clad warders took cue from the prisoners. They were all Islamic brethren even if some had wronged. The two prisoners were butted with rifles and kicked until they hobbled. They kept going by supporting each other.

They were bundled into another almost bare room and pushed on to a long wooden bench which lay along one wall. Barred windows let in sunlight which, over the years, had partially bleached a plain wooden table in the centre of the room. They were left there with four armed guards who sniggered and talked to each other in guttural Arabic.

For three hours they were kept there. Every time they tried to change position they were threatened with a rifle butt. The threats weren't idle: the guards were looking for the slightest excuse to maim them. The ordeal of sitting on hard wood in virtually one position was agonising.

Long after the sun had gone down and the heat in the room had begun to abate, the light was switched on. A man entered, his face shadowed by the peak of his military cap. He stood looking down at the two prisoners, the fingers of one hand splayed on the table top. The two guards with him had drawn back to join the others. There were now six armed men in the room. The man straightened, the light falling more clearly on to the uncompromising features of Ibrahim Kawar.

Wilson and Shearer recognised him as the man who had shot Haddad but they had no knowledge of his identity. Nor did he now enlighten them. Yet his authority was obvious.

Nobody pushed a chair up for Kawar, as if they already knew that he would not sit down. He continued to stare at the prisoners thoughtfully, without anger or malice. It was more unsettling than if he had shown his feelings.

"Tell me about the threat Haddad was under in London."

It was left to Wilson to answer, to avoid the added complication of Shearer's American accent. "We're only employed bodyguards. There were threats. We heard there were letters which the police took seriously. Mr. Haddad was in favour of extra bodyguards before his operation."

"You didn't see the letters?" Kawar was speaking in slow, careful English.

"No."

"We would not normally allow European bodyguards to come here like this. I find it most strange."

"Mr. Haddad insisted that we came. At one time he pleaded with us. The visas were rushed through by your consul. What can I say? The school we went to trains your own bodyguards. We're the best."

"Are you saying Haddad employed you?"

Wilson quickly saw dangerous ground. "No, sir. The British Government employed us, as I understand it. I can't be sure. They must have believed the threat to be real."

Kawar switched his gaze to Shearer. "You say nothing. You think your American accent would make me wonder?"

"I've lived in England a long time." Shearer showed no surprise at the Arab's knowledge.

"Of course. Tell me why Haddad's surgeon was killed?"

"Medlip? He's dead?"

The reply was so spontaneous that Kawar hesitated. "Not Medlip. Professor Murton, who was supposed to have operated."

"Never heard of him."

Shearer quickly added to Wilson's claim. "It's over our head. Murton means nothing to us. Who operated is not our scene."

"Why are we being held?" Wilson was uneasy at the way the questioning was going. "We've been bashed about. All we did was to make sure Mr. Haddad got back alive."

"Is that all? Then what was it you whispered to him just before he killed our beloved leader?" Kawar was glaring now, his fervour showing, his tone accusing, his gaze switching quickly from man to man.

"I only asked him if there was anything more he needed us for. Our job was over. We wanted to get back. And I didn't whisper."

"Haddad reacted immediately after you spoke to him."

"It was nothing to do with me. The Colonel was coming forward. That might have triggered him. Who knows? We're here because you need a scapegoat."

It was risky to say, but Kawar suddenly smiled. Placing both hands on the table so that he was leaning on it, he glanced over his shoulder at the guards and then looked back at the prisoners. "Mr. Wilson, you are quite right. None of the men behind me speaks a word of English so try not to look surprised by what I say. I'm going to send you back because I don't want to upset certain people, but I cannot do it quite so easily. I must give some show to please my people. You will be proved innocent but that cannot be done at an interview like this. The truth must be prised out of you. You understand?" He straightened, not very tall but solid.

"If you torture us it could have the wrong effect." Shearer's mouth was dry.

Kawar inclined his head. "I will ensure that you won't say the wrong things. You will only be beaten. Someone I trust will be briefed. But I must put on a show. I thought an explanation might help your suffering. When you leave the people will know and will see that I have been satisfied."

"So we get tortured for doing nothing?"

"Nothing? Mr. Shearer, if you really believe that then you, too, have been programmed."

Wilson and Shearer went cold yet they sweated. They were afraid to say another word.

Kawar went on. "My easiest course is to have you executed. The only reason I don't is because I want to avoid international pressure and criticism at this stage. It would be difficult to give an entirely satisfactory answer and at the moment that's important to me."

He stepped back a pace. "Gentlemen, you should be grateful. I give you the lesser of two evils. Scream as much as you like. It will be better if you are heard." He stopped as he saw their reaction; both had a look of recklessness about them. "And please don't try to grab me now. It is written in your faces. The guards would club you to death." He stepped back again. "For you to be killed while escaping would solve some of my problems but it could be embarrassing at this time. You see how reasonable I am? Hold out for a few days and I will have no further reason for detaining you." He suddenly spoke rapidly in Arabic and the guards came from behind him towards the prisoners while Kawar disappeared through the door.

The days became prolonged, meaningless. Day and night lost form; heat and cold alternated. What made it worse was being always taken singly to the torture chamber. Had they suffered together they might just possibly have bolstered each other, formed a rivalry of two flags that might have helped sustain them. They might, perhaps, have tried not to let themselves down in front of each other.

The fact that they had been told by Kawar that it would terminate helped at first but was soon lost sight of as excruciating pain and increased privation drove out all thought except that of facing the next session.

One might be huddled in a corner after being dragged back to the cell, while the other was manhandled to the chamber. And as the wretch who had just suffered lay there, still feeling the pain and glad only that he could openly show his fear and suffering while he lay alone, he would have even this crumb of comfort taken from him as the nearby screams penetrated the cell.

Barely a word passed between them during this time. Pain, hunger, debility and shame took away their pride. They almost lost sight of what they were holding out for. Questions were asked for the sake of record and no real answers were expected. Had they been capable of taking stock of time they might have held on better but a tortured, feverish mind has little knowledge of time.

They knew it had ended when nobody came for them any more. There was a point when they glanced tentatively at each other in subdued hope and disbelief. Would Kawar keep his word?

They gazed at each other not knowing what to think and not daring to think too far. Had they been closer friends they could have better tolerated their present position. As it was they each believed they had let themselves down in front of the other.

That night they fed on hot meat balls and rice. It was their first decent meal since their imprisonment. But even now they could not openly discuss their position for fear of a trap.

They were left alone that night. They shivered with cold. Both had lost weight and the dropping temperature aggravated their raw weals. But they would rather convulse from the cold than suffer again in the way that they had.

The next morning they were stripped and were given rough but clean prison clothes. This left them in a high state of anxiety until razors, soap and water were brought. Hard stubble was shaven off and they had stand-up baths, helping, with infinite care, to wash each other's backs. They began to speak again, shame melting in the face of realism.

Their cleaned clothes were returned that

evening and they dressed carefully. Even a shirt touching a back was painful. Within an hour their passports had been returned and they were flown to Rome with their original luggage. Before landing they were given a typed message and on its instructions they waited after customs clearance and were met by a florid, middle-aged American who drove them to the Excelsior Hotel where a twin-bedded room had been reserved. They were handed single, first-class tickets to London for the following afternoon.

Whoever had made the arrangements must have collaborated with Kawar, which they found odd. One fact stood out above all others; no newsmen had even remotely approached them. Their arrest in connection with Rachid's assassination had completely slipped through the media network. Kawar must have enforced heavy censorship.

By the time they reached their hotel room they were exhausted. They bathed, changed felt a little better. They had money but found the tab was being picked up. They did not ask by whom, but were encouraged to eat well and they had a late dinner at the hotel and indulged themselves almost to a point of gluttony.

They drank a lot—and it helped them to forget what they had suffered. As drink and food relaxed them they came round to the subject they had been afraid to voice.

"When we get back I'm signing off. I'm in bloody agony and my pride has suffered." Wilson's words were slightly slurred.

They were sitting facing the almost empty lounge with a bottle of Scotch on the table in front of them.

"You'd be wise to do exactly what you're told to do."

Wilson eased his chair back so he could see Shearer better. "Don't try that with me, mate."

"Ray, it doesn't worry me what happens to you. But I'm concerned about what happens to me. Get it through your head that what happens to one happens to the other."

"So you sign off as well?"

"Goddamn it, are you as thick as you seem to be? Professor Murton, was it? This guy who was to operate on Haddad and was killed? How do you reckon we equate with him? If they'll knock off a top surgeon they'll exterminate us with barely a thought."

Wilson moved uneasily, then reached for the bottle. "I was hoping that you might come up with a better line. We're in trouble, aren't we? They picked us out."

"Someone who can do the job but least likely to be missed."

Shearer stared at the almost empty bottle, before pouring the remainder into his glass. "The whole Western world wanted Rachid knocked off. He was a menace. But think of the reaction if the truth got out. Kawar's walking a tightrope. If that particular boat is rocked it's back to square one. The slightest suspicion of the truth and the whole Arab world will go crazy. And we weren't supposed to see it happen. We weren't supposed to know."

"Well, that's great. We may as well take our chances now."

"There is no chance. Nowhere we can hide."

Wilson suddenly turned to look Shearer in the face. "We'd better get to trust each other, matey."

Shearer nodded slowly. He grinned suddenly and held out his hand. They shook hands firmly. "I've good reason for being the way I am but I guess it's no excuse. If we can drum up another bottle I'll give you my life story."

Joseph Marshall received Sir Maurice Higgs in a private house not far from Grosvenor Square. The house was owned by the United States Government, enjoyed no diplomatic protection, but had the most up-to-date de-bugging equipment which included elec-tronic vibrators to prevent internal dialogue from being picked up from the houses either side.

"I've always like this house," said Higgs as he accepted the cigar and cognac and seated himself. "It's a delightful terrace. I hope to God they don't demolish it." He gazed round the room, at the porcelain, the paintings, but his mind was elsewhere, his eyes weary. He slipped one plump leg over the other and sipped his cognac appreciatively. "I wish I had your expense account."

Marshall smiled. He filled the wing arm-chair, grey hair toning with the antique leather his head rested upon. "So Kawar let them go."

"I can see his point. Executions would raise questions. We still need them."

Marshall replied cautiously, "They saw it happen. *They know*. It wasn't supposed to be like that."

Higgs gazed through the cigar smoke.

"They have always been expendable." He shrugged. "I agree it makes their silence more imperative. We must choose our time carefully."

"We've no time to replace them, Maurice."

"I don't think there's need. Ever since we were instructed by your President and my Prime Minister to find a clandestine solution to Arab blackmail over oil supplies, this sort of risk has been on. But we did get rid of Rachid. If only the rest goes well."

Marshall nodded. It worried him that the method of the killing was now known to others. "The arms for the invasion of Iran are ready. It's not been easy. We've selected the generals. We want to finish the job the Iraqis started in 1980. They've long realised that they can't do it without considerable help, with three Iranians to every one of them. They're a mixed bag. The Shah's old secret police are in the line-up, and the old body-guard troops. A large number of Kurds are included. No Western forces at all."

"How will the Russians retaliate? We could be committing suicide, Joe."

"We will be if we let them get the Gulf. We might as well surrender and get it over with. Put up the white flag. They've been worming away inside Iran ever since the Shah left. Let's not chicken for God's sake. We must get stability out there."

Higgs waved a hand through the cigar smoke. "You're angry because I've echoed your own doubts. A third world war. The final holocaust. The alternative for us is slow strangulation. Oil prices have caused chaos in too many countries; many are near bankruptcy. Look at Turkey."

Marshall stabbed a finger. "I'm sick and tired of being hamstrung for fear of what the Russians might do. Sure it's a gamble. They gamble all the time. And they win."

Higgs changed the subject. He felt the same as Marshall but emotion was dangerous. "I gather the arms are still in the old border barracks? The big stuff; tanks, field guns and so on?"

"Much of it. Some is secreted under the guise of Iraqi equipment. And there's an offshore freighter loaded. We've got to arrange the release of arms to the invading forces. Your man out there seems to know what he's doing."

Higgs smiled briefly. "A brilliant rogue. If we want to make sure the stuff gets properly distributed and some of it doesn't slide off elsewhere we'll have to use Wilson and Shearer, using the local man as advisor. It would be far too risky to use an accredited arms agent. You have faith in Shearer? Wilson will be of little use on that side."

"Shearer's had that sort of experience. A good all round man."

"And the oil pipe line? It will be highly dangerous to allow Wilson and Shearer over the Russian border now, knowing what they know. Rogov would squeeze it from them."

"We mustn't stop the destruction of the Russian pipeline. It will distract them and give them a fuel supply problem at a crucial time. We only need a short respite, after which it will be too late for them to do anything. There's also the propaganda advantage to show the waverers that the Russians are not invulnerable. I rate it not only worth it but essential at that time."

"Then Wilson and Shearer must stop at the border. They can train the saboteurs while they travel."

They stared at each other silently before Marshall said, "Are we making too much of it, Maurice?"

Higgs shook his head slowly. "We're being

squeezed to death. Let's at least make the effort."

The wind was blowing hard across Dzerzhinsky Square. It was ridiculously cold for the time of year even for Moscow. Collars were up, covered heads sunk down into them as people hunched against a wind particularly blustery on the corner of the square. Lubyanka prison was part of the building on the corner. The rest was K.G.B. headquarters which continued into the newer and bigger structure to its right, built by captured German soldiers from World War Two.

The two men in a fifth-floor office were looking through a Georgian-style window at the bleakness of the Square. Both men were out of context and one was head of the First Chief Directorate, foreign operations, which was housed in the massive, curved block outside Moscow.

General Rogov preferred the old building and it still housed a small section of his department. He was apt to think that the brain work was done in this building and the paper work in the new. He also found more privacy here.

"Summer," he said. "Unbelievable." And

then, "So they got Rachid. They were clever."

He sat down heavily and stared at the much slimmer, dark-haired Panovich across the desk.

The assassination of Colonel Rachid had shaken the Politburo to its roots. Russia had survived many frictions with Libya but in ways that really mattered their co-operation had been invaluable. Rogov held a certain admiration for the killing and he knew far too much about psychiatric drugs to be misled by it. As always he was thinking ahead. "What do we know about Kawar?"

Panovich held a batch of notes. He waved them without referring to them. "He's one of ours. Trained here."

"Was or is?"

Panovich shrugged. "Only time will tell. I don't like the way the British escort for Haddad was set free. Although they suffered first."

"I've never heard of foreign escorts being used like that. There must have been a reason."

"Someone threatened Haddad, so we're told. It's too early to see anything clearly."

Rogov sat back, cigar in fingers. "Panovich, there's a smell. Find out who the escorts were. They may be unimportant but do it quickly. Put someone on to them. Let *Pravda* make its usual rumbles; but I don't want speculation, nothing to indicate we're suspicious."

Wilson had expected an Englishman, Shearer an American. Shearer was right. His name was Marvin Brown. They met for lunch at the Savoy. It was three days since the return of Wilson and Shearer to London. They had been taken under guard, straight from London Airport to the house in Surrey. Another kind of prison, but one they could bear. They lived there shut off and guarded, each with his own room, and licked their wounds in luxury. Neither wanted to move from the grounds. They built up strength, had what they needed and enjoyed it, even knowing they were under sentence.

With Marshall now in America, Higgs had seen them alone and had briefed them. He hadn't mentioned one word about the Rachid murder, as though he recognised that to do so could only leave much unsaid and raise other questions in their minds. He did ask how they felt after the torture, but even that was voiced in an automatic, only-polite-to-ask way.

They knew they were getting in deeper at a time they wanted to cut loose. Whenever they could, usually out in the open, they had discussed breaking with Higgs. They always wound up convinced that they were well trapped in the snare he had deviously created. The only way out was through the same door Haddad and Professor Murton had taken. They believed that would be their fate whatever they did. But if they held on, made no rash moves, something might turn up. Hope springs eternal; it was all they had.

Higgs had blandly asked them to start another war in Iran and to blow up a Russian pipe line. They had listened carefully to what he had to say; knowing that as things stood their lives were in his hands.

So now they were with Marvin Brown, a tall, leathery, cold-eyed Texan, some ten years older than they. Brown was an oil man. They did not know which company he represented but he talked in millions of dollars as a matter of habit, and he clearly carried the authority to back his talk. He needed no reference to switch vast sums of money.

He talked generally at first about the

problems of Iran as they appertained to him. He talked of oil pipe lines, of where they ran, the likely number of pumping stations in different kinds of terrain. In the massive desert stretches they could be as far apart as a hundred and fifty to three hundred miles and this would be very relevant to what Wilson and Shearer needed to know.

Brown talked of the 1979 oil find by the Russians in the Caspian Sea, some of which was now flowing from offshore wells. There had been delays on others that should have been ready by late 1982. There were always delays with off-shore drilling.

Brown was one of those men who could talk endlessly but always with something to say. He never indulged in idle chatter. Remarkably, while Wilson and Shearer hardly uttered a word, Brown was never behind with his meal; he had developed his skills of eating and talking together as an inoffensive fine art. And he ate like a horse. He did not like being called an oil tycoon but that's what he was. He'd never known anything else but to be involved with oil. He knew what he was talking about, and the day he suspected that he didn't he would retire.

By the time lunch was finished, late in the

afternoon, Wilson and Shearer had built up a picture of what they had to face. Except in one respect they did not want detail but an image.

After lunch they went up to Brown's suite and he produced a map which he spread over the bed. He lit a long cheroot which fouled the air but which he clearly enjoyed.

"Now you boys look at this." A long finger pointed to the east side of the Caspian Sea. Both Iran and Russia pincered the Caspian; Iran just the lower portion, the giant share above being Russia's. The finger stabbed again. "There are the oil fields at Kotardepe. The pipe line comes up from there and joins the one from Krasnovodsk. Get it? Then it comes right down at an angle here, where it's marked, to Ashkhabad. Right? What would you say? About ten miles from the Iranian border? Very close to Iran along that sector."

"The Iranians aren't exactly friendly to us."

Brown wheeled on Wilson. "Nor are the Russians, sonny." He lost some of his steeliness. "Sit down, boys. Spread yourselves." He sat in a leather armchair, long legs crossed, and faced them. "This isn't easy, I know that. But nothing's for nothing. You boys come very highly recommended."

"Anonymously, we hope." Shearer could be acid, too.

"Sure, anonymously. I don't know your names, and it would be an embarrassment to me if I did." His cheroot had gone out and he groped for matches. "Okay, so we oil companies like to wield the big stick. We're used to getting our way. It's said we run governments and start wars. I've no comment to make on that. But I'll say this; the Arabs have the oil and it would still be under the goddamn sand if it hadn't been for us. They still need us, and those who say they don't are talking crap. We taught them all they know, and most of 'em are still learning. So we got rich. So did the sheiks."

Wilson and Shearer said nothing to this. It was a sudden outburst from the heart.

Brown apologised. "I guess I get carried away. You'll have noticed I have strong feelings on the subject. Okay. We'll pay you a hundred thousand dollars each for a week or so's work. Any bank, anywhere, in any form. You can have it in gold if you want."

"What if we don't come through?"

Brown had already considered the

109

question. "We'll pay in advance. What happens if you don't survive is a matter for you to arrange. We don't wanner know."

"You'll need our names for payment."

Brown held up the still extinct cheroot. "No way. I don't want to know your names. Not ever. All we need to sort out is a bank account number."

Wilson and Shearer exchanged glances. Their spell of silent communication in the cell did not fail them now. Who was their boss? Higgs and Marshall had started out to be; now they were being passed on to an oil company—perhaps a consortium. "What do we do," asked Shearer drily, "for this 'nothing's for nothing' money?"

"We want the oil back. It's no secret that we'd like to see a civil war in Iran with the right faction winning. We've put a lot of money into it. We want the pipe line over the border in Russia blown up to keep them off our backs. You organise it. If you can get at some of the new rigs in the Caspian it would be a bonus, and we'd pay a helluva lot for it. If that's too difficult you might be able to get at the land rig further south of Niettechala on the west side of the Caspian. It's about sixty-odd miles over the border."

"It's easy," said Wilson. "No bother, mate."

Brown stiffened. He didn't like flippancy and had been unsure of Wilson from the outset. He couldn't categorise him.

"You don't like the idea?"

"Instant death? Would you?"

"I'm not being paid a hundred thousand dollars."

"That's not six months' salary to you. Without putting your life on the line." Shearer stood up and wandered into the bedroom to take another look at the map. "What help do we get?" he called through the doorway.

"Are we talking business?" Brown followed Shearer in and Wilson joined them as Shearer answered.

"We're talking business." It was almost as if Higgs was hiding somewhere in the room waiting for the reply.

# 6

THEY stood at the end of the bar in a pub in Wardour Street. It was early and the place fairly empty. They were drinking bitter.

"I think I'm going barmy," said Wilson. "You sure we have to go through with this?" He glanced round to make sure they could not be overheard.

"Could you live behind the Curtain?"

Wilson's face hardened. "I hate communism."

"That's your alternative. Spill to them. They'll take us like a shot."

"I'd rather be dead."

"We're going to be dead anyway, the way things are."

Wilson sipped his beer. "We've had a tail since our return to London."

Shearer showed no sign. Without looking at Wilson he said, "You sure?"

Wilson grimaced. "It took time to spot them. They're not a bad team. The inside man is the character with the tweed hat. Looks like a bookie's runner."

"Who, I wonder?"

"Higgs's crowd? What's it matter? It answers my own question: we're hooked." He added thoughtfully. "I'm going to see Jennie."

Shearer slopped his beer as he raised it. "You're mad. They'll know."

"If we're being topped I'm seeing her before it happens."

"You step out of line and they'll wonder why. They can't take chances. Don't be a fool." Shearer finished his beer.

Wilson said, "If I've got to go it'll be with a smile on my face. Besides, I owe Jennie. She'll be worried sick."

Shearer ordered another round. After pocketing his change, he said softly, "Do you want what happened to Murton to happen to your girl?" Shearer had been looking at his beer; he turned to Wilson and he raised it. He got as far as 'cheers', and he stopped. He lowered his glass slowly. He had not seen Wilson like this before. The whole frame and face were granite; the eyes would have made Brown's appear weak. He'd struck the main nerve.

Tonelessly Wilson said to him, "If any of them lays a finger on Jennie while I'm alive I'll sing like a crowded aviary. And I'd let a lot out before they could stop me."

Wilson picked up his drink and Shearer thought the handle of the tankard would snap off. Wilson was showing another side. The easy-going character had gone. "You tell 'em," he added. He put the tankard down very carefully. "If I were you I'd go to the cabaret club round the corner. The fun stops tomorrow."

Shearer met his gaze. The cold fury of Wilson was barely contained. "I'll see you at the hotel."

Wilson left and Shearer noticed the man with the tweed hat was undecided whether to follow Wilson or stay with himself; he followed. Shearer turned moodily back to his beer. Wilson was being a fool but he'd learned more about the Englishman in the last two minutes than during their whole enforced stay together. Suddenly the club round the corner sounded attractive. Why not? A condemned man was entitled to a last fulfilment.

Wilson set out to lose his tail without finesse.

He was angry and deliberate. He was also very quick on his feet. After half an hour he was satisfied that he was no longer being followed. He slowed his pace, letting the cold air cool him.

He didn't go in the block by the front entrance in case it was being watched. He went up the fire escape and unlocked the back door on the tiny metal landing where Jennie kept her flower pots. Once in the kitchen he called out loudly so as not to alarm her by stealth.

"Jennie! It's me. Ray."

All the lights were on because she hated being alone. He switched off the kitchen light behind him. She came running into the small hall and he could hear the television as she left the lounge door open. She flew into his arms, housecoat trailing and clung to him as if afraid to let him go.

"Oh, Ray. Oh, darling. Where have you been?"

They stood there rocking and he felt her tears against his cheek. God, it was starting all over again. She trembled and he realised she knew it too. He cradled her waist and led her back to the lounge, switching off the television and settling her on his knee. They kissed passionately and when they broke she was half laughing, half crying. "You stink of beer," she said, wiping her eyes with the back of her hand. "You going to tell me?"

"I told you I'd be away for a bit."

"You didn't say for how long, where or why."

"I couldn't, love."

"The business will rot. You shouldn't leave it."

"It's okay, and you know it." He paused. "I've got to go away again."

She leaned back from him looking infinitely sad. "Why do you do it, Ray? Why to me? These last years have been wonderful."

"For me too, Jennie. You know I couldn't deliberately hurt you. You know how I am."

"I thought you'd changed."

He looked guilty. "You know I'll never change. The gaps might widen, though. That's not so bad, is it?"

She nuzzled him, trying to fight down her fears. "It all started from that blasted letter. I sensed it was trouble. What is it this time?"

"You know you'll get nothing out of me. So why don't we go to bed?"

"I'm too worried."

"Weren't they always the best times?"

"As if it was our last? I thought it was different now. We're getting older. I don't want to keep thinking I'm going to lose you."

He tried to keep it light, grinned, aware that he wasn't deceiving her. "Lose me? You're kidding. But you've reminded me of something. Something I've meant to tell you for some time but keep forgetting. There's a bank account in Switzerland I haven't told you about. I'll leave the number with you."

"Oh, God." She slowly rose, stood in front of him clenched fists to mouth. "I remember the last one. What it meant."

He reached for her hand. "I'm here, aren't I?"

She nodded slowly, thinking back. "For how long have you forgotten to tell me? A day? Two?"

"Aw, come on. You can trust me." He stood up beside her, held her.

"In some things I can always trust you. But not in this. You're up to your neck again. I don't want money when you're dead. I want you here and alive, now."

"A few days," he said. "That's all I need." He paused, trying to control his feelings. "And then it'll be over."

She clung to him again, her nails biting in. "Come on," he said. "Bed."

She didn't resist. She was almost listless as she went with him. "Yes," she said. "Something to remember you by."

He did not reply.

Shearer looked at the head on the other pillow, bleached hair fanned out, lipstick almost worn off the opened lips. She breathed slowly in sleep, red-nailed fingers lightly clutching the sheets, shadowed lids closed; traces of mascara seeping from under the eyes. She must be twenty years younger than me, he thought. He lifted the sheet and eyed the naked, slightly heaving young body, trying to visualise her in twenty years' time. He didn't like the image he conjured up of her and lowered the sheet again.

The drink had worn off with the passion. There were gaps he couldn't remember. He hadn't done this since just after Joan had left him.

He gazed round the room surprised, somehow, to find it so nice. A woman's bedroom, and a lot of care had gone into it. He sat up slowly, sorry for what had happened, not because he hadn't enjoyed himself—the girl was pretty, and had been fun—but because of the girl.

He swung his legs out slowly, found the bathroom, filled the tub. The apartment was warm and friendly, and he wondered how many others had thought so and how long she could last. Longer than he; he had barely any time left at all, and what little there was would be disaster.

After he'd bathed he returned to the bedroom. The dressing-table lamp was still on. Neither of them had felt inclined to climb out to turn it off. Its pink glow had been more than enough.

He dressed slowly. The girl stirred, opened her eyes blearily, then sat up as she realised he was leaving. Her young breasts were exposed and he felt another pang of sorrow for her. It was no use lecturing; she couldn't raise her kind of money any other way—and he certainly had no right to tell her what to do with her life.

"Breakfast is included," she said, blue eyes widening. "Was I that bad?"

"You were fine, honey. But I must move on."

She glanced at the clock. "You'll have a job getting a taxi."

119

He smiled at her. "I don't need a cab. My hotel is just around the block. You take care, now."

She felt his concern. It was something new. She smiled back and tousled her hair. "You're not bad for an oldie."

It was three a.m. when he left and the warm night air closed round him. When he got back to the hotel he could just see the shadow of the two heads across the way. They'll be relieved, he thought. He entered the room to find Wilson still missing.

Wilson rose at five a.m. He showered and shaved and then dressed in the dark. Jennie didn't stir, but he knew she was awake, listening to him. It was her way of not wanting to say goodbye, to avoid visible tears and to make it awkward for him. She had gone into their association with her eyes wide open; she had known how it would be. But it didn't make him feel better. She should have left him years ago, but he was glad that she hadn't. Far too late, he thought of marriage.

When he was ready he bent over the bed and kissed her cheek lightly, thinking, as he always thought, how beautifully soft it was. "See you, love," he whispered.

He thought he heard her stifle a sob as he moved away but he kept going, closing the door quietly behind him.

Shearer was already up when Wilson entered the room. Neither said much. They went downstairs for an early breakfast and the car called at seven a.m. They sat in the back together, still sombre, lost in their thoughts, the darkened windows of the car cutting out the morning. It was some time before Shearer said, "There was a car outside last night. Two men. They were cut off just now."

"I saw it when I came in, too. If they were cut off they can't belong to Higgs."

"Nor Marshall. It's great to know you're blown before you start."

Wilson suddenly turned. "How can you see through this stuff? All I can see are shapes."

"I noticed as I climbed in."

They were driven to the R.A.F. airfield at Northolt, and taken to a low wooden hut away from the main complex. They went inside. Higgs was already there, drinking steaming coffee from a thermos flask. He did not offer them any. He sat precariously on the edge of a trestle table and eyed them blearily.

"The R.A.F. will fly you to Oman. Your first contacts will meet you there. Friendly place, very pro-British. Good spot to start from."

Higgs stared at Wilson. He shook out the drops from the plastic top and screwed it on to the thermos. "That was a very stupid thing you did last night."

"If you couldn't trust me then, you can't now."

"And that's a rather silly thing to say. You realise how you endangered Jennie Palmer? We simply cannot take that kind of risk."

"There was no risk."

"Had you taken her out instead of staying in we would have had to do something about her."

The chill took Wilson slowly. Higgs had been mild, but he always was. "You bastard," said Wilson. "You have bugged her place. You listened in. Christ, how low can you get?"

"It was as well that I did. It saved your Jennie. Don't ever break my instructions again. You should have done what Doug Shearer did, take a harmless tart to bed."

Wilson could hardly contain himself. Shearer held himself ready to intervene if Wilson went over the top.

Higgs didn't move from the table. "Be

your age, Ray. Taking me apart won't alter the situation one bit. You could do it easily, I know that. I won't even attempt to stop you. I'm really too old for aggro."

Wilson kept down his temper. He might say too much, and that could cause problems before he was prepared for them.

Higgs said, "Let me recap. There are masses of arms hidden and camouflaged in safe areas waiting to be released by us to the commanders designated. In Oman there is a man called Mukhtar, who has lists of these arms. It's up to you to release them to the sections of the secret armies that need them."

"We're not generals, Sir Maurice."

"I daren't use a general, Doug. You'll find it easier than you think. Mukhtar will be of immense help. He could do it, but I can't guarantee that he won't do secret deals along the line and we need all there is. You two are the symbol of fair play. They won't argue with you, for if they do you give them nothing. The power will lie in your hands. Listen, take heed of Mukhtar, and use your common sense."

"How do we release them?"

"Mukhtar has release certificates. The quantities and type of arms are to be written in. There is a coded release to insert which Mukhtar will give you."

"You trust this guy?"

"When he's under control. He has vast experience and contacts. But he needs the rein of your presence. He's still answerable to you and he knows it. When that's done he will help you cross to Iran where another group will meet you. From there you go to the Russian border in the north-east of Iran. *You do not cross the border*—we cannot let you fall into Russian hands. Before the group goes over make sure that they know how best to use the explosive. Pass on the knowledge Brown gave you about the oil pipe line. Teach them how to do it. Their methods can be rough. What we want is success. Teach them all you know, and remember every bit of Brown's advice. Organise them. Questions?"

There seemed little point. They'd have more questions than they could cope with once they were in the Middle East.

"No? Then you'd better go. I'll walk you over to the plane."

When they reached the steps of the R.A.F V.C.10, Higgs said, "This is a deadly seriou business. We want you both to be successfu and to return."

The same thought occurred to both of them. Neither voiced it.

Like hell you do.

Rogov and Panovich drove back to the older building in Dzerzhinsky Square. Once in his office Rogov rang for coffee. He went behind his desk but did not sit down. When mentally agitated he invariably stood and, because he did, Panovich stood also. Rogov roamed behind his desk, hand raised, forefinger up to emphasise his points. "Wilson and Shearer openly had lunch with Brown." He suddenly interrupted his own thoughts. "You know, Panovich, these oil giants cause enough trouble, but let us be grateful that they haven't the Cubans to run around for them." He stood still for a moment. "They had lunch openly, yet at any other time they have been protected. Isn't that so?"

Panovich made sure he got it right. "We *think* they went to Surrey. We don't know. We only know that each time we have tried to follow them we have been stopped. We *think* they were in Libya—the bodyguards' description fits them—but Kawar is proving something less than a friend. We cannot be sure."

"In other words, it begins to fit. You'l have to do much better, Panovich."

"It's not easy. Comrade General. Higgs knows we are watching. What makes it so difficult is that D.I.6 is watching them, too so we have to tread very carefully."

"Watching or guarding?"

"Perhaps both. They left their hotel next morning in a closed car."

"You don't know where they went?"

"No."

"Yet we are allowed to witness them dine with Brown at the Savoy. What is Higgs up to?"

"Perhaps he wants us to believe it's abou oil when it's not."

"And perhaps he wants us to believe they're operating for the massive oil combines when they're not. You say Wilson has a girl friend? What about her? Has Shearer a wife?"

"She left him some time ago."

"It might be better to work on the woman."

Panovich looked doubtful.

Rogov growled. He pulled his chair back but still did not sit down. "You know Panovich, my feeling is that we should issue descriptions to the P.L.O. right through the Middle East."

"You think they could be so important?"

Rogov accepted that the question was not a challenge; Panovich was simply testing his line of thought.

"Two men. The British have an aptitude for the low profile and for using a minimum of numbers. They haven't the resources of ourselves or the Americans. I think, on the issue I am beginning to believe is at stake, that Higgs and Marshall would be forced to use an absolute minimum for security reasons. We haven't had a whisper back from any of our implants throughout Europe or in America. That can only mean there is nothing to come back, or that Higgs and Marshall are dealing with it exclusively. Don't underrate the size of the American back-up these two agents would have. If we could get hold of one of those two we'd have the truth very quickly."

"I'll get the P.L.O. on the job at once."

"And don't ever forget that the death of Rachid was well executed. They're aiming very high, Panovich. We *must* stop them. We've already lost out in Libya."

# 7

THE plane flew above the Gulf of Aqaba to the Red Sea, a bright blue cucumber strip beneath them.

The seats were utilitarian, with little cabin comfort. The crew had supplied flask tea and sandwiches; that was all. The two men were left to doze and to think.

Shearer was worried. The Red Sea finished at the Gulf of Aden, and that held the People's Democratic Republic of Yemen: controlled by Russians and East Germans. The Red Sea also narrowed to a bottleneck at its base. To deviate only slightly one side or the other meant flying over South Yemen or Somalia. Both were communist.

In Aden, the capital of South Yemen, the Russians had cruisers and destroyers in harbour. Nuclear submarines were there, as were T34 and T54 tanks and Ilyushin bombers and MiGs; Russian pilots and crews. The East Germans had a torture chamber full of electrical gadgets. And there were Cuban troops everywhere. All this next door to the country from which he and Wilson were to start out. Oman had a few old R.A.F. aircraft and a few hundred British troops and military advisors. It was true, the Americans had developed a naval base there, but the Omanis had insisted on restrictions; it was a foothold in comparison to the military might down the coast.

Wilson noticed Shearer's agitation and it temporarily took his mind off his own problems. The plane banked noticeably. Sea and sand filled the window view.

Wilson leant across Shearer to peer out but the angle wasn't good. The plane had levelled out and was now heading for the Saudi coastline. Wilson transferred his gaze to the starboard side. The sea was still immediately below; he knew how pleased he would be when finally they had land under them. He could see the tiny image of a ship. Ahead was a coastline, dun-coloured in the sun. The heat below could be sensed even at this height. They seemed to be moving slowly.

At the altitude they were flying land height could be deceptive. It seemed flat, but as they crossed the coast what appeared to be foot-hills were in fact a long coastal strip of mountains which stretched just inland down to the Gulf of Aden.

As the plane whined on Shearer lost some of his apprehension. He'd been behind a desk too long. The pilot knew what he was doing, and it was not long before both men had the feeling that the plane had been detached from all semblance of life. Below them the landscape was vast and frighteningly lifeless: mile upon mile of nothing. They were too high to pick out the sparse number of oases. Once they caught a suggestion of movement and saw the minuscule shadow of their own plane moving like an ant over the sand.

Shearer sat back, not satisfied but at least reconciled. They were flying over the Ar Rub Al Khali. The Empty Quarter. With or without permission no longer mattered.

They maintained height until they were over the Oman border, then dropped like a stone. It was descent all the way now and the plane was scudding above the uninviting barren hills towards the Gulf coast. They crossed the coastline into the Gulf of Oman. Ahead was Iran, but they circled over the sea and came back in to land at Muscat.

It was as though nobody knew of them or

wanted them. A ground crew trundled up some steps and the two men went down them on to an apron that looked like part of the Empty Quarter. The heat was blistering. Wilson was holding his nose and blowing, trying to remove the pressure from his ears. They stood there waiting, but it was clear that nobody was going to meet them.

"Great," said Shearer in disgust. In the distance were the usual low airport buildings. They walked towards them, carrying their grips, loosening their ties with free hands. After the London weather they were sweating within a few steps.

As they neared the buildings, Shearer noted an Anglo/French Jaguar aircraft. Further away was a near-obsolete Hunter. He spotted a Strikemaster and a B.A.C. 111 transport. One helicopter. It might not be all, of course, but he could not help reflecting on the pathetic showing in comparison with what he knew the Russians to have in the adjoining South Yemen.

They went through the nearest open door and were stopped by uniformed Omanis for a customs and passport check. An R.A.F. flight lieutenant detached himself from a group of Arabs. "You the radar chaps? Shouldn't have landed here. You're wanted at the Salalah air base on the Dhofar coast."

"They didn't give us parachutes, mate, or we'd have dropped off."

"The sand's soft enough for a free fall. Can't get you down there until tomorrow, though." The young officer smiled. "Follow me. Put you up for the night."

As they followed the officer he called back over his shoulder. "There's an outside chance we may be able to fly you down before sundown but don't bank on it. Wait in here while I find out where you're quartered for the night if you have to stay." He opened a door and they went in.

A traditionally-dressed Omani was standing by a window. As they entered he closed the shutters so that the daylight was halved and the view cut off. Bars of bright sunlight made a grid across desk and chairs.

"Sit down, gentlemen." He was British-educated and softly spoken. The Omani stroked his beard thoughtfully. "I apologise for the lack of reception. It had to be that way. The arrival of technical advisors is not uncommon, though most are nearer the Yemeni border at Salalah. The flight lieutenant believes you to be exactly what he called you." He gestured again to the chairs. "Please. Welcome."

He sat down at the side of the desk so that all three men were close together. "The Sultan himself would have liked to see you, but you will understand he does not want to draw attention to you. Palestinians are everywhere, which is why you were granted no privileges. The Sultan sends his deepest regrets."

He spread his hands apologetically. "We are a small country by oil standards. Out there"—he pointed in the rough direction of the Gulf—"a tanker passes along the whole length of our coastline every eighteen minutes. We are flanked by trouble, and we no longer have the British Special Air Service who were of such enormous help against the Marxist guerrillas of South Yemen.

"Even so, we manage. We are not cowards, but you understand why officially we must keep out of what you are doing. I can pass you on to others. No more."

The Omani had spoken with truth and dignity. The political pressures on them were enormous. If Russia seized control of the Gulf what then would be the fate of a tanker every eighteen minutes?

The Omani rose and held out his hand to Wilson and Shearer in turn, a limp handshake in the occidental way. "It's important that we are not seen together." He picked up the telephone and spoke rapidly and low.

Within a minute there was a polite tap on the door. Nobody entered. The Omani said, "You leave now. Go with the person outside. Allah be with you."

They reached a humble villa they had been allocated near the sea on the fringes of the town. Palm trees grew from crude holes in the crumbled concrete of a rough-walled yard. Broken flowerpots littered the yard; in a few, along one wall, cacti grew.

The rooms were small, the atmosphere close. An old Arab, his face creased from wind, sun and dehydration, took their grips into two separate bedrooms where there were old-fashioned, brass-knobbed beds. There was one bigger room, with a wide, open verandah which faced the sea; already the twinkle of lights could be seen from dhows and larger ships. They stood and watched the distant blaze of lights from a massive tanker.

The old Arab servant was called "Farid", the only information he was able to convey to them after a long struggle in Arabic. He cooked them a meal of rice with meatballs which they ate with their fingers from a communal bowl. They were hungry, but also they realised the urgent necessity of fitting into their environment.

As soon as it was dark Farid closed every shutter in the villa. Air could get in through the slats and the outside gauze but no one could see in. After the first mugginess the air slowly cooled. They sat in low chairs and studied the duplicated lists the man called Mukhtar had given them in the car which he had driven here. They had washed and had eaten but they were tired, unwilling to concentrate on the lists. Until they started to read them.

They did so quickly, flicking over the stapled pages, unable to believe what they were reading. The inventory had been carefully arranged in catchment areas.

"This is bloody stupid." Wilson threw his list down.

"Go through it," said Shearer, not looking up.

"There's no point. I'm in over my head."

"Just read it."

"They must be mad to saddle us with this.

It's out of my league." Wilson stood up angrily, pointing to the discarded list on the tiled floor. "There're millions of pounds worth of arms there. How would I know how to cope? It needs a military mind."

"You were in the British army, weren't you?"

Wilson suddenly laughed. "Sure. A warrant officer in the Commandos. They need a brigadier general at least."

"Read it, Ray." When Wilson still refused Shearer added, "And then leave everything to me."

"You'll cope with it?"

"I'll cope with it."

Wilson pointed to the list. "Machine-guns, submachine-guns, automatic rifles, grenades, explosive. Thousands of the bloody things. Millions of rounds of ammo. Even tanks, for God's sake. Transport, gun carriers, spares. There's enough for a major war, spread around. In Iraq, Iran, an offshore tanker. All pugged up and ready to go." He aimed a kick at the list and missed.

"Leave it to me."

Wilson sat down broodily. He snatched the list from the floor and disconsolately went through it. It became meaningless, the enormity of it totally confusing. Every item had a maker's name and approximate date of manufacture was submitted with each batch. They must have been accumulating for years, waiting for the day. *If* they still existed; if they hadn't been plundered. How could such an enormous quantity of arms, even though split up into several areas, be hidden from inquisitive eyes or kept safe from the sticky fingers of greedy men who must realise the enormous wealth it could bring? And why were he and Shearer dealing with them when there must be others more qualified?

"You weren't kidding when you said that London was your patch." Shearer was watching Wilson's agony of mind.

"Higgs is raving mad." Wilson shook his head in resignation. "But we don't get marks for knowing why he's using us instead of an arms agent."

"I keep telling you. *I know*. Impressive, ain't it?" Shearer was smiling slightly, for the moment enjoying his ascendancy. Wilson was a strategist and basically a loner.

The first man to arrive was the diminutive, lively Mukhtar, dressed now in Western garb.

"Mukhtar the Magnificent" they were to

call him later and they were soon to realise his value. They did not discover his surname. He was a link man of considerable experience who clearly Higgs had decided not to trust completely. He spoke adequate English with an atrocious accent and he understood it better than he spoke it. He talked in a bird-like way, picking quickly at his words as if they were seeds he sometimes missed.

It was he who explained what would happen, he who brought the blank release documents for the arms, he who explained that the arms would stay where they were without the coded releases. These documents were typed on plain, high-quality paper, which Wilson examined against the lightbulb.

"A water mark," he exclaimed in disgust. "It might as well be a trade mark. Look at this."

Shearer rose to look. A special job. The water mark was an oil rig elaborately etched. If supplied by an oil company would they be so careless? Or was someone deliberately pointing things that way?

Mukhtar talked of the arms dispassionately as if he'd been organising wars all his life; he probably had. He did not need to refer to the lists to understand the general magnitude o what they contained. Shearer began to feel superfluous and said so.

"No, sir. We need you. You are boss. With you, no problems. They know me as arms dealer who did deals during Iraqi invasion before and will expect me doing deals again. I will not, of course, but I understand their feelings. You are not Arab. You represent the West, money behind arms. They will accept what you say. They know the power that stands behind you and they know that this time they go all the way."

The shrunken face screwed into a yellow, long-toothed grin. "You understand? I can help, advise, but the moment I tell them what to do they would be suspicious. If they do not agree with you they are finished; their war is over before it begins."

Shearer said uneasily, "Let's hope they are not suspicious of each other."

"Please do not worry. Some other Arab nations are embarrassed by what is being done under the name of Islam. They have a shadow government ready."

"Can a revolutionary army win?"

"Oh, yes. With this support. Provided *foreign* troops do not set foot in Iran. If that happened the country would unite in a com-

139

mon hysteria. The armies sheltered by Ira
have been ready for a very long time. Thi
time the job will finish."

"Okay. Who's calling?"

Mukhtar was sitting crossed-legged. Fo
one so active it was a strange position an
most animation came from his arms. His eye
too were bright and lively and his fac
changed shape with each expression. H
broke it down for them. "Three men only
General Dajani, who is commander-in-chie
of the whole campaign. One of the Shah's ol
generals. And two high-ranking subordinate
One is a Kurd, Rahid, who will command th
north-western front. General Dajani will tak
the middle sector, and the third man th
south-western sector. It is merely a matter c
priorities, of best distribution and effective
ness of arms."

"What about east and north-east?"

"The Russian border. That is where w
will go to blow up their pipe line."

"You don't think that will provoke th
Russians?"

"Since when have the Russians neede
provoking? If they see opportunity they wi
take it regardless of what the rest of the worl
think. All we can do is to show they are not a

140

invulnerable as they think they are. Keep them occupied as long as possible. Give them a real problem."

"We'll need help and explosive."

"Of course. I will be with you, but a Kurd will lead our group."

"They know the odds?"

Mukhtar smiled. "The Kurds have been fighting the odds all their lives."

"Opposition to the main forces?"

"The Iranian army will split its loyalties once it has suffered defeat and is under pressure. It did so before. The army is schizoid—it can be fermented one way or the other. Once it breaks up, again as it did before, it will be over."

"The worst of it."

Mukhtar shrugged wearily. "It will take years to sort out. Perhaps not in my lifetime but at least with a new situation the oil, with Western help again, will be flowing properly, and if the Russians move against the oil countries they will know that America will have to come in to survive and World War Three will start."

Shearer held out a hand. "You've been a great help, Mukhtar. Now we need your advice on distribution."

It had been tortuous at times, Mukhtar's choice of words, or absence of them. But he had always stopped or corrected himself to ensure that, in the end, the right sense came out, that there could be no possible misunderstanding. The little Arab had proved to be an asset that London and Washington must have cultivated over a long period.

During the whole of this time Wilson had said nothing. He was content to let Shearer do the talking, but notwithstanding, he was impressed by Mukhtar's grasp of what was a complicated subject. While not relishing the difficulties of complex organisations of scattered armies he had been fascinated by Mukhtar's appraisal: the Arab had a firm understanding of the problems, if not their solution.

When the three commanders arrived each was solemnly introduced to Wilson and Shearer, each shook hands, and one by one they squatted round the walls, their backs against it. All were bearded; their dress was an assortment of traditional and Western. But that did not matter.

These men were dedicated. They had been waiting for this day as if it would never come. They had been promised arms before and had been let down, and when they hadn't been there had never been enough. There was something of restraint in eyes that had seen it all, and behind them justifiably lurked the thought that this might be one more let-down. They were attentive in a relaxed but suspicious way, but they were hopeful too. Was this the moment?

All eyes were on the two Westerners. These two men were the power that could set war moving. Everything depended on their say-so. The arms were there, mostly under the protection of the Iraqis. All that was needed was for these two men to set them free. And once more Wilson and Shearer shared the thought of why such power had not been given to more qualified men.

Wilson and Shearer could feel it. The concentration on them was unwavering and intense. They were suddenly aware that, through delegation, they might be holding the fate of a country in their hands. It was a new sensation. Neither cared for it, and each wondered if he were up to it. It made no difference. The situation existed even if it overawed them. They squatted as the others did.

Shearer said, "Do you all speak English?"

They assured him they did.

"Okay. The maps?"

Mukhtar unrolled a map of Iran which showed the bordering countries, Russia, Turkey, Iraq, Afghanistan and Pakistan. It displayed the Gulf, the Gulf of Oman, through which tankers were passing even now, and the Arabian Sea. All oil fields, land and offshore, were marked clearly.

This was a political map, showing boundaries. Mukhtar was yet to use a physical map, showing the terrain they had to conquer.

Shearer asked each man in turn about his own particular forces, where they were waiting, how many, what arms. Each man said his piece, sometimes, when his English faltered, through Mukhtar who would improve it slightly.

Knives had been placed on the four corners of the map like paperweights to stop the edges from curling. With his arms list in his hand, Shearer started talking. While he talked, slowly, emphatically, Wilson studied the faces one by one and decided he would not want to make an enemy of these men. All eyes were on Shearer as if they were willing him to put a foot wrong. The silence, beyond

144

Shearer's voice, was total. It was broken once by a ship's siren in the Gulf. Nobody seemed to notice.

Wilson, listening to the American, knowing the pressure, the personal lack of preparation, the enormity of what he was handling, could not but respect him. Shearer had grasped the situation and computed its problems with evident acumen.

It was late when they finished. There had been no haggling. It was evident that General Dajani not only had overall control but also the respect of the others. As it was there were more arms available than they had expected. Their dream was in sight.

There was a bright light in their eyes when they left. They ghosted away, as carefully and as singly as they had come, leaving a feeling that the meeting had never happened. Shearer knew that it had. He felt depleted and worried.

"You did all right," said Wilson grudgingly.

Shearer rose shakily. "I told you I'd handle it," he said. "And your turn will come."

There was still work to do. The release papers had to be apportioned. Quickly as Mukhtar worked, it took time. Eventually each one went through the releases, and finally Wilson and Shearer endorsed them with the code. They would be handed to emissaries of the generals in Iran.

"It's like signing our own death warrant,' commented Wilson wearily.

They needed sleep but there could be no rest. They took their guns from their grips, a Colt for Shearer, a Browning for Wilson— their individual flag-carrying went that far— and strapped them on.

It was too late and too far to leave for Iran that night. There weren't sufficient hours of darkness left. In any event Mukhtar pointed out that Muscat was not the best place from which to leave. Instead they would travel by coastal road to Shinas near the border of the United Arab Emirates. And from there by fast launch to the tiny club-shaped peninsula of the second part of Oman which separated The Gulf from the Gulf of Oman. It was also the nearest point to Iran.

They switched off all lights and left the villa by the back door. There was a door set into the cracked wall of the yard but Mukhtar led them to the opposite side where the flowerpots stood. Some were huge, two or three feet in height. Mukhtar, small and nimble, climbed onto the wide rim of one of these to reach for the top of the wall.

Wilson and Shearer watched and felt the danger around them. If Mukhtar was taking this kind of precaution there had to be good reason; the little Arab had courted danger all his life. They saw Mukhtar pull himself up, a dull outline on the top of the wall.

A shot thundered beyond the wall as Mukhtar was about to jump down to the other side. The Arab swayed, steadied, then fell outwards clutching his middle.

# 8

SHEARER sprinted to the end of the wall, hurled himself at the top, gripped, swung and rolled over in one continuous movement. Wilson, noting his direction, had raced to the other end.

Shearer landed with surprising lightness. He dismissed the inclination to go to the aid of the crumpled Mukhtar; Wilson was much nearer to the Arab.

For perhaps three seconds he stood still, gun now in hand. There was no moon but trillions of stars shone brighter than lanterns. They were not far from the twinkling lights of Muscat, but visibility was poor. The back-cloth was a rugged barrier of rocks and sand. Tall and squat palm trees formed an irregular line, only just visible, the fronds stationary. To his left was the sea, hidden by a continuing line like some darkened, gigantic rockery.

Of one thing Shearer was certain: to shoot anyone in this light meant close range. A rifle would have been no good without night sights and the shot had sounded near. He heard

Wilson at the other end of the wall. It was what he wanted. Someone took advantage of the sound Wilson made and Shearer picked up just the faintest of noises ahead and to his right, roughly midway between Wilson and himself.

He raced forward, crouched and light-footed, knowing that he had the wall cutting out any possibility of silhouette. He had difficulty over the rocks and had no idea how far they went but he kept moving, pausing occasionally for the barest split-second to listen to the sound of scurrying panic ahead of him.

The ground began to even. He saw the repeated flash of passing headlights and realised that he was heading for a road that curved away from his sight. Momentarily he caught sight of a shape ahead of him, just a blur. As oncoming traffic reached the bend, headlights swept the wasteland. He ducked quickly each time.

There was little traffic, just the isolated car, but he did not want to be seen. He was gaining rapidly now, and the man in front turned and fired wildly. Another pair of headlamps picked out a parked car which had no lights on. After the beams flashed past

Shearer saw the parking lights of the stationary car come on, then the dipped headlights. The man was running towards it, and the fringe of the beams picked him out.

Shearer quickly saw that he would lose him, not because of distance between them which he had narrowed considerably, but because the car represented more enemies, and his lungs were already searing. Anger drove him on. He stopped, dropped to a crouch, waited for the dipped beams to pick out the now-slowing form more clearly, aimed two-handed, held his shaky breath, and fired twice. The man fell flat, arms flailing. He did not move.

Shearer flattened himself on the ground, gun held out. By lying prone he had lost some vision but he could still see most of the car. Out of range of the lamps shining across the uneven, gorse-covered waste ground obliquely to him, he waited. If a car door opened on his side he'd see it. There was still no movement from the man he had shot.

It became a waiting game until the next vehicle, the next sweep of beams picked out the stationary car. Possibly it worried its passenger, for a few seconds later the engine started and the car moved off.

Still Shearer waited. When the road was empty again, the darkness back, he rose and took a circuitous route to where the man had fallen. It was difficult to gauge the position. The ground was a mixture of hard sand and gorse. Headlamps finally, and briefly, showed the hump, gorse clumps shadowed in porcupine spikes across the form.

Shearer advanced cautiously. He had no flashlight and he couldn't see the man's gun. He approached ready to fire at the slightest move. He crouched, rammed his gun at the base of the spine and with his other hand groped for the man's wrist. There was no pulse.

Shearer sat back on his heels and cursed. He looked around, got direction, waited for another car to pass. He lifted the body, obtained a fireman's grip and started back for the villa. The rocks were difficult and he had to take a chance to call out to Wilson before the Englishman might decide to fire.

Wilson had Mukhtar sitting up against the wall.

"Is he okay?" asked Shearer as he clambered down.

"He says he is. But he's stopped one. He's in pain."

"This one's not." Shearer dropped the body at their feet, and searched it, finding nothing that identified.

"A pity he's dead." Wilson had padded a wound in Mukhtar's side.

"He lost a lot of blood?" Shearer bent the other side of Mukhtar.

"I think so. Difficult to tell. We'd better find a hospital."

"No." Even the single word was painful for Mukhtar. "I'll be all right." He gathered strength again. "There's a car. I'll direct you. We must get away from here."

"Okay, but you need attention." Shearer was worried.

"I've been shot and knifed before. There's no time."

For Mukhtar's sake they did not argue. Shearer helped Wilson climb the wall to retrieve the grips from the yard. Wilson rejoined the others and, with Shearer's help, lifted Mukhtar to his feet. The Arab was plucky. Realising they had the grips to carry he made the effort so that only a minimum of help was required from them. He gave them directions towards the sea.

Mukhtar's own precautionary measures now went against him for they had some

152

distance to walk before joining a side street off the main road. He refused Shearer's suggestion that they dump the grips, as he did not want the traceable ownership of them connected with a dead Palestinian. He also continued to refuse their pleas of getting him to a doctor. But it was increasingly obvious that he was making a supreme effort.

The car was parked behind a low derelict building. Mukhtar insisted on sitting in the front to give directions. Wilson drove.

It was after midnight and they had about two hundred miles to cover to the northern border. The road clung to the coast. Wilson drove well within himself, the Gulf of Oman to his right. They had the windows down, the humid air sweeping in. Once they were travelling at a steady seventy, Wilson said to Mukhtar, "Why don't you get in the back. Lie down. I can't go wrong on this road."

But Mukhtar would not move and Wilson picked up a nuance of suspicion from the Arab's stubbornness. "You expecting trouble?" And when Mukhtar didn't reply, "Why are you doing this?"

"Money."

"It must be a helluva lot to put up with this."

"It's what I'm best at."

Noticing the effort, Wilson said no more. Mukhtar was in pain but his judgement was still cool.

Shearer, sitting in the rear, noticed Mukhtar's head moving. The Arab had his eye on his wing mirror and was giving the occasional glance over his shoulder. He said to Wilson, "He *is* expecting trouble."

"I know. You'd better be the eyes in the back of our heads."

Mukhtar smiled in the darkness. He put a hand against the dashboard to ease his position. "They will know we have to reach Iran. They might try to get us on the road."

"You keep quiet, matey. We'll keep our eyes skinned."

Wilson briefly turned his head and noticed the gun in Mukhtar's hand. He drew out his own and laid it on the driver's shelf. Shearer had also drawn his.

Yet the road was sparse of traffic and the further from Muscat the lonelier it became. Occasional headlights swept towards or came from behind them. The sea was a black, sluggish mass to their right, betrayed by the tang of salt and by the masthead lights of silent dhows and the streamer lights of tankers.

"This is it," observed Wilson drily. There was a car in front, slow in spite of the empty road.

"How'd you know?" Shearer was leaning over the front bench seat.

"He's too slow. Been waiting for us."

"What do you think?"

"I'll blind the bastard. Get a reaction." Wilson had been racing up on the car ahead. Now he braked, falling in behind it, full beams on. Mukhtar and Shearer had their guns ready.

The silhouettes of three men in the front car were quite visible as Wilson closed up. The driver adjusted his central mirror in an effort to cut out the blinding glare. But the reflection was also bursting from the wing mirrors as Wilson moved from side to side.

"I hope you're right," bawled Shearer.

"I'm right," said Wilson with certainty.

Mukhtar said nothing but was ready.

The front car suddenly accelerated but Wilson closed, holding his position, keeping the distance just right. When the other driver suddenly braked Wilson was ready for it. Tyres screamed. Wilson held on, Mukhtar gasped with pain.

The next step was foreseeable enough. The

155

speed settled again, two silhouettes moved to opposite windows and leaned out with guns. Wilson closed up, almost nose to tail, making the angle impossible for the gunmen to be in any way effective. They could neither see the gun flashes nor hear the gun cracks above the engine noise, but Mukhtar's wing mirror cracked as a bullet struck it.

"Satisfied?" said Wilson drily.

"Never doubted you," lied Shearer. "Now what?"

"Just be ready. On your left side. You too, Mukhtar."

Nothing happened for a while. The car in front tried swerving, swinging from side to side, but Wilson swung with it, dropping back a little, knowing that the erratic movement precluded accurate shooting. They tried braking again but Wilson was up to it.

The frustration of the other driver increased. He could be seen gesticulating and it seemed that all three were arguing as hands waved. Wilson knew the situation could not last. He could feel Mukhtar's anxious glance at him and Shearer had already expressed his doubt. "Be ready," he said again. "There's only one thing left for them to do short of crashing."

Wilson was just sufficiently behind to swerve if necessary. And then suddenly he stiffened and the others with him sensed it. The two gunmen were belatedly smashing their rear window with gun butts. Now was the moment. "Get them!" he bawled and swung out across the road as the gunmen poked their guns through the rear window.

Wilson accelerated with a tremendous burst, drew alongside, braked and held steady for Mukhtar and Shearer. It was out of his hands from then on. The other driver tried to pull away as Mukhtar and Shearer fired but Wilson had been expecting it and did not lose ground.

The crash he had been avoiding almost came. The other driver suddenly slumped and the car swung towards Wilson. He risked a touch of brake, swerved, braked again, and the other car hurtled in front, off the road and down the dip towards the sea. Wilson braked hard, tyres screaming, tail swinging. Timing it carefully, he turned the wheel and the tail swung round in a U-turn.

It was clear where the car had gone over. Its lights were still on, pointing down and out of sight, but the reflection filtered up from the dip. Wilson swung the car round so that they were facing north again, stopped, pulled on the handbrake, left the engine running, then dived from the car yelling at Mukhtar to stay where he was. Shearer was just ahead of him in getting out, having just inserted a new clip.

They separated by a few feet, then knelt at the edge of the road. The car was visible because of its lights but elsewhere it was pitch black. The road had been built high, stone falling away from its edge towards the sea which caught, and threw back, some of the headlamps' glow. Placid ripples quietly lapped the sandy shoreline, giving contrast to the horrible grind of the still-running engine.

Wilson and Shearer worked their way down either side of the car, which had fallen into a depression, its nose almost buried. The depression had saved it from the sea.

The two men flattened as they closed in. They crept up, one each side, the engine drowning any sound of their approach. To Wilson it sounded as if the fan was catching on its cowling where the radiator had struck. It was surprising the headlamps still worked.

On Shearer's side both front and rear passenger windows had been smashed by gun fire. It created opaque shields pitted with holes, from each of which spread webbed patterns. He kept slightly to the rear as he released the door catch and pulled. Nothing happened.

There was no further point in stealth. Wilson threw open the other rear door. He had a better initial view because the glass his side was uncracked apart from one hole where a bullet had gone right through. One man was slumped over the front seat as if he were searching for something. The second gunman was a dark heap on the floor between front and rear seats.

Shearer crept up to the driver's seat. The man had his head on the wheel, his arms hanging straight down, apelike. Even in the bad light Shearer could see the blood down his face, and then the source of it; he'd been shot through the head.

Wilson cautiously pulled at the man on the floor and there was a terrible moan. He called to Shearer, who leaned over the dead driver, to switch off the engine and to find the interior lights. Wilson was able to confirm that the man draped over the front seat was dead. Shearer came round to give him a hand with the remaining one who was still alive.

The man screamed as they each got hold of an arm and pulled. They closed their ears to his agony and dragged him onto the sand. He screamed again and swore in Arabic.

In the bad light they examined him as best they could. He'd been shot in the face and through one hand. A flashlight suddenly bore down and they jumped back in alarm. It was Mukhtar. He stood swaying, the light wavering about the prone body. They could all now see the bloodied froth on the lips of the gunman.

"This is the one who screamed?"

"The others are dead," said Shearer.

"We want information from him."

"He's almost dead. And in a lot of pain. You'll get nothing from him, old son."

Mukhtar propped himself up against the car. They thought he was going to fall forward but as they prepared to catch him he said, "Leave him to me." His tone was cold-blooded. They eyed him silently. The gunman was going to die, that much was obvious. Nor could he die painlessly—his low groans were escaping from the moving lips, part hidden by the welling froth. The question was, would he die in more pain than was necessary?

"Don't make it worse for him. He's finished anyway."

Mukhtar looked back at Shearer. He was still holding his side. "You will never get done what you have to do with that attitude." With the prospect of reprisal Mukhtar's voice had strengthened. "This is not London or New York. These lands are cruel by your standards. He will expect it. And I must do it."

They could have stopped him but they couldn't argue with his logic. It was by no means certain that Mukhtar himself would see the night out. Everything he had done since being shot had called on reserves unaccountable in one so small.

"Search him. Then leave me." What had happened to the slightly subservient tone Mukhtar had used at the outset? Even his words were falling into place better, his accent less tortuous, as if he knew that he could not waste the energy on mistakes and repetitions. To their surprise, Wilson and Shearer dropped to their knees without further argument and searched the dying Arab. That brought screams too and they found he'd been hit in the chest, his clothes soaked with blood. He was drawing in air from the wound in his lung which formed the pink froth on his mouth as it mixed with

161

blood. The man had nothing on him, not even a coin.

They rose and without speaking went to the car to search it. They had to pull the bodies out to make it easier. They were soon wishing they were miles away. The screams burst through their ears and they looked at each other as they knelt. They made no attempt to stop Mukhtar. Information *was* vital. These men *had* tried to kill, and had almost succeeded. They had to tell themselves this over and over, as they tried to shut out the screams that carried across the Gulf. This was how things were done here, and it would be done to them if they were caught.

Such common sense did not help. They finished as quickly as they could, finding nothing but road maps and odd scraps of paper. These they collected, then they climbed back to their own car.

They could still hear Mukhtar's harsh guttural demands as they reached the road. They believed they heard the last pitiful whimper of the wretch who was too far gone even to scream any more. When the headlamps went out behind them they knew they had.

In spite of their revulsion they felt compelled to go back and help Mukhtar. Perhaps, in his place, they might have done the same. They helped him up the slope and into the car, engine still ticking over, and drove off. Mukhtar had learned nothing.

They arrived at Shinas, near the border at four in the morning. Considering the hold-up the timing was good. On Mukhtar's instructions they drove on to a village just off the coast and almost on the border. He directed them to a house, low-slung and in an alley.

In the darkness the village appeared poor, the road narrow, a mixture of sand and stone. Wilson drew up, switched off the lights that had made a tunnel of dirty, plaster walls. They helped Mukhtar out, held him while he knocked three times on a rough wooden door which quickly opened a few inches. A lamp was held near the gap.

The lamp was put down and Mukhtar was being hugged, then helped into the house. Wilson and Shearer were ignored but nobody stopped them from entering. They followed a narrow, airless passage which held the smell of cheap cooking oil, into a room where mattresses were laid out. A woman, still adjusting her robe, stared uncertainly until she saw Mukhtar. Her face broke into a smile. She uttered sincere and quick greetings in Arabic. They lowered Mukhtar on to a mattress, still warm from the woman's body. Mukhtar had friends as well as enemies.

In the light of a pressure lamp the toll on Mukhtar could now be seen. Life seemed to be draining from him as if all his effort had led to this point. He lay back with eyes closed, his breathing shallow.

The man spoke to the woman who slipped on some sandals and, with an expression of apology to the two Westerners, left the room. The man turned and said something rapidly to them. Neither understood, and after a while it was clear that he spoke no English. He indicated they should sit down, but they'd been sitting for hours and remained standing. The man knelt beside Mukhtar, stroking his brow and muttering soft incantations.

There was nothing to do but wait. The car was still outside, a give-away if recognised, but neither Wilson nor Shearer knew where they might safely hide it. They were in the hands of Mukhtar for almost everything. If he died their lines of communication died with him. Which was why he had been shot. Without Mukhtar the whole project could collapse.

It was only minutes before the door opened

again. An Arab in a European suit preceded the woman; he was carrying a bag. A doctor. The man held the lamp while the woman boiled water. Feeling superfluous and confined in the small room, Wilson and Shearer went outside into the narrow, silent street and leaned against the wall, watching the stars reflect back dully on the dust-covered car.

The mood of escaping from the gunmen had gone and even that relief had been tempered by the cruelty of what had followed. They were despondent, and all too clearly saw the odds against them.

Wilson limped into the unfailing safe mental harbour of Jennie back in London. This time he didn't expect to see her again. She would have to stand without him, and from this distance he could understand how agonising that would be. His thoughts were not conceited but a realistic view of what would happen. Jennie would be heartbroken and would curse him for the financial legacy he would leave, when all she had ever wanted was himself.

Shearer stirred against the wall, the cheap distemper rubbing on to his jacket. He reflected quickly on his ruined marriage and then on Wilson and the uncertain future he had to face with him. The inevitability of their dying together was not easy to accept.

"Thinking of Jennie?" he asked.

"Yep. Doesn't do any good."

"No. Sorry you got into this?"

Wilson rolled on the wall to face Shearer. "That's a silly bloody question. Trapped into it. When I started I thought there was a way through the tunnel."

"Both ends are blocked."

"If we were like Mukhtar we wouldn't worry whether we lived or died."

"He worries. It's simply that the bastard doesn't know how to die. He'll do it when he's ready."

The door opened beside them and the doctor slipped out. He left it ajar and approached them. "I've got the bullet out. Did you hear anything?" His English was good.

"No. Why?"

"I had to probe." He tapped the house. "These walls are very thick. He needs a blood transfusion, but he won't go to hospital."

"Will he be okay?"

The doctor shrugged. "He's all skin and bone and sinew. And there's not much of that. But he's so tough, that one. His will is incredible. Anyway, you must judge for yourself. He wants you back in there. Perhaps you can talk him into resting. I must get back. Good luck."

They could talk Mukhtar out of nothing. His wound had been dressed and strapped up and he was sitting against the wall, his face pitted and pale like a dried fig. He looked weak, but then he always would. The fact that the doctor had treated him and removed the bullet had recharged his batteries. His rest was over. He insisted that they move off. They were behind schedule.

"We'd better get out of these clothes," said Shearer.

Mukhtar nodded. "It has not been forgotten. Follow Ahmed."

They were taken to another room, and by the light of an oil lamp took off their crumpled suits and slipped on djellabas and sandals. They returned to Mukhtar who had been helped up by the woman.

"You're crazy," said Shearer. "Not fit to move."

"I do not argue. I've told Ahmed to burn your clothes. He will do it."

It was an act of implicit faith when Ahmed

well needed the money he could have got for them. Ahmed and his wife saw them to the car; the farewell was emotional.

They drove to a completely deserted area on the coast. Wilson took the car as near to an old jetty as he could and from there they walked across soft, still-warm sand.

The jetty was long and narrow, two planks side by side, supported underneath by stanchions that needed reinforcing. It would have been easier had they been able to separate into single file but Mukhtar needed their help.

Reaching the end they eased Mukhtar down into a fair-sized launch and climbed down after him. Shearer took the wheel. Mukhtar told them the course and Shearer started her up and eased her out to sea. They had about sixty miles to travel to the northern section of Oman.

Wilson got Mukhtar into the cabin and was told where to find waterproof bags and submachine-gun. When he located them he searched for the makers' mark but could not understand it. He thought they were old Thompsons.

"PPD40s," explained Mukhtar. He managed a wry smile. "Ironic, you call it.

Russian. Old but good. Seventy-one rounds in the drum. Eight hundred rounds per minute. Velocity, one thousand six hundred feet per second." He drew his breath in sharply.

"You must know a lot about arms. And don't answer if it hurts."

Shearer, in the cockpit, had got the launch up to full speed, her bow lifted, the spray spattering back like crystals. All he could see ahead was blackness and he was using no lights.

Resting on the bench seat Mukhtar showed no sign that the motion upset him. And he wanted to talk a little.

"I can tell you the capability of all the small arms on the list from the French PMQs, to Italian Beretta M1938As, Spanish Laboras to Erma EMPs, Finnish Suomis to your own Sterlings. Mausers to Uzis. Old and new. I have dealt with arms all my life." Dedication for his subject came through as Mukhtar spoke, slowly and with long pauses. But he was coming to life again.

Wilson handed over the waterproof bags and Mukhtar carefully inserted the various arms releases, one to each bag, and sealed them. The Omani was a meticulous man.

Wilson familiarised himself with one of the Russian PPD40s, left three of them out on the seat, then joined Shearer in the cockpit.

At first he could see nothing after the light in the cabin. After a minute or two he picked out the luminous dials, and the phosphorescence of the bow wave flashing past. There was nothing else except the stars, as if the moon had taken a night off.

"It's uncanny," said Wilson. "I can't see a thing. Just black. And the pale edge around the boat. How long?"

"She's fast," said Shearer watching the dials. "A good boat. But it will take another two hours, maybe more."

"It'll be daylight when we get in."

"It'll be dawn any time now."

Minutes later the first wavering greyness appeared along the horizon to starboard. For the first time that night the sky showed signs of being prised from the sea.

Wilson stayed with Shearer as the sun pushed the changing dawn ahead of it, flooding both sky and sea with varying colours at first dull, then brilliant and breathtaking. Then the deep red cascade of the sun itself shivered on the horizon, beautiful, vacillating. It overflowed along the sea edge as if blood had been spilt and bleached the remnants of darkness from the sky.

"Compensation," observed Wilson.

"It's about all we're likely to get."

# 9

WHEN Wilson returned to the cabin Mukhtar was sleeping. Wilson went back into the cockpit and he and Shearer talked the time away. Neither had slept, yet tiredness had left them as if they had gained a second breath against fatigue. Yesterday morning they had been in London.

As the knots ticked off Shearer needed new directions and Wilson reluctantly roused Mukhtar. But the little Arab awoke instantly. He and Shearer pored over the chart, got their bearing and bore well to port. Mukhtar had obviously gained from his short sleep.

The coastline wavered into sight some twenty minutes later, partially hidden by the morning haze which hung above it like thin cloud. And through this cloud there was a sudden burst of expanding flame and smoke that continued high before mushrooming. They all heard the explosion even above the engine noise.

"What the bloody hell is that?"

They were gazing forward but it was Mukhtar who had to grab for support. When the others turned to him they were startled to see how grey his face had gone. Mukhtar's obvious shock was the only indication that the explosion might in some way be connected with them. He made no explanations and soon recovered his poise. But for some minutes he gripped the rail for support and his face remained drawn. "Hide the guns." Mukhtar's voice was terse. Wilson went into the cabin and locked the PPD40s away.

Guided by Mukhtar, Shearer eased the launch into a small harbour filled with dhows, fishing boats, a small yacht or two and rowing boats. Most were moored to buoys, others were alongside the small quay. Shearer swung in near the shallow steps, took a rope and climbed up to the quay, mooring the launch to a bollard. He called down for Wilson to climb forward and drop two plastic balls between the boat and the sea wall. He helped Mukhtar up the few steps.

The reason for the empty quay was obvious. About half a mile inland was the billowing aftermath of the explosion they had seen.

"Wait in the launch." Mukhtar was back in command again.

"You're going to see what's happened? Alone?" Shearer looked across at Wilson, seeking support to stop the Arab.

"They will see you as strangers. Your eyes are not Arab eyes. People may have been killed. They will look for culprits. Please wait in the boat. The quay will not stay empty. You will find food in the lockers."

They watched him go, for they knew he was right. He had coped so far.

A cluster of Arab shops, not yet open, lined the back of the quay. They were almost holes in the walls. Behind them a small, dusty township spread out. Two laden camels were led behind the quay. Another camel was in an open shed to the left of where Wilson and Shearer stood. The beast was fixed to a horizontal pole which came out from a central axis, and he went round and round endlessly, turning a huge grinding stone. To prevent dizziness the beast was blindfolded. Here this kind of treatment was accepted: a matter of priorities, human or animal. The terms could be harsh for both.

As Wilson and Shearer made themselves watch their thoughts were similar. They too were bound to a treadmill from which there was no escape. When they turned to board the launch Mukhtar had disappeared behind the buildings.

They went through the lockers systematically. They found tinned meat and vegetables, coffee, and two jerrycans of water which they boiled in a copper kettle on a small, single-ringed primus. There were mugs and plates, forks but no knives, sugar but no milk.

They cleared up, keeping the empty cans for later disposal but wrapping them to stave off the rising flies.

As the heat began to build up confinement to the launch became more difficult. The small cabin was stifling and the deck a hot plate for the rising sun. The sea shimmered, reflected, threw back the heat and the harbour began to turn into a steam bath. Flies searching for food found moisture in the sweat of the two men's arms, necks and faces.

Both Shearer and Wilson had considered it safer to remain in the cabin with door open and small windows drawn back. But there was no breeze, no answer to the sweltering sun. They took a bench seat each and tried to sleep. Sweat flooded from them almost immediately and soon their clothes were soaked. There was no rest, no peace from the flies, and instead of feeling better they felt worse.

They longed for the comparative coolness of evening, still hours away. Deprived of sleep and cleanliness, forced to endure the acute discomfort of increasingly oppressive heat, and condemned to what they were doing, they had no alternative but to suffer it. They began to bicker.

Wilson wiped his face again on a towel already wet from sweat.

Shearer was grinning. "Interesting to know we have the same dodgy parenthood." There had been a short stage where they had called each other bastard incessantly.

Wilson laughed. "Before this is over we might know the difference between English bastards and American bastards."

"About three to six thousand miles, at a guess. I wonder if Mukhtar has gone to a mosque or something. His wound hasn't stopped him dropping to his knees in prayer at the allotted hour."

"I hope he puts one in for me, mate."

The activity around the quay and in the harbour had increased considerably. Boats were moving in and out. The launch must

ave been noticed as a new arrival and the
wo agents felt more keenly the necessity to
tay in the cabin. They began to worry about
he Omani. He had now been away for over
our hours.

When Mukhtar finally returned he came
board so quietly they did not hear him. As
oon as he entered the cabin they could see
omething was radically wrong. He seemed to
ave shrunk even further, a diminutive
uppet with some of the strings missing. The
nergy that had always surfaced through his
lark eyes had faded. They helped him to a
ench seat but it was an act of consideration
ather than one he wanted.

He raised a hand helplessly.

"We should have sheltered in a house
oday. Slept. Eaten. Washed. Refreshed our-
elves for the night journey to Iran. The
ouse was blown up—two more alongside it.
They used far too much explosive for such a
mall job."

"We'll rough it here, mate."

Mukhtar looked up tirelessly. "My friends
nd my brother went up with it. There was
othing left of them but chunks of flesh and
hreds of cotton. No heads, no arms; just
its."

177

They realised then the depth of his feelings; he was too proud to show them.

There was nothing they could say. They sa down opposite him, separated by a fixed plastic-topped table on which their coffee mugs still stood.

"Who are 'they'?" asked Shearer after a pause.

It was the best remedy for Mukhtar—ge his mind back on the job, fill it with the need for revenge. Mukhtar flattened his hands on the table: dehydrated flesh formed valleys for the veins. He shrugged. "Palestinians. They are agitating through the Arab world. Someone has warned them, but not in time for them to be completely organised. There must be lack of communication. I think two things they thought we would be in the house, and that we probably arrived in the night."

"It means they know you, your brother and friends. That's not so good, Mukhtar."

"Everyone knows me. Killing me doesn't help them. They would only kill me if they knew I was involved in a specific plot against them."

"What we're doing is not specifically against them."

"They have been told to do it."

"Who by?"

"Moscow—who else? They would not do it without instructions."

Wilson and Shearer felt cold in spite of the heat. If the Russians knew, they were fighting on all fronts. They couldn't win.

Suddenly Wilson said, "We're sorry about your brother and your friends."

It came out unexpectedly and at the right time.

Mukhtar reached across the table and grasped a hand from each of them. "Thank you." He sat back. "They know we go to Iran. They don't know where."

"Will they have seen you?" Shearer asked.

"We haven't shown ourselves since you left this morning, but binoculars could have picked us out."

Mukhtar agreed. "We must assume that they have seen me."

"Will they attack us here?"

"By now they will know they failed. They might try again, but in the harbour it is more open, more difficult for them."

"Except at night, I guess."

"We move out of harbour as soon as it's dark."

"That leaves an attack at sea."

179

Mukhtar nodded gravely. "No trace."

Shearer said, "Have you still got contacts here?"

"What do you want?"

"Limpet mines. Diving gear. One full cylinder will do. Flippers, mouthpiece. Don't worry about the suit. No time, and the water's warm."

"A *mine*?"

"Can you lay your hands on one?"

"I wish I had known in Muscat."

"So do I. Can you get it or not?"

"I must go back on shore."

"I'm sorry about that. I don't fancy putting out to sea with the thought that some bastards with more fire-power are going to sink us."

Mukhtar rose unsteadily. Wilson asked, "Will you be safe?"

"In daylight, yes. I still have many friends out there."

"Do you need us?"

"No. Stay out of sight. I will have help. I have arranged for petrol." He turned to Shearer. " 'Gas', as you call it, and some other supplies." He stopped by the door. "We were to change boats. It will be here in the harbour somewhere loaded and ready, but my brother would have kept the knowledge to himself. To make enquiries could be disastrous. Now we must continue in this."

"This is okay," said Wilson.

"But they will know it by now." Mukhtar looked at Shearer. "Limpet mines? The diving equipment is no problem. There is diving along the coast. Coral and tropical fish."

He was gone so long they began to worry again. The sun was sinking, an orange flare in the west. The heat had decreased too, but their clothes felt as if they had been dipped in lukewarm water.

They were alerted by the sound of the rattling of cans. They looked out to see a dilapidated van with wooden sides crossing the uneven quay. There was a string of cans tied at the rear. Steam escaped from under the rusted bonnet. In the driving seat sat Mukhtar.

Three bare-legged Arabs carried supplies down to the cockpit and returned to the van after a quick interchange with Mukhtar, who started the launch engine. One of his friends cast off from the bollard and Mukhtar let the rope trail in the water while he went slow astern. It was clear from his actions that he still wanted Wilson and Shearer to stay out of sight.

The launch swung in an arc, and Mukhtar headed slowly out to sea, the sun following across the surface like a creeping flame. Still in sight of land they swung to starboard, south, in the direction from which they had come. The sun slipped away spreading its glow across the sky. But the twilight would be brief. So near to the coast there was a reasonable amount of inshore traffic, any one car of which might be interested in them.

It wasn't until it was dark that Mukhtar joined the others in the cabin, having locked on course. When the reverse might be expected it was clear that his continuing action had restored some life into him. Rest was something for others. It seemed that he had completely forgotten his wound, though it must have continued to be painful. He told them what he immediately wanted done and they went into the cockpit.

Because they were still travelling south, away from Iran, the navigation lights were on and so, too, were the cabin lights with the curtains drawn. Wilson climbed forward to pull up the plastic ball fenders and fastened them on deck. He pulled in the trailing rope and rolled it.

They switched off the engine and Shearer filled the fuel tanks from the jerrycans the van had brought. Because space was cramped they filled the emptied cans with sea water and let them sink. The fuel was timely; the tanks had been almost empty. By the time they had finished they had two full cans in reserve. Oil was checked. The engine was restarted, Wilson taking the wheel while Shearer and Mukhtar went into the cabin.

Mukhtar laid a crude sack on the table. Grain scattered over the surface and Shearer blew the chaff away. The Arab groped in the sack with some care. Item by item, he laid them on the table, looking at Shearer as he did so, noting the blank disappointment on the American's face.

"This it?" asked Shearer. "This all you could get?"

"I was unable to get a limpet mine. I need time and much of that we have already lost. I'm sorry."

Shearer gazed along the row which Mukhtar had carefully arranged. He did not at first touch anything. Then he said, "Plastic explosive, a couple of detonators, fuse wire, a couple of clocks. Great. What am I supposed to do with them?"

"Make a time bomb. Our people do it all the time."

Shearer resisted a smile. "Under water?"

"I have electrical wire. A battery. You can't do it?"

Shearer did not reply for some time. Eventually he said, "You got any more of those waterproof bags? Big ones? And nails and a hammer?"

Mukhtar was quick to see the way Shearer's mind was working. "I have them. You want to make a bomb?" He touched Shearer's hand. "I knew they would send resourceful men."

"It won't be so resourceful if we run up against something with a metal hull."

While Shearer worked Wilson kept their speed down. If they went too far south they would lengthen the distance between themselves and Iran, and that was better to avoid.

Shearer worked as fast as he could but bomb-making was not something to be hurried. When he had finished it was an ugly, untidy-looking apparatus. The plastic explosive had been taped together, the detonator wedged in, the trailer wire emerging to fit the battery which in turn led to the back of one of the clocks. The contact wires would not be connected until he was satisfied how much time was needed.

He fitted the crude bomb into the largest waterproof bag Mukhtar could find and checked that the opening would close sufficiently well for it to be sealed with the special strips Mukhtar had used on the arms release bags. When that was done he asked Wilson to check it all while Mukhtar took the wheel.

Wilson went over it. "I just hope we don't have to use the bloody thing. How will you fix it?"

Shearer pointed to a hammer and some nails. "Along the strip where it'll be sealed. The water shouldn't get in."

"You're joking."

"Got a better idea?"

"How much time do you think you'll have?"

"How can I tell?"

Wilson looked at it again and Shearer was niggled by his silent criticism. "Can you do better?"

Wilson shook his head, "It's certainly no limpet mine."

Annoyed, Shearer went out to the cockpit to check the diving gear. He stripped down to his briefs, adjusted his harness and tried on the flippers. He found he could wedge the hammer in the harness and the nails were held in the elastic waistband of his briefs. He would have to carry the bomb itself. Meanwhile the bag couldn't be sealed until a timing device was set. He wound the clock up and stayed in the cabin with his djellaba off. The three S.M.G.s had already been produced again and they developed the habit of always carrying one.

Prepared for attack, it was now time to change course, and Wilson and Mukhtar pored over the charts again. They were to make for a point between Misk and Jask on the most southernly and comparatively straight stretch of coastline which joined up with Pakistan, some two hundred and fifty miles to the east. The immediate coastline was just above sea level but behind it the hills began to rise with increasing steepness into Iran.

Exactly five miles to the west of Jask, in a sheltered position off the road, emissaries should be waiting for three consecutive nights for the arrival of Mukhtar and the

Western agents. If they failed to arrive during that time then it would be understood that the whole scheme had failed and they would disperse and hope that there would be another call. One night had already passed.

Before changing course Mukhtar explained the next part of the plan. The main road behind the coast was about a mile inland of where they should land. If arrival was not pinpointed then they would miss the transport that should be waiting there for them. Once the emissaries had the arms releases they would leave and most had hundreds of miles to travel. It would take some of them days to reach the clandestine depots: over the Iraqi border, just inside the Iranian borders, and, the one at sea. Long before then the three generals would be back organising the deployment of their armies.

Once the arms were delivered, the road to bloody conflict would be swift. By the time Mukhtar's group reached the Russian border the secret armies should be on the move. All that was needed was the match to light the fire. Some match.

Mukhtar, still gaining strength, had reverted to his original torturous English, but he did not burden them with unnecessary detail to remember. Events could unfold and explain themselves. The vastness and ruggedness of the territory they had to cross were only now emerging, and at once seemed hopeless. Far more than the terrain was against them.

When the briefing was over they doused the lights and turned to port to start across the bottleneck stretch of the Gulf of Oman to Iran. At its narrowest it was about twenty-four miles; but they would be covering another fifteen to twenty to reach the point they wanted.

With the lights out the sea closed in. There were a few distant, scattered lights but it was like moving in a void, the engine sound an intrusion, the swish of the low bow wave sometimes audible above it.

Strangely the darkness removed the boredom. It brought home the immensity of what they were trying to do and spotlighted the near-hopelessness of their position. They had felt some of this the previous night, but that was on the way to a staging post.

There was an additional problem. They were now heading *across* the sea lanes, with the constant flow of tankers coming broadside on. If they were too close radar might no pick them up and even if it did they would not be seen with the naked eye without lights.

It was no coincidence that now all three were in the cockpit, constantly looking out to sea. Searching for trouble. It came in strange form.

The one piece of equipment they lacked, that Mukhtar had either overlooked or had been unable to obtain, was a pair of binoculars, but night glasses in particular. He had done so much else and so much had been left to him that they did not mention it except to check that there weren't any. In this particular instance the use of night glasses might have blinded them, for the concentration from the brilliant light that appeared ahead would have been sight-robbing.

It was difficult to judge its proximity. At first it appeared like a distant lighthouse, the beam shooting across the water intermittently. The size of the orb and its nearness to the sea suggested it was some distance away. Its brilliance did not.

The light was moving. Not a great deal, for the sea was placid. It was also difficult to detect because the light was not constant. A lightship then?

Mukhtar was sceptical. He explained the

189

lack of need for a lightship there. Behind them, in the Gulf, offshore rigs stretched back as far as Kuwait and south-west Iran. In front of them there was none. And the light was ahead.

Wilson hove to, wondering what best to do. If they could gauge the range it would help, but distance at sea is deceptive. Each time the beam fingered out it washed the launch on its periphery. Wilson switched off. They could hear nothing. If it was a ship then it was stationary. The silence and darkness, combined with their total isolation, were unnerving.

Shearer eventually said, "I'm going to get the bomb ready."

"You'll need the cabin light, and it will be seen."

"They'll have seen us already."

"Okay. We'd better push on and see what happens."

They were a sitting duck. Wilson started her up, and the craft moved slowly ahead. For a few moments the light continued to blink, then suddenly cut out, the beam pulling back to its source as if sucked in.

Wilson cut the engine again and now picked up the sound of another. Powerful.

increasing revs. He drew the bolt back on his gun. So did Mukhtar. Shearer was inside, still working on the bomb.

"Full ahead," said Mukhtar.

Wilson nodded, agreeing. It wouldn't make it easy for Shearer but it was the sensible thing to do. He opened up the engine, the bow lifted and the launch gathered speed. He tried to steer slightly to port of where they had last seen the light, but it was a gamble. From the height of the light and the sound of the engines he guessed it was a big boat.

If they were being scanned, speed was the best line of defence. Once at top speed he kept her there while Mukhtar leaned out of the cockpit, trying to peer forward, spray stinging his face.

The light came on again, nearer and slightly to starboard. Mukhtar wanted to fire a burst at it but guessed it to be out of range of an S.M.G. They did not yet know whether it was hostile. Mukhtar did not need to know. It should not be there, and for him anything not understood was the enemy.

Again the light went out; each time this happened it played havoc with their sight. And now a searchlight beamed down at a lower level. It was easy to guess that the original beam had been fixed to a masthead, and the searchlight was operating from a deck.

Mukhtar fired at it but with no result. Return fire thudded into the launch. Wilson and Mukhtar dived below the gunwhale but it was limited shelter from a heavy machine-gun whose range was superior to their own. Wilson reached up, handling the wheel unsighted. The searchlight flooded over the boat, holding her, moving with her.

The gunfire was controlled on the illuminated target. The wood splintered and two windows in the cabin shattered. Shearer swore fiercely as he dived under the table, the bomb in his hands.

He squatted, listening to the impact of the bullets. The curtains over the smashed windows were flapping wildly. He crawled to the door, opened it and bawled out. Wilson called back.

Shearer returned to the table, leaned back against a metal leg, pulled his knees up as a support for the bomb, steadied his shaking fingers and then set the crude timing device. He crept up to the cockpit, shielding the bomb as best he could. Prone on deck, he wriggled into the harness with Wilson's help.

managed to get on the flippers, wedged the hammer and put the nails in his waistband.

They had all settled on the port side, as far away from the firing as they could get. Each worried about the damage being done below the water line.

"Ray, can you go straight at her?"

"If we hit we're dead."

"If we stay like this we're dead. I can't go over with the goddamn light on us."

"Right. It'll narrow the target anyway and that'll give us the protection of the bows."

Mukhtar approved. "Then I can get their light."

"For chrissake, whatever you do don't do that. Not until you think I've had it. That goddamn light is the only guide I've got."

"Okay. Get ready." Wilson crawled forward and swung the wheel. By now most of the small windows had been shot out, and as the launch pulled round to face the firing they enjoyed a temporary respite. Keeping his head down Wilson used the beam, as a direction-finder and aimed directly at it, only momentarily raising his head to see how near they were and to avoid collision, and he could hear the whine of bullets.

Wilson's eyes were just above cockpit level.

Bullets thudded into the hull and ripped into the plastic ball fenders. One whined off the handrail. Blinded by the light, Wilson screwed up his eyes, guessing at their position. "Now!" he bawled.

Sheltered by the angle of the bows and the shadow cast over the cockpit, Shearer flattened on the side and rolled over into the sea. He struck a maelstrom as the stern scudded past his head, the screw thrashing the water. He was rolled over and over but fortunately away from the boat. He surfaced uneasily but Wilson had swung to port to take the beam with him. Getting his bearings on the light, listening to the thudding of the guns, more noticeable now without the engine noise, Shearer sank below surface and struck out in the direction of the beam.

He thought of Wilson as he held the bomb in front of him. It might be better for the Londoner to keep as close to the ship as possible. It would be more difficult for those on the ship to angle the searchlight. He did not know that Wilson was doing precisely that, but for another reason: he'd found that the beam aimed more closely down, illuminated the water in a way that Shearer could easily follow.

Shearer kicked his legs rhythmically. He could only keep going, keeping a check on the light. Once he had to surface when all went totally black and he found the beam had been switched to the other side. Something knocked his legs quite hard and belatedly he began to worry about sharks. He was not sure whether there were any in these warm waters.

The rumble of engines reached him and he was afraid that if the ship moved away from him there was no hope. It had to remain stationary or dead slow.

On the surface Wilson, too, was well aware of this. He was making it difficult for the gunners, keeping close in, circling the ship at speed with Mukhtar getting off the odd burst, careful to avoid the light he would be happier to see extinguished. The Arab's firing had no effect on the ship itself but it kept a few heads down and made the machine-gunners nervous, slowing their own rate of fire.

The screw was barely turning when Shearer reached the ship. The captain evidently wanted his engines running at dead slow. He swam alongside, rose, touched the hull. At last he was forced to admit to himself what he had known for some time: the ship was too big for anything but a steel hull. There was no way he could fix the bomb.

# 10

SHEARER trod water, letting the hull glide slowly past. Apart from the searchlight the ship was in darkness. He rocked as the wash from the launch caught him as it came racing close in. He grabbed at the hull one-handed, almost dropping the bomb. A dark shape passed above him and he guessed it was the platform of the accommodation ladder. It was far out of reach.

As the stern passed the screw barely moved, churning the water into faint phosphorous streamers against the rudder. He struck out fast and dived, coming up against the rough edges of the bilge keel. Still nowhere he could fix the bomb. No way of getting on board. And the deck was too high out of the water for him to attempt to toss the bomb on to it.

He tried to suction one-handed again so that he could go with the ship but the rusted steel tore at his palm. He would have to let the bomb go and try to reach the launch. How he would do that was itself a problem. It had all been too hasty. The sinking of the launch was now only a matter of time.

He kicked back towards the stern, still on the surface, hidden by the swell of the hull. He eyed the screw again, and knew what he had to try to do.

Kicking forward, he dived just under the surface, came up sideways on to the rudder and worked his way along it, all the time conscious of the screw being too near to him. If he was caught by the screw, however slow its revolutions, he was finished.

In the shadow of the hull, with the ship barely moving, reflection from the searchlight no longer helped him. It was so dark that he mentally screamed for light. Having to do everything by touch could be fatal.

Twice he failed to get an effective grip and had to let go, then chase after her and start again. He lost any sense of time. In a cynical way he thought it might be best if he went up with the bomb. Either that, or his oxygen tank would empty and he would eventually drown. He tried again.

His resignation to failure possibly helped him. Another attempt was almost casual, but this time he managed to get a hand behind the rudder which was straight at that moment. If the rudder turned towards him he would be pulled on to the screw, now rotating very near to his head.

He held on, working blind, and explored down the back of the rudder, sinking further to find its base. The rudder was hinged on to the stern post which, he knew, at the bottom went at right-angles back to the hull.

He could not check it all the way because of the screw, but he groped along far enough to find what he wanted. Grabbing the stern post near its lowest angle he was now in a better position and was literally being dragged along with the ship. For the moment he was also out of danger from the screw.

Gripping the angle one-handed, he lifted the bomb, and, very carefully, eased it over the horizontal lower section of the stern post. The turning screw was much too near the bomb for comfort. He could not see it, nor could he judge it without getting a hand severed, but he knew there was precious little gap.

He transferred the package to one hand and felt the contents separate. Quickly seeing the advantage he was able to get the explosive and battery one side of the post and the clock the other, using it as a rough saddle. There was some form of crude balance. The swirling water from the screw would almost certainly dislodge it but there was nothing else he could do.

He had done his best. He made a last check by touch, then dropped away, aided by the mild wake. He surfaced.

Before he could glance round he was blown from the sea by a massive blast that struck his legs and back as if he'd been hit by an enormous sledgehammer. The tank pressed against his back with such force that he could not breath.

Half-conscious and in great pain, he re-entered the water back first, the weight of the tank twisting him in mid-air. The sea he struck was different from the placid one he had left. He was now in a raging storm, waves breaking over him, being tossed like a piece of driftwood, with no control over his movements. With bursting lungs he realised his mouthpiece was missing. He couldn't find it, and thought it must have been blown off. He could feel the tank was at a strange angle, dragging him sideways and down.

He was drowning. His ears were screaming from the explosion, and now there was a terrific suction dragging him. Tossed in the massive currents he fought to release the harness, and as his fingers worked awkwardly he guessed that part of the strapping had already gone. Letting the tank drift he struck out blindly, buffeted and tossed, but aware at least that his legs could move.

He broke surface, popping up like a bottle, gasped, and was sucked down again. He needed more air than that and he tried again. The pull against him was changing. The sea was still hammering, but easing now, as if settling into a pattern. But the suctioning was most severe, and he had to fight for his life.

Surfacing again he was able to hold it longer this time, aided by his flippers which somehow had stayed on. There was far too much surface movement for him to get sight of the ship. He managed to shout at the top of his voice before being dragged down again. He tried to swim away and this was slightly easier as he surfaced again.

The whole world was black. The searchlight had gone, so had the ship. He didn't expect to see any sign of the launch, for the sea was rising too high and he needed light. It was impossible to judge direction.

He shouted again. He risked treading water for a second or two as he heard an answering shout. And then he realised it was not answering. It was a voice in torment, a wail of despair. Then there were others backed by a repetitive, piercing scream that died, only to start again.

Where was the ship? As the heaving sea gradually steadied to erratic swells he tried to gaze round, but he could pick nothing out at all.

With the eerie sound of disembodied cries, the frantic appeals made in a language he did not understand, Shearer still felt isolated and lost, floating in a strange, unfriendly void that was wet but invisible.

The spotlight cut across the water and almost immediately picked up the ship. It was not powerful but it was enough. The beam followed the line of the ship *perpendicularly to the sea.*

He was fascinated. The bows were sticking up straight, and the huge sea swells were reaching up to amidships. In the traversing light he could see the crusted hull. For a moment he thought she would crash back on her spine, but the water pressure below surface kept her in position, as if she were performing some bizarre dance. Clouds of steam rose from the surface, but through this spectral cloud he could see a huge rupture in the hull. Had the engines burst?

His immediate problems forgotten for the moment, he was filled with the exhilaration of success. I must have blown the bloody stern off, he reflected. To a degree he was right. The ship was old and had already suffered stern damage some two years before. It had literally been patched up before being sold off. She might well have survived for many years to come in these waters but the bomb had taken the rudder right off, blasted away the screw and created a massive gap in the weakened plates above it.

The ship was going down at an unbelievably fast rate. The spotlight held her as if those operating it wanted to be absolutely certain. Was it from the launch? Had the launch's spotlight survived the machine-gun attack?

Shearer called out again but there were the other shouts. The spotlight left the ship to its dying misery and started to traverse the waves. It picked out waving arms here and there as the seas parted into troughs or someone crested a swell. It came his way, lingered on him and he waved frantically. The light passed on but its beam was narrowing as the launch drew closer.

Relief hit Shearer slowly. He began to believe he would escape and as he did he heard, above yells, machine-gun fire. He turned cold. He struck out towards the light before he realised that the firing was coming from its direction. Suddenly there were more screams, one finishing abruptly. The spotlight was searching for heads and someone was firing at each one it picked out.

Shearer was sick. The knowledge that the survivors were being picked off struck him hard. He floated while he tried to get his feelings under control. The bloody murder had all the cold logic of Mukhtar about it.

Angry and disillusioned he struck out again. A good deal of his power had gone. He found he had to take it easy.

The launch was cleaving through the diminishing swells, creating bow waves like ethereal wings. The light bounced across the water, searching relentlessly. It played again on the hull, which had now almost submerged. As if the old ship commanded some silent respect, the launch slowed and kept the light on the black, rust-caked mass as it finally slipped under the surface, suctioning with it two of its crew whose final screams ended in gurgles.

That did not satisfy Mukhtar. The search started again. Shearer called out but realised he could not be heard above the engine noise. The launch circled, its spotlight working erratically as if animated by blood lust.

Shearer swam on, then trod water. The launch was moving away from him. Machine-gun fire crackled across the settling sea. And again, prolonged bursts with short intervals. A longer gap followed, and Shearer guessed that Mukhtar would be changing magazines.

The launch traversed the area where the ship had sunk. Wilson's navigation was noticeably more methodical than Mukhtar's firing. Then the beam swung round towards Shearer and he waved both arms. The launch came round in a wide skid, picked up speed and came bouncing towards him, its beam alternately illuminating the sky and the sea.

Shearer, suddenly nervous, kept waving. The launch did not slow. He could just see the faint reflection of a white djellaba behind the deck-mounted light and then he heard the crack of the gun and the whine of bullets.

"You mad Arab bastard!" Shearer screamed, but the gun continued to rattle. He dived, surfaced further on. The launch had veered but was coming again. The gun had just started again, the light full on Shearer when the launch skidded in an acute arc, the light sweeping madly, the shots going wild. The launch slowed and then the engine cut out.

Across the water Wilson's voice called out. "Doug! Is that you?"

"You stupid bastard. Who the hell do you think it is?" His voice choked with frustration and anger.

They came up slowly beside him. One of them had put on the navigational lights, and the spotlight was kept on so that he could see more easily. Mukhtar put out a hand to help him but Shearer shook it off angrily. Nor would he accept help from Wilson. He climbed over awkwardly on his own, trembling from fury at what had happened. "You murdering bastards," he said. "They never had a chance."

"Would you have preferred we left them to drown? To die slowly?" The ever-logical Mukhtar.

"They could have taken their chances." Shearer was rubbing himself down with a towel Wilson had thrown at him.

"They had no chance. We could not take

them aboard. They were fanatics and there is no room."

"I'm surprised at you," Shearer shouted at Wilson. "Cold-blooded murder."

Wilson answered angrily, "He's right. Don't you think I'm just as appalled for chrissake? We can't let word get back to Oman or to Iran. *We had to cut the line.* For our own protection."

Shearer didn't reply. It didn't help to know. His reaction was emotional, he knew that. But the price seemed too high.

Mukhtar said quietly, "You did a wonderful job. We are both so happy to see you back alive."

Sitting in the bulwarks Shearer towelled away, still angry, partly at himself.

Mukhtar added sagely, "We respect your feelings. You have saved us. So we will also respect your wishes." He indicated the vast stretch of sea. "There are one or two more out there. If you listen carefully you might hear them. We will let them take their chances as you suggest."

Shearer had no answer. He glared up balefully. They did not remind him that it was he who had planted the bomb. They did not need to.

Captain Kimura was on the bridge of the ninety-thousand-ton tanker, the *Chiyoda-Ku* when he received the report of the blips on his radar screen. He crossed to take a look for himself. There were two: a small ship sometimes converging on one appreciably larger. They were on his course.

What he found strange was the larger blip was stationary and the small blip must be circling her like a fly. From time to time it disappeared behind the shadow of the larger ship. The other mysterious feature was that the larger blip was shortening. The captain turned to his duty officer. "Check with the radio room."

A telephone check revealed that no distress signals had been received. And yet another curious factor roused the captain's interest. Although he had instructed his duty officer to use his binoculars on the wing of the bridge nothing could be sighted. No navigational light came in view.

The radar scanner lost the larger blip altogether. It was as though a ship had gone down, yet the small blip was still there, moving across the screen erratically; still there was no kind of report. The weather was perfect. No atmospheric reflections could account for what was on the screen.

The duty officer called from the bridge wing. He had now sighted a light. The distance was too great to judge what was happening but he could pick up the faint beam which seemed to be flashing everywhere. The captain ordered the chief engineer to reduce speed.

A tanker cruising at full speed can take up to two miles to stop. Once on collision course it would be virtually impossible to avoid one within a mile and the gap between the Gulf and the Gulf of Oman was like the pinched section of the glass of an egg timer.

From the size of the blip he knew that he need not be concerned for his own ship. But he did not want problems or delays. There was also the human angle and the law of the high seas. Sailors in distress must be helped.

A half-mile further on a mounted searchlight was used to help the lookout. Nothing untoward came to view. The smaller blip had also vanished from the radar screen. Navigational lights were picked up but were too separated and too distant to be connected.

The sea where the bombed ship had sunk had settled and there was no debris or oil slick. The *Chiyoda-Ku* passed over the spot and swept powerfully on with the captain and officers still mystified. An entry into the ship's log was made of this very strange phenomenon.

What they had missed were two injured and near exhausted crewmen from the sunken ship who lay beyond the fringe of the search-light. Their faint cries were not heard above the steady thud of the tanker's huge engines.

It was Mukhtar who saw the distant tanker. He switched off all lights and warned Wilson to get back on their original course fast. When the tanker's beam came flooding out the launch was well out of range. The same doubt was in all their minds: would the tanker spot and pick up survivors?

They saw it ghost past, a sunken-bellied apparition moving slowly, and clearly searching. When it didn't stop Shearer was the first to admit that he sighed with relief. The business of the shooting was not mentioned again. And they had been left with other problems.

The launch had taken on water, partly from the upheaval of the explosion but more ominously from a leak below decks. The hull had obviously been holed by the machine-gun fire but it was difficult to assess how seriously, and impossible to predict if it would get worse.

Because of Mukhtar's wound he was left to navigate while the others baled. Shearer said nothing about his back and Wilson could not see his suffering in the dark. There came a point when Mukhtar put the lights on again and it was then that Wilson noticed how drawn Shearer had become. He made no comment. There could be no respite if they were to keep afloat, and the intake was hampering speed.

They neared the coast of Iran about midnight. Even now there were problems. They had to reduce speed, and a deserted coastline had been selected for secrecy. That meant no lights either on land or on the launch. Mukhtar was satisfied with his navigation but he had to be deadly accurate. They could not land without help.

The temptation was to use the spotlight to pick out the shore, illuminate the hazards. The launch was barely moving but still the baling could not stop. The navigational lights had been out for some time, and there was the grave risk of inshore currents and rocks. The noise of the engine was a danger in itself, but it could not be switched off for fear of drifting ashore. Mukhtar switched on the deck light for perhaps a second. They waited, peering towards land.

Nothing happened. Mukhtar switched the light on again, held it for a second longer. Still no response.

In the cockpit they had got used to working on voice positions and the nebulous shapes of each other. The launch had been blacked out for so long that they had picked up, in crude form, the senses of the blind. Even while Wilson and Shearer were still baling they were aware of the disappointment and puzzlement of Mukhtar. The little Arab could not see where he had gone wrong.

Wilson said without complaining, "We can't bale all night. Doug's suffering. And my arms are dead."

"I know. This is the place, I am sure." Mukhtar took the risk of flashing the light on and off, finishing with a prolonged flash. Suddenly an answering flash came from the shore to their left. It was a pinprick of light, as if miles away.

Mukhtar shouted with satisfaction and set course at dead slow. Occasionally he flashed to show his changing position. Each time he did this he now received a response.

The launch, noticeably listing, crept in towards the shore. White patches were dotted in front of them and with tremendous relief to the three, helping hands were on bows and gunwales guiding them in. Low, friendly voices expressed clear welcome. Wilson and Shearer threw the balers down in relief.

Before it reached the shoreline the launch began to sink. By then everything the three men needed had been collected—guns, charts and the arms releases. They had to wade before being helped up shingle, along a narrow path through a high rock cluster, on to a stretch of sandy gorse. They had about a mile to walk. The guns were being carried for them.

Some twenty minutes later they crossed a deserted and dark coast road and then continued inland for a while before reaching a rock shelter. Hurricane lamps were placed around and they found themselves in a bowl of pale light. Some of the men gathered excitedly round Mukhtar to congratulate him.

From Wilson and Shearer's point of view they were now in the most hostile territory that could be found.

The leader was a black-robed Arab who sat on a rock close to Shearer and plucked the fears straight from his head. "You must be very careful. You have many enemies here."

He turned, puzzled by the timbre of the voice. It was not a kaffiyeh he was looking at but a chador. Not a man but a woman.

# 11

"SO far so good," observed Higgs. "They've done well, those two. And that Arab you conjured up from Oman."

"Yes." Higgs crossed to the window to peer out at the London scene. "It's the ramifications that worry me. If Wilson and Shearer are caught the truth will be tortured out of them." He turned to face the seated Marshall.

"They don't know the truth. Anyway, no one will believe the Iranians. Only those who want to and they're already converted."

"Unless the Russians get hold of them. That's always been my worry since it went slightly wrong with Rachid. Rogov will put on a show trial. And this time it would be the truth: the Middle East would explode in our faces. We could lose the lot."

Marshall shrugged. "But they're not going over the Russian border. They are there to advise and to pass on what Brown taught them. The stability of their presence is vital.

Shearer's first class at organising and that's what's needed so badly."

"I'm not arguing. What about the next stage? Sheik Marroum's visit?"

"For the moment the Saudis have suspended it. They've got trouble enough. The timing has to be absolutely right. We have to be sure to get him."

"Have you found your assassin?"

Marshall suddenly looked around the room as if afraid they could be overheard. "I'm seeing him tomorrow. There's another lined up if he won't do it."

"We're on the thinnest of eggshells, Joe. I can smell war."

Marshall said nothing for some time. Then quietly, but with considerable feeling he replied, "Don't I know it. As carefully as we tread I can feel them cracking under our feet. Wilson and Shearer will only die. We could finish up wishing we had."

"*Two men*? The same two who were in Tripoli?" Rogov almost snarled into the scrambler. He listened impatiently. "Then you'd better make sure, Panovich. You might believe they are at the bottom of the Gulf of Oman but that's too convenient for me."

Rogov paused, thought quickly. "Tell the P.L.O. they had better not slip up again. Get on to Ben Waffa in Teheran. See that he gets what he needs and do it now." Rogov hung up without waiting for a reply. He glared icily at the scrambler as if it were responsible for the bad news Panovich had just imparted.

Marshall went alone to the Tombs prison in New York. Nobody but the Warden knew of his visit. He had arranged the appointment in person. When he entered the huge detention centre the Warden met him personally and escorted him, asking no questions at all.

They went up in an elevator which was divided into two parts. Two separated cages, Marshall considered it. His side of the wire contained himself and the Warden, and even then he did not believe there was too much room. The other side was crammed with prisoners, mainly black, whose hostility could be felt even in the safety of Marshall's own section.

They'd like to lynch me, he thought. String me up and watch me die. The malevolence of their thoughts came from their eyes, fastened on him unflinchingly. Barely whispered warnings reached him, the white enemy. He considered what caused such hatred and he felt both guilty and uncomfortable. Perhaps, in their shoes he'd feel the same.

He was glad to get out of the elevator, the feeling of danger and hatred still strong. They walked to the end of a platform, to a plain steel door with a closed spyhole in it. Before the Warden opened the door Marshall asked, "He in there?"

"Yes. He's dangerous."

"I want no-one in there with me. And I want no one near this door."

The Warden was uneasy. "Have you a gun?"

"I don't need a gun. And if I had one this guy would have no problem taking it from me and blowing my head off. Just open up."

"I hope you know what you're doing." Still doubtful, the Warden lifted the keys. "Bang hard or shout if you want me."

"Don't worry. I can yell pretty good."

The Warden opened the steel door, swung it back and went in first. He stood, blocking the doorway, scanning the cell before standing aside to let Marshall in.

The Warden closed and locked the door behind Marshall. He had never liked this level. For some reason it was quieter than the other floors, as if the inmates knew there was less likelihood of them being heard. He could feel eyes on him, sense the strength of feeling. But he was used to it. Right now he was more concerned why the head of the C.I.A. was seeing one of his prisoners alone and using him, the Warden, as a lackey.

He knew one thing for certain, though. If news of this meeting leaked out it could only have come from himself or Marshall. The prisoner was, and would remain, isolated. The Warden did not need this incentive for secrecy but he did recognise that it guaranteed it. It even muted the tempting speculation of what it was all about.

Inside the cell a table had been temporarily placed longways from the door. At the further end sat a slight, sallow man of about thirty, with dark receding hair. His eyes were pale agate, hard and shining. He wore a short-sleeved vest, his thin arms bent at the elbows, forearms and hands resting on the table, the wrists manacled.

Marshall pulled out a chair and sat with his back to the door, placing his hat on the table. "You Rafael Calvera?"

"Yeah. You Jesus Christ, man?"

"Not yet. I'm working at it."

"You're too big, too fat."

"As fat as your lip, maybe."

The hard eyes brightened. Calvera held up his wrists. "You see these? I could crush your head in with these."

"You could. But you're not going to because I'm the only person who can get you out of here."

Calvera gazed at his visitor balefully. He was interested but totally mistrustful.

Marshall continued, "Do we sit here insulting each other or do we talk?"

"You can get me out of here?"

"Without a doubt."

"Who are you?"

"You've already told me. And so far as you're concerned that's who I am. I can work miracles for you."

The eyes stared. The tip of a tongue touched the thin, long-lipped mouth.

"What do I have to do?"

"Kill again. Once more."

Calvera grinned sloppily. He did not know what to make of it. "Hey, man that's weird." His fingers intertwined and his tension showed in their grip. "You come into this place and ask me that? They *showed* you in? You're the devil."

"Make up your mind. Either way I can get you out. You interested?"

"Sure I'm interested. If I believe you. I'm the one who's supposed to be crazy."

"Not crazy, Rafael. Frustrated. I understand how it was. A judge and jury won't, but I do."

"Yeah? That's what I keep telling 'em. I was in the queue, out of gas. I couldn't go another hundred yards. Know what I mean? out dry, man. I was the next in line and then his guy put a hood over the pump and says he's now out of gas, and to wait for the next delivery. I told him he was a liar. He ignores me. Turns his back on me as if I wasn't there. I call to him. He walks away. The other cars are moving on. Some of the drivers shout and wave fists but this guy takes no notice."

Sweat beads formed along Calvera's upper ip as he relived the moment. "I shout again. He goes to his office. I climb out of the van, run after him. I see him through the window and he doesn't even look up at me. His door's ocked. I tap his window. He's reading a newssheet. I tap again. Call. He's in another world, man. I shoot him straight through the glass. I break open the door, take the pump keys and help myself to gas. The fink was

lying. He'd been keeping gas back for h
friends or for black market."

The hands came up to wipe his lip. The
were quite steady. "I didn't leave any cas
'cause he didn't need it any more." Calver
banged the table with his fists, the chai
rattling against the wood. "They called
robbery and murder, man. That bastard wa
doing the robbing. I shot a black-marketeer.
did Uncle Sam a favour."

"Well, that all ties in with your statemen
Rafael." Marshall kept the scepticism fro
his voice.

"That's how it was. I keep telling 'em."

"Of course, that was the second one."

"The second one? What you trying to pul
miracle man?"

"The first gas station job. Brooklyn. Yo
remember. Only that time there was no g
involved. Just money. A double hit. The wi
was D.O.A."

Calvera pushed his chair back, stood u
his manacled hands held in front of hir
"What you trying to do? I was cleared of th
job. They tried to pin it on me, the lyin
bastards."

"Sit down, Rafael. It makes no differenc
*Sit down.*"

Calvera sat cagily, sideways on, head turned. "You be careful, you hear?"

"The only reason I mentioned it was because with all three people you only needed one shot each."

Calvera wasn't sure whether it was a compliment or a trap. "I only needed one shot for the black market guy."

"Straight through the head. One shot. With a Saturday night special. Like the others. What could you do with a real gun?"

"I didn't do the others. You stop trying to say I did."

"Okay." Marshall spread his hands. "It was just that the shooting impressed me," he said truthfully. "That's pretty good shooting. How do you do it?"

"What d'you mean?"

"Aim? Hold it? What's your technique?"

"I don't think about it. I just fire. Instinct."

Calvera suddenly thought he might have committed himself too far. Marshall, seeing his expression, waved him down. "Forget it. No trap." He stood up, tapped his pockets, opened his coat. "No tapes. No records. Just you and me. You can deny anything you've said, and you haven't said much."

Calvera looked relieved. "When are you going to get to the point?"

"I want to be satisfied on how good you are with a gun."

Calvera grinned, showing bad and uneven teeth. "Give me one. I'll show you."

"Ever used a rifle?"

Calvera was suspicious again. "Maybe."

"Come on, Rafael. I mean since you were kicked out of the army. You were a top marksman for the short time you were in. Have you kept in practice?"

"I was framed. Yeah, I've had the odd practice. I'm still good."

"I might want you to practice again."

"How do I get out of here? Spell it out. Who do I hit?"

"Does it matter?"

Calvera gave it due consideration. "Not if you're levelling." His eyes narrowed as his suspicion returned. "There's something crazy about this. You can get me outa here to waste somebody? Then what? I'm back for life?"

"You'll be out for good. Unless you do something stupid. A pardon."

Calvera stared down the table. He was thinking of the evidence against him. "How can you do that? How do you sew up the D.A., the cops?"

"Don't worry about it. How am I here at all?"

"You're really something. Jesus Christ. Yeah. You're worse than me. You preach good and bad, you bastards, but you're no better."

"We all have our cross," said Marshall easily. "One hit. Then you're free. Do you or don't you?"

"You give it in writing?"

"Would you?" Marshall looked at his watch then glanced up. "I can't give you much longer to make up your mind."

"This hit, is it for Uncle Sam?"

"No, it's not. It doesn't matter to you who it's for. It's for me. Okay?"

Unexpectedly, fear flecked the agate eyes. "Not one of the Organisation?"

"No. Your time's up. You're not the only candidate." Marshall pushed his chair back, put his hat on.

"I'll do it but I need to know more. You haven't told me a thing."

Marshall took his hat off again. "One hit. One shot. I'll set it up, make it easy for you. I'll tell you where, when, who. When you've done it I'll give you a sum of money, enough to set up a small business, a café, something like that. You'll have a new identity. Cut off the past and start again. A new life. That's pretty good reward, isn't it?"

Calvera's eyes were bright. "You can do all this? How do I know?"

"You don't. You use your brain. You ask yourself how I can offer this. And you keep your mouth shut. The first whisper in here and the deal's off."

"How can I whisper in this pen? I'm in solitary."

"There are ways. Just one word and you'll have an accident here. Understand?"

"Yeah . . . When do I get out?"

"This afternoon. I want to find out if you're as good with a rifle as you are with a hand gun." But Marshall already knew.

# 12

THE heat was blistering. The Land-Rover, covered in a crusted mixture of salt and sand, heaved and lurched like a camel along tracks created by the desert beasts over countless years.

Mukhtar had handed out the arms releases, satisfied with the credentials of the agents who took them. They were all aware of the immense risks.

The emissaries had started on the long journeys to various parts of Iran and beyond her borders. Once the arms were released the war would begin, most of it along the whole western boundary from Turkey to the northern tip of the Gulf.

During this time Shearer had been impressed by the girl's efficiency. The Iranians took orders from her without hesitation. But there was much more than that which attracted her to him. He was drawn both physically and emotionally so quickly that he was disturbed by his own reactions. He believed those sort of feelings could never return to him.

The strange thing was, there was so little of the girl to see. The robe covered her body, showing only a suggestion of breasts beneath the black garment. He thought she was slim by the way she walked and moved, but it was her face and quiet manner that always seemed to hold his attention. Her eyes were so deep yet bright, lively and humorous at times when she caught his interested glances. She did not discourage him.

She had told him her name was Leila and he would have liked to continue talking to her, believing that she felt the same. But time was against them and she could not afford to lose her authority. They had to keep on the move.

Fires, oil lamps were doused, signs of habitation removed, even though the area was remote. Two old Land-Rovers remained after the general exodus and these were to make the long journey north to the Russian border on the east side of the Caspian Sea.

Wilson and Shearer were denied the relative comfort of riding in the front with the drivers. By the time they moved off, dawn was not far away, and seated in the cab they would be too identifiable. Although the whole area this side of Iran was sparsely populated, covered by huge tracts of both sand and salt desert and by long ridges of barren mountains, the dangers were still there.

It was already proven that the P.L.O. were looking for them. They wouldn't stop now. At best there might be a respite but that possibility had to be ignored. There could be no let-up.

The Rovers carried arms and explosive, and old grenades discovered to be useless because the fuses had corroded. They were dumped for being too dangerous. There was food, petrol, oil and water, with little room in the back for passengers. Wilson and Shearer hacked out space and found blankets on which they could lie. They could have travelled separately but preferred not to, perhaps feeling a security in the presence of each other.

Leila had climbed in with them, a black-cloaked figure crouched near the tail board, bounding up and down and yet uncomplaining, as if the violent jarring were an everyday part of her life. Wilson was quick to notice the exchange of glances between the girl and Shearer. In the back of the second Rover were two more Iranians and Mukhtar, so the total number, including two in each cab, was ten.

They had been climbing ever since leaving camp, as they rattled and ground their way up, it grew noticeably colder. They drew blankets around themselves but could not stop shivering. Conversation was difficult with the bone-shaking movement and above the noise of an engine constantly in low gear.

As the falcon flew they were about a hundred and fifty miles from the nearest road, Leila told them in quite good English. But on the camel tracks, the route so erratic and difficult, it was clear that two hundred miles would be nearer the distance. Perhaps more.

They were using full beams for it would have been impossible to cover the terrain without lights. Transport did not move at night along these crude tracks. The Rovers were sturdy but were taking a battering.

Shearer's back still hurt, and Mukhtar's wound was in danger of opening again. Leila had been quick to notice the uncomplaining suffering of both men.

Their route took them north-east, which meant at times leaving the camel tracks and travelling over virgin country, eventually to pick up another track. The lead driver, Houshang, seemed to know exactly what he was doing and nobody argued.

When they eventually stopped Houshang came back to speak to Leila, who translated for the others.

"We will have to wait here for dawn. It is too dangerous to go on." She did not immediately explain whether they expected an ambush or whether the terrain was too difficult.

They climbed out, taking their blankets with them. They were on an acute slope and the two drivers wedged rocks under the rear wheels. It was dark, the air bitingly cold and they huddled in a tight circle, shivering.

Leila explained, "We really need to go north but if we do we will run into Hamum-e-Jaz-Murian, a huge salt lake. There is also another lake to the east of it. So we are forced off course. The driver has stopped because the camel tracks are fewer here."

"I don't know how he's got this far."

Houshang, getting the gist of what Shearer said, grinned in the darkness. "Much practice," he said, "But now, dangerous. Mountains. Very big. Only wait an hour or so."

And he was right. The sunrise Wilson and Shearer had seen at sea was mediocre to the spreading colours that split the mountains to the east. It filtered first through the Siahan Range in Pakistan before cascading over the border and separating the peaks and isolating like a golden crest the peaks of Kuh-e-Birag.

As the mountains were silhouetted with an orange and yellow backcloth the valleys filled with purple, ever-moving, ever-changing. Wilson looked back down the gradient they had climbed and marvelled at Houshang's driving. The terrain looked impassable, and he was glad now that he hadn't seen it exaggerated in bouncing headlamps from the cab.

There was no sign of human life, and any village was tucked away in the folds of the hills. Water holes did not exist in this region, so they had to rely on their own supplies. The river beds were dry. Leila explained that the flow was seasonal only. Sensing that Shearer wanted to talk to her Wilson edged back to the second Rover where the others were gossiping in Arabic. He indicated that he'd like to check the explosive equipment, and once they grasped this they were quick to let him. This was something with which they all had an affinity.

Shearer leaned against the rock face, the best of the dawn now gone. "I've been wanting to ask you," he said. "How come you are in this, risking your life?"

"Because I'm a woman?" Leila laughed, her olive skin tinged by the brightening sunlight. "It is *because* I'm a woman. The Mullahs have cast us back to the dark ages. We were getting nearer to equal rights." She smiled and her dark eyes shone. "Not as near as the Western woman, but we had been fighting and gaining some ground. Now it has all gone. We have been reduced to chattels."

"Yet you dress traditionally?"

"I am a Kurd. Kurdish women have much more freedom, and we do not wear veils. Nor are we secluded from male company. But in this part of the country I do not want people wondering what a Kurd is doing here. I must fit in." She smiled suddenly. "I will answer the question you are too embarrassed to ask. Why is a woman leading a group of revolutionaries? Isn't that on your mind?"

Shearer felt caught out. Leila was amused at his discomfort. "Some Kurdish tribes are ruled by women. There is even a tradition of matriarchy."

"That's interesting. Your English is excellent, by the way."

"I was educated in England."

He gently teased her. "Perhaps the English tainted your views."

"I did not notice their horns."

"There's a lot against us. Much more than is going for us. You're young, beautiful and you should be somewhere safer."

"You are a considerate man, Mr. Shearer. Perhaps we wear our age better and I'm older than I look. In any event, I am committed. I cannot sit back and watch my country destroyed by the ignorance and vanity of old men, and the stupidity of some of the young. If it's to stay like this I'd rather be dead."

Shearer did not answer. That sort of conviction was one he held himself. He was suddenly amazed to see her slip out of her robe.

"Take off your shirt, Mr. Shearer." Leila smiled as she caught his expression. "I believe your back is hurting. I will massage it, but I cannot work hampered by this." She pushed the robe with her foot. "Put your hands on the tail board."

As he turned he realised he had been right about her figure. When her cool fingers

234

touched his back he forgot the pain and was aware only that her near-naked body was precariously close to his.

Without warning Houshang drew up under an overhang on the edge of an escarpment and yelled back, pointing down. Wilson looked out over a sheer drop of fifteen hundred feet to the valley below. He saw a small grey shadow gliding over the rocks. As the engine was switched off and the second Rover closed up tight, he, like the others who were riding in the back, knew that it was not the difficulty of the road that had forced them to stop; Houshang had seen the shadow of a plane.

They were well protected under the overhang and unless the plane came down into the valley they would remain unseen. Wilson confirmed what they had all concluded. "He's searching. It's too erratic for a flight path."

The droning persisted, faded, returned, came lower. Was the pilot descending into the valley? The wait became uncomfortable, made worse by fatigue.

The engine faded but still the group waited. They were losing time, but to play anything but safe would be foolhardy. They remained for half an hour after the last sound of the plane. The decision to move on was mutual but their mood was muted.

Distance did not improve the conditions. They were constantly forced east to avoid the big areas of salt desert. By late afternoon they reached camel tracks. This made the going more predictable and they ran into a camel train bivouac; small children ran in and out of the tethered beasts.

With Wilson and Shearer still hidden in the back of the first Rover the rest waved at the traders. It was unusual not to stop to compare notes in so desolate a place but it would be unwise to do so. Children had a habit of exploring.

The track followed an erratic course through rugged country which often meant doubling back and constantly moving away from the required direction. The tracks had been used for centuries and were well tried and trusted routes. Just before sundown, they arrived at the road to Bampur which they skirted to join it again just beyond Iranshahr.

If it wasn't the best road in Iran it had a surface which seemed to them now the smoothest silk. It meant both speed and the right direction. Before reaching Kahonan they stopped to refuel, eat and stretch their legs. By common consent they moved on using headlights now but covering the miles at speed.

The road was virtually empty and they made good time. Wilson and Shearer began to doze but there was no comfort and they were racked with pain.

Their objective was to reach the town of Zahedan before dawn. This was very close to the Pakistan border, but it would be necessary to take on more fuel and food supplies to sustain them for the long journey north. Beyond Zahedan the area was even more remote, and they had to keep to the eastern fringe of the Kavir-e-Lut, the massive desert covering much of the interior.

The drivers changed over now they were on an identifiable road but the Westerners were still not permitted to enter the cabs. The journey diminished apprehension by the sheer painful monotony of it. It was easy to reach a point where care was discarded, but these young revolutionaries had seen too much bloodshed already entirely to forget the rules of caution.

They reached Zahedan about three a.m.

and traversed its empty dusty streets slowly. The sand-splashed headlamps washed the crusted off-white walls and the dark gaps of the offshooting, narrow labyrinths as if it were a ghost town. All that stirred were hobbled camels and outcasts curled in shadowed doorways. Once on the northern outskirts the trucks gathered speed, left the road a few miles clear of the town and ventured over the rough ground until they were reasonably sure of seclusion.

Leila roused Wilson and Shearer, apologising softly but explaining, "You can sleep between the jeeps. A few hours, no more. But it will be more comfortable for you."

They clambered down, feeling wretched. They had not had a night's sleep since reaching Oman. Exhausted and battered, they lay in the gorse, folded djellabas for pillows, blankets pulled round them and they fell into feverish sleep.

The young group of Iranians, each with a submachine-gun, formed a rough perimeter of sentries. They too needed sleep but they had not endured what the others had suffered; they were content.

Ben Waffa awoke with the certain conviction

that someone had passed over his grave. One moment he was asleep, the next awake, his mind clearing rapidly as he quickly wondered what had roused him. A noise? A light? He sat up on his mattress, one hand on the concrete floor.

The small room smelled of staleness but nothing as bad as a hijacked plane full of European passengers after being isolated for a week in the blazing Middle East sun. That had stunk.

He was alone in the room. He could not hear anyone sleeping too near to him, not even a woman. The Turkish pilot, Riza, and Ben Waffa's own companion, Naim, were in the next room. The pilot had complained bitterly at the poor accommodation, but the fanatical Waffa resented any form of complaint.

Ben Waffa had roughed it so often it was part of life. Sleep got in the way of pursuit of his ideals and kept him from his enemies.

He would wake at the slightest sound or excuse. He rose now, and began to pace the floor in his bare feet. It was pitch black in the room. He did not need a light; that too could be an intrusion, for his sight had feline qualities.

Ben Waffa, at thirty-five, had followed a violent way of life since he was twelve, which was when he could first hold a gun and shoot straight. A Palestinian, he had become a hero very early in his young life. He had shot dead hostages in foreign embassies without remorse and had become a living legend by the time he was eighteen. People feared him, and with good cause. They had quickly learned that so far as Ben Waffa was concerned if you were not with him you must be against.

When the request for his services reached him, via the Soviet Embassy in Teheran, he was overjoyed. The source of the request came as no surprise: he had been trained in Moscow.

Quick to grasp essentials, he realised from the outset that time was against him. An Englishman and an American with an Arab arms dealer had left Oman for Iran in a launch. That much came to him quickly. He had made so many similar journeys himself that it was easy for him to guess that in a boat that size they would take the shortest possible sea route. The ship that was supposed to intercept the launch had not been seen, nor could radio contact be established.

The Russians had provided a twin-engined Cessna, owned by a dummy Turkish trading company. They had no need to provide arms.

The Palestinian located Naim, a man he could work with well, no friend in the true sense but someone with similar aims and one who had also grown bored due to neglect of the use of his skills. They had loaded up, the many arms and explosives stacked in boxes so as not to worry the pilot, Riza, and took off from Teheran at first light on the morning the launch had reached the southern coast.

They flew to Esfahan, directly south of Teheran, refuelled and then crossed first a range of mountains and then the Kavir-e-Lut, the desert Leila's party had avoided, to an airstrip at Zahedan. By the time they had arrived the two Rovers had already been travelling for some time.

Ben Waffa had given Riza no rest, and the Turk, seeing the fanaticism of the man, chose not to argue. After refuelling again they were airborne and searching.

At first the search was haphazard. They had flown to the coast, covered the area where the launch had sunk and had been unable to spot it. Ben Waffa had then told Riza to concentrate on caravan trails. This had paid off quite early. By dropping low they had picked out the Rover tracks, but realised this in itself could be inconclusive. They could be old, used by anyone; but it was a start.

Fuel was always a problem. It was about three hundred and fifty miles from Zahedan to the coast, a round trip of seven hundred miles. It left little room for a squared search.

When Naim had claimed that he'd seen something move in the hills they had set off in that direction. They found nothing. Ben Waffa got angry at the lost time but Naim was adamant that he'd seen movement. If he had, it was not repeated. With fuel getting low and Riza complaining that his oil pressure too was falling, the disgruntled trio had been forced to return to Zahedan.

Waffa had expected that they would refuel and take off again, but Riza was insistent on finding mechanical help. Waffa had fumed while Riza worked on the plane. By the time the repairs had been completed it was too late to go up.

Ben Waffa and Naim had gone round the town checking on whether any strange vehicles had been seen. In a small Iranian town so remotely placed the question was not so odd. The problem was that Ben Waffa did not know how many or what kind of vehicles there were. He did not even know if the launch had arrived safely but if he took a negative view of that he had no task left.

During his enquiries he referred to two Americans. Americans out here would attract as much attention as a Jew in a mosque. While he was sounding out the local populace he was also marking those he might rouse as a search party, should one be needed. Ben Waffa was a past master at inflaming emotions, and in a country suffering high emotional cross-currents he saw no problem.

Eventually, as the town closed its doors, the street babble died and the animals were at last released to rest, Waffa was forced to eat and then to sleep. Largely he had lain thinking, pondering the possibilities. If the enemy had landed they might well head for the Iraqi and Turkish borders to Kurdistan, where they were most likely to find help. It was difficult, therefore, to justify his own movements, of searching east instead of west. All the action was west. And what could they possibly do in the east?

Waffa had gone east acting instinctively. But now he had to think it out. Something had woken him. In the darkness his high-cheek-boned face tightened. He looked at his luminous watch. Three-thirty in the morning. The Rovers had passed by some fifteen minutes earlier.

Leila let Wilson and Shearer sleep on while her companions stripped one Rover of arms. They emptied all their fuel cans into the tanks, topped up with oil, checked the tyres and did some minor servicing. Unarmed themselves, two young Iranians then took the stripped-down Rover into Zahedan for supplies. They presented themselves as young palaeontologists, on a sabbatical from university, out to establish links between the animal and plant life with Iran and Afghanistan. They obtained their supplies with a minimum of fuss, paid, and left town again. They were in town for perhaps an hour. By the time they rejoined the others the plane, without Ben Waffa but with his friend Naim, had been in the air an hour. It had flown south again.

Ben Waffa's reason for not going with it this time was inexplicable. His waking in the night still rankled. He wandered round town and he learned of the Rover at the shabby petrol station that had filled the cans. He got no detail from the man who made the sale—there was little information to give. He curbed a rage, feeling he was close but conscious too, that he was a Palestinian and that the Iranians did not consider themselves Arabs; he needed their help, not their antagonism.

He hired a battered Cadillac and tanked up. There was no shortage of fuel here. He checked on the direction the Rover had taken, but not even that had been noticed by the indolent attendant. He went back to his room, loaded a PPS-43, an old Soviet S.M.G., with a spare magazine, and drove north.

At this stage he had to reason instead of relying on blind instinct, and this was much more difficult for him. What would Western agents be doing here anyway? To incite revolutionaries against the regime? It was the wrong part of Iran to make impact.

Waffa hated to be baffled. It never occurred to him that the young Iranians with the Rover might not be part of his problem. He did not believe in that sort of coincidence—not in this part of the country. So he kept driving, occasionally noticing his own dust cloud in his rear-view mirrors.

Well aware that he might be driving the wrong way he at least felt better doing something positive. Just when he needed the plane it was not there. He drove at speed, the steering wheel trembling under his grip, the worn suspension suffering badly. Quick to pick up signs either side of the road, he was looking for any turn-offs. According to the pump attendant he was a good two hours behind the Rover, and he began to think he was wasting his time. They might have continued straight on. He slowed, momentarily confused. Up ahead he could see the low dust of a camel train coming towards him, off the road; a hazy mirage of knock-kneed, ungainly beasts with heads raised high in almost narcissistic hauteur. He pulled over and stopped, switched off the engine.

There was little traffic: the odd car, but more often huge sand-cloaked trucks carrying materials and personnel balanced on their cargo. Out of the general silence came a hum like a mosquito. It took Waffa a little time to realise what it was. *The plane was returning.*

# 13

AT first the drone of the plane seemed an intrusion. Apart from faint streaks of cloud the sky was clear, bleached, pale blue. Waffa could not see the plane but its engine noise became persistently louder. He climbed from the car quickly, excited and impatient.

The plane came from behind a mountain range almost as if it were following its contours. It looked small and vulnerable despite its speed, and appeared hardly to be moving. Ridiculously, Waffa waved his arms above his head. As he watched the all-too-slow approach, he saw that they were veering away from him, to the west.

His immediate reaction was to race back to the airstrip, to reach it before they did if he could, so that they could be airborne again immediately. When he saw that they weren't heading for the air-strip he began to lose his temper. He needed the plane *now*.

It was Naim who first located the Rovers, a reflection on steel or chrome.

He shouted to Riza who had also caught the flash but was slower to react to it. It was well off the road, which made it suspicious. He banked and made a slow turn so that they could take a long careful look. He maintained altitude.

Leila's group were reloading the Rovers when they heard the plane. Their first reaction was to rush to their arms.

One of the men trained his S.M.G. on the approaching plane but Shearer grabbed him quickly, forcing him back against the Rover. "What the hell do you think you can hit at that range?" Shearer's words needed no translation. The Iranian nodded slowly, lowered the gun.

"It's the same plane as yesterday," said Wilson.

"Okay. So it's the same plane. They can't know who we are."

"They don't have to," said Leila. "You saw the reaction of Khaled." She indicated the youngster Shearer had just released. "He was about to fire." She stared at the circling plane. "It's the same with them. They will be satisfied that we are the enemy. That's how things are here."

"If you're satisfied we'd better try to shoot

t down then." Shearer smiled at her keeping his voice soft, showing his feelings for her. He knew that the others had long since noticed his interest in Leila but he did not care, nor could he stop himself.

"You've already said that they are out of range."

"Don't forget the semi-automatic armelite rifles in the back."

Leila stared up at the plane, shielding her eyes against the glare with cupped hands. "We need to get her lower. She's keeping distance."

"The best way to entice the pilot closer is to ignore him," said Wilson. "Just carry on loading. No hurry. Don't pay it too much attention. Keep those guns right out of sight. Move off when we're good and ready. No signs of panic."

It was the only way. There was no doubt now that the plane was interested in them, banking like an eagle.

"He's waiting to see what we're going to do," Mukhtar agreed. "He wants our direction. Let us give it to him." He still held an arm close to his wound.

Leila quickly explained to the others, and they continued the loading without haste.

Guns were carefully packed out of sight. They drank coffee, scouring the mugs with sand when they'd finished.

The plane had pulled away further to the west, as if the pilot had realised he had made his interest too clear. Finally they climbed aboard. Wilson and Shearer separated this time, one in each Rover. They sat well back under the canopy, each with an armelite rifle.

The Rovers moved off slowly, heading north-east obliquely towards the road some few miles ahead. The uneven ground and the constant obstruction of rock outcrop reduced their speed, but slowness was also part of their strategy.

The young Iranians were near the tail boards as look-outs to keep an eye on the plane. At first there was no sign of it and their own engines covered its sound. They carried on, Houshang the lead driver, working his usual miracle in country not designed for this kind of transport.

They had to stick it out. To crane from the back would be a mistake. They had to sit and wait and see whether the plane would return. At the moment their route was inconclusive, directed mainly by the wildness of the country.

They did not know that the plane was running short of fuel and was only continuing at Naim's insistence. All he wanted was to check that on reaching the road the Rovers would head north and to be reasonably certain that these were the people they were after. Once that was established Riza could go straight back to the air-strip to report to Ben Waffa.

Riza brought her up beautifully. He gained altitude while Naim used the binoculars. There was no way those below could see them unless they got out or hung out over the tail boards. Riza placed the plane high above and behind the Rovers which climbed over boulders too big for them.

And then he brought her down in line with the tiny convoy, as if he would sit on them. His timing was perfect. For the first time he was enjoying himself and Naim admired his skill. It was true that Riza had complained of the fuel level but as Naim always believed he exaggerated, *he was forced to do just that*. They had enough fuel. And now he was flying instead of driving a bus.

"What do you expect to see?" Riza shouted as he eased her down.

"Anything. Arms. Panic. The Americans."

"You won't see much."

"Can you bring her in directly behind them? So I can get a good look into the back with these?" Naim held up the glasses.

Riza shouted back. "I have to be careful o the rocks. It's much more uneven down ther than it looks. I'll do my best." It was challenge he enjoyed. He raised his voic again, "I'll try a dummy run. Not too low a first." When Naim looked doubtful, Riz grinned, and added, "They won't see me."

And they didn't. The plane lost altitud rapidly and Naim's heart was in his mouth. I was like coming down in a fast elevator an suddenly stopping. Riza timed his descen perfectly, keeping just above stalling speec At two hundred feet, roughly midwa between the two Rovers, he powered th engines and pulled back, rising at a stee angle with Naim seeing nothing now but th glare of sky, and feeling sick. Riza ha spotted a ridge ahead of the Rovers that h must at all costs avoid at the next descent. H pulled away and banked, circling and gainin height. "Next time," he bawled, glancin quickly at the drawn Naim, and wonderin why he had not made him suffer before.

In the Rovers the plane had not been see

out its roar had been heard as it soared up. Even then they were not quite certain. It was Leila who saw the plane's shadow again, touching Shearer's arm to draw his attention to it.

"Stop the truck," Shearer shouted. He thumped on the cab and climbed to the rear, jumping off before he could be stopped. He landed badly, jolting his back again. As he rose he bawled out to Leila, "Keep going slowly. Get Ray out."

Leila scrambled forward and hurriedly gave instructions to the driver, who flashed his lights. The first Rover stopped. Leila looked out her head and shouted to Wilson, who now saw the plane climbing away, banking slowly preparatory to another run in. He caught a glimpse of the limping Shearer climbing over rocks with his armelite rifle and jumped down to join him, shouting to Houshang to continue on.

Wilson raced in the opposite direction to Shearer. He'd spotted an outcrop and he knew that time was against him. Once the plane levelled he would be in view. He hurled himself head-first into a narrow crevice and straightened himself out quickly.

He gazed around. Shearer was nowhere in

253

sight. The Rovers were moving forward again slowly, the reduction of speed helped by the ascent to the ridge Riza had seen as hazard. If the plane took too long to return the gap between the Rovers and Wilson and Shearer would be too great to be effective; they wanted the plane as low and as near as possible.

Wilson searched the sky. At first he thought the plane would not return at all it had climbed so high, a dot in the pale blue. Then the dot lengthened as it continued it turn and the engine note changed. The plane was coming back. Wedging himself in Wilson adopted as comfortable a firing position as he could. Somewhere across the gulley Shearer would have done the same.

From this position Wilson could appreciate the pilot's skill. The plane wasn't diving but sinking rapidly, its nose up, its approach directly behind the rear Rover, which appeared almost to have halted. Wilson had the safety catch off his rifle, the first trigger pressure taken up. He knew the chances of stopping the plane were low. The nearer approached the more noticeable would be it speed and the more difficult it would be t hit.

Nor would it be of use simply to shoot at the plane. He needed to hit the engines or the fuel tanks. Once the pilot knew he was being fired at he would pull out and take with him the certain knowledge that he had located his enemies. Suddenly firing at the plane did not seem such a good idea. Again he wondered whether Shearer was feeling the same.

The plane was now much lower, the sun reflecting on her windscreen. She was almost gliding down. Wilson aimed, waited. He glanced quickly to his left. The Rovers had created too big a gap: the plane, still descending, would pass too high.

The feeling of defeat had a calming effect, as if none of it mattered. He watched the plane dispassionately, noticed the red-painted flashes streaking away from the white nose and narrowing towards the high tail. The plane was coming at him too fast, much too fast for accurate shooting. He closed one eye, aimed carefully, trying to swing the rifle ahead of the plane.

Now! He started pumping away, swinging the barrel, twisting his body in the crevice until he could turn no more. The plane shot past with a roar, came up just behind the Rovers, gave the optical illusion of hovering

255

over them before pulling out, nose up and climbing away. Wilson, having changed positions repeatedly, fired after her until his magazine was empty. There was no time to reload. He laid the rifle down; they had failed.

The plane banked, starboard red flash quite visible. Wilson could even see a face trying to peer down. Suddenly the starboard engine burst into flame. The plane dipped, then held as Riza gave the port engine more power. Flames were streaking back over the wing but the starboard engine was shut down as Riza reacted quickly.

It was touch and go. Wilson rose from the crevice because there was no longer need for cover. He watched fascinated, heard a yell and saw that Shearer, too, had come from his cover. It was Shearer who must have hit the starboard engine.

Riza was gaining altitude slowly. He knew he hadn't enough height but he was on full throttle on one engine and there was nothing else he could do. He had to keep his head and coax her up. The air stream was helping to keep down the flames. If the fire didn't spread there was a chance: he could land on the road if he could reach it, but he'd have been happier to have more airspace before turning.

Riza shouted, "You got your wish. Now we know."

Naim was too petrified to answer. He was afraid to look at the flames bursting back over the wing. And he was praying, lips moving, mentally promising that if Riza got them out of this he would never criticise the pilot again.

While Naim prayed for survival and Riza was using all his skills to achieve it, Leila's party were pondering their own fate. If the plane got back there was little point going on. Escape itself would become impossible, as forces were mustered against them. All they could do was to watch.

The plane was lifting slowly, wings wiggling, gently banking. The flames had noticeably diminished and the plane was heading south-west.

Leila shouted, "He'll try to land on the road. We must get there."

Wilson and Shearer lingered on, watching. They knew that by the time they reached the road the plane would be clear. Once it was over the road it would follow its course south back to Zahedan, ready to use it as a runway at the slightest sign of extra trouble. There would be a radio on the plane, so help was probably already on its way.

In fact Riza had not radioed. He knew that success or failure was in his own hands. Nothing could help him but his own prowess. *And luck*. He would certainly need that as well. So far so good. Even Naim was beginning to stir as he realised that Riza was coping; the Palestinian licked his lips, began to look about him, began to believe again. His restoration of faith was short.

Riza had noticed the sudden drop of revs in the port engine. He used the throttle, with no response. For the first time he felt himself to be losing control. The wrong kind of luck had struck him. At a time when Naim was gaining faith he, as rapidly, was losing his.

To those watching on the ground the plane seemed to be well on its way. Then the engine coughed, the port wing dipped and the plane plunged disappearing behind a rise. The terrible sound of the crash rose above the high ground a fraction after the engine cut out. It was like a bomb, and with the explosion came the gush of flame and over-lapping smoke. Through this appalling mass shot pieces of metal, screaming as they whirled through the air. The feeling of triumph to those who watched was squashed by the awesome sight; they had become too involved in the pilot's efforts. For a while they were rooted by the horror of what they saw, then, silently, they returned to the Rovers.

Ben Waffa had been watching the antics of the plane ever since it had sighted the small convoy. From where he stood it was difficult to gauge precisely what had happened. He was miles away. It would be better to watch and to wait. The Cadillac was not built for cross country.

When the plane first came down to examine the Rovers he lost sight of it behind high ground. It was, in any event, a small image from this distance, but he was quite certain that he had identified it correctly before it had veered off.

It soared up again, and he lost sight of it. He reached into the car and put on dark glasses. The plane came into sight again and he watched it descend out of his view. He could just hear the engines but they were muffled by the intervening low hills. At one stage he thought he heard shots but the sound was inconsistent and he was not sure. There was still no sight of the plane and he began to be concerned, not for Riza or Naim but because another plane would be difficult to find.

He did not see the plane again but he did see the spiral of black smoke squeezed out above the lower skyline. At first he didn't connect the two; the main smoke was hidden from him and the top of the cloud was eddied. Eventually with the plane not reappearing, he began to think the worst. He waited a little longer, then accepted that the plane had crashed.

Getting back into the Cadillac Waffa felt his fury rising. Riza and Naim had bungled it. More importantly, they had lost a plane. He felt no remorse: they had deserved to die for being so stupid.

Waffa headed back for Zahedan. He passed the camel train, shooting a cloud of dust behind him for them to choke on. But at least Riza and Naim had served some purpose; they had located the Americans, that was clear. And the Americans must have fire power unless Riza had been careless enough to strike a hill. He must get back and organise a strike force. Quickly.

# 14

THIS time they met in Bermuda. Marshall had been in Florida and Higgs took the opportunity of a short break. With a direct flight from London and the proximity of Miami, Bermuda was convenient to both.

They sat in the sunshine under striped umbrellas, idly observing the bikini-clad women who graced the sands. With umbrellas as sentinels and bodyguards discreetly placed well back, their privacy was complete.

Higgs had brought some English newspapers with him. As he sat with feet up, a John Collins by his elbow, he passed them one at a time to Marshall. "It's stirring nicely," said Higgs mildly.

Marshall read the headlines. "Of course, it's nearer to you. You make more of it."

"Don't you think it's time you did? There's a great big world beyond America's shores."

"They're beginning to grasp it. Slowly. The holding of hostages in the American Embassy in Teheran in seventy-nine made a lot of them sit up." Marshall flipped the front page of the *Daily Express*. "When the fanatics took over the Grand Mosque at Mecca that same year it registered, too. And that wasn't religious as the media reported. It was political, a deliberate attempt to get King Khaled."

Higgs looked quizzically at Marshall. "You're covering up, Joe. Reminiscence won't increase your present news coverage." He pointed at the news-sheets. "We're doing our part. Get your press to give it equal coverage. The pot must simmer."

Marshall was apologetic. "As I say, you're nearer to it. Your press boys play on it as a matter of course." He went through the head-lines again. "I can't get them going without them smelling a rat. I can't tell anyone. There's you and me and that's how it had better stay. Don't push me, Maurice."

"I understand your problem. The irony is that those headlines have been created by your people. The taking of the Grand Mosque was the turning point for you. You were able to get your feet under the table once more. The Saudis know their enemies—God knows there are enough—and they're afraid of them. They daren't come out into the open." Higgs reached for one of the newspapers. "Anyway, good work. I'm just surprised your media haven't made more of it. You need the constant pressure."

Marshall knew Higgs to be right, yet there was little he could do. They aimed for total secrecy, but it could never be maintained for long. They could kill off every agent involved and events themselves could be a give-away. If the Western press claimed one thing *Pravda* would claim another. Nothing was ever as it seemed. But they could *try* for secrecy. Destroy the sources of knowledge and your enemies are left with nothing but conjecture, however shrewd.

Marshall placed the papers at his feet. There was no breeze to make them stir. They all stated the same view in different ways, some more soberly than others, but they did the job that was needed and they had done it without pressure.

The riots in Saudi Arabia *had* apparently got out of hand. The Grand Mosque *was* again under siege. The country *was* near to turmoil. Certain countries believed what they preferred to believe, and were delighted because they wanted it to happen. It was not yet civil war, but the possibility of one breaking out was strong.

*Secrecy.* The planning, collusion, the colossal problems that had gone into making the ferment. Marshall himself had flown to Riyadh under the greatest secrecy and had met only one man there, the man who mattered most. Every single phase had to be controlled before the great act of betrayal. If the Saudis invited the Americans in now there would be eruption in the Arab world. The reasons weren't yet sufficiently strong. The timing, as always, was crucial. And the supreme sacrifice had to be made if the bitter pill was to be accepted, no matter how reluctantly or begrudgingly or even hysterically, by those who condemned it, as long as the need was seen to be there.

*Secrecy.* Marshall had nightmares about it, and so too, he suspected, did Sir Maurice Higgs. As things simmered, no matter how well, a slight change of heat could send them to boiling point. If events boiled over it was war. They both knew it. Behind the stolid, sometimes relaxed attitudes of these two men was another kind of turmoil, the torment of carrying too great a responsibility, a certainty that if the news leaked in any way they, too, would be sacrificed.

Neither had complained and, once committed, it was always too late. So far they had met with a great deal of success, which in itself was unnerving. With so far to go how could they expect their luck to last?

"What of Wilson and Shearer?" Higgs interrupted his thoughts.

"Strange, that. I always think of them as Shearer and Wilson."

Higgs smiled. "That's nationalism for you. Nothing your end?"

"Not a thing. My guess is they didn't make it."

"Shouldn't we have heard?"

"Communication's difficult." Marshall lowered his sandalled feet and moved his chair so that he could face Higgs more squarely. "I've the feeling that I should've asked the first question. The contacts are yours, not ours."

"I thought you might have picked up something. The only report I have is that their northern Omani connection was blown to bits. They left by a launch which hasn't been seen since. But then nor has an old Greek island cruising ship which the P.L.O. has been operating in the Gulf."

"You holding back?"

"My information is that armies are on the move. Some arms undoubtedly have been received, which indicates that our men sorted things out with Mukhtar and the arms releases were given to those who need them."

"That might have happened in Oman."

"The final arrangement was for Iran."

Marshall crossed his legs slowly, his ankles reddening from the sun. "They might have got there?"

"The releases did. There's no radio contact they can make if they did land. They'd be virtually cut off, on their own with a small group of Iranians."

"Not much of a deal."

"It was the best we could do."

"You're hoping that their group will reach the Russian pipe line?"

"I'd have settled for an invasion of Iran. Neither of us believed they would ever reach the Russian border. Perhaps they won't. But I'm beginning to hope they will."

"Don't get too fond of them. Nothing's changed."

Rogov could not escape the reception. All the foreign ambassadors would be present. So would those holding the highest Soviet awards. Ballerinas, dancers, musicians, artists and writers would attend. Every year it was the same. From a professional point of view the reception was a waste of time: nothing was ever learned from it.

Everyone was watching everyone else. He had only to have a few words with an ambassador and rival eyes would swing towards them. Everyone knew he was the head of the K.G.B. He didn't mind that, but he did object to non-productive receptions.

And he hated wearing his uniform, with its high stiff collar and its gold, red and blue epaulettes. He was a general, yes, but to him that meant no more than a standard of living and the authority to run things as he wished. The rank itself was meaningless.

He had received the message just before changing. Panovich had decoded it personally, and it had somewhat worried them both. At a time when they needed to discuss it they had been forced to put it aside.

It was important to be on time, he recognised that. His absence could cause more comment than his presence. So he went and he mixed and he drank vodka prodigiously to the amazement of his enemies and to the envy of his friends.

The chandeliers sparkled, the orchestra played discreetly, the noise of mixed voices, mixed tongues, was canopied by rich cigar smoke. It would be unwise to seek out Panovich in such a crowded hall under so many watchful eyes.

They had to wait late into the evening before Rogov could safely catch Panovich's eye and raise his gaze to the first landing.

Rogov was first up the staircase, leaning over the galleried landing, watching the farewells, the beautiful gowns, the too-polite goodbyes, the empty promises of tomorrow. He'd seen it so often. He spotted Panovich coming up, made sure his subordinate saw him, then turned into the facing corridor.

He opened a white door which had ceramic finger plates and entered the room beyond, leaving the door slightly ajar. There was little in the room except elegant gilded chairs and a magnificent Boulle desk, all of which would have raised a small fortune in foreign auction rooms. He crossed to the tall, draped windows, and a moment later heard Panovich come in. He turned to make sure the door was closed behind him. Only then did Rogov put a match to the unlit cigar he had been holding in his hand for the last ten minutes. He laid the extinguished match in a tray on the desk and unbuttoned the two hooks of his collar.

"These parties, Panovich. How I can do without them."

Panovich smiled. "They are believed to be necessary, Comrade General."

Rogov wasted no time.

"I'm worried about the cable. There's something wrong."

"About Wilson and Shearer? I don't see how they can escape."

"But what are they doing there?"

Panovich had considered the point but had come up with no answers; Rogov now voiced what he'd been thinking himself.

"I can accept them as being resourceful. At least Ben Waffa survived, and we still need him. He's the type to stick at it, and he won't like being beaten. But I don't like the way he used an open telephone to Teheran."

"He was careful—the signal confirms that. We can't be sure that the two Westerners are alive. It might not have been them."

"It's them." Emphatic. "But I did not expect them to stay in that part of Iran. To head west, north, I can understand. There is much stirring along the borders, and the Kurds are doing more than rattling sabres."

"We have our own problems with them that side of the Caspian."

"Why, Panovich?" Rogov struck the air, leaving a trail of smoke. "Why there? There's nothing but desert and mountains. All the oil is the other side. There's nothing where they are, not even trouble. They are hundreds of miles from the real unrest. From where they are Teheran is a planet in outer space."

"Perhaps they know that they can't survive on the western side. They could not remain hidden indefinitely. It would be extremely dangerous."

"So having done what they came for they would return to Oman. Why wander north-east into nothing land?"

"A decoy? To keep our eyes on them when we should be looking elsewhere?"

Rogov nodded slowly. "Perhaps." But he did not really like the idea.

"They are holding our attention quite a lot."

Rogov sighed. "That's true." He stood still for a while then added, "There are problems all along the borders. There are arms there—they've got them through under the closed eyes of the Turks and Iraqis."

"It won't affect us. We have two thousand five hundred tanks along the northern Iranian borders. A mass of troops, wire, lookout posts. It won't overflow on to Russian soil."

"I was hoping it would. We need an excuse to go in before any kind of civil war. It's difficult—not like Hungary or Afghanistan or Czechoslovakia."

Panovich kept his counsel. Rogov had immense power, but he was overstepping his bounds. A military suggestion from him would raise the hackles of army command. The Politburo would listen—he had too much on too many of them for them not to—but the President and the Secretary would be difficult to pressure.

Rogov knew what Panovich was thinking. He said, "What have we along the other Iranian border, Panovich? East of the Caspian?"

"No concentration of troops except at Ashkhabad. Constant patrols, of course. There's no need. The problems aren't there, and there is the natural barrier of the Reshfehye Allah Dagh—the long mountain range. It would be madness for any army to try it. The other side of the range, our side, is the Tsentralnyye Karakumy; nothing but desert."

"And the Karakumskiy Kanal," added Rogov. He rarely asked questions to which he did not know the answers. Panovich knew himself to be constantly on trial.

Rogov continued, "I want high altitude surveillance planes over the border. Some photographs might be useful."

"We already have an abundance of surveillance photographs. There's the problem of the radar station at Mashhad."

"I want more." Rogov crossed to the desk to clear the ash from his cigar.

Panovich said, hesitantly, "We'll need clearance, Comrade General. It's a delicate area."

Rogov gave Panovich an icy stare. "Not delicate enough to stop American interference. We've lost ground there. At one time we had the Ayatollas who mattered under our control. We helped Khomeini in Paris, and what have we in return? Confusion. Fanaticism. I'll speak to the President myself."

Panovich looked relieved. "The contro

will come back. We have enormous support there. It's a matter of waiting only."

"No. This time we can't wait. That way we lose what we have. We can't send an army in to support a regime at the moment indifferent to us. But the slightest sign of American or British involvement and that will change everything. Wilson and Shearer must have some answers. I've changed my mind about them. They're that side of Iran for a reason. Perhaps as decoy, but I'm not convinced. I want them alive. I want the truth squeezed out of them—quickly."

The studios were small and dilapidated and formed an almost isolated section of the group. Some television films were still made in the main sector but they belonged to a company now trading on a name established during the heyday of Hollywood. It was not difficult for continued success.

Part of the complex had been sold off to another company and was in process of renovation. Concrete mixers lay back in line to provide for the huge cracks where weeds and grass had shot up through the old, neglected roadways.

At the moment it was quiet. There were no

workmen, no actors, directors, or movement It was Sunday. The skies were blue, the Cali fornian sun at midday height. Seen from the higher ground the sea moved restlessly as i waiting for the next earthquake.

The trucks drew up at the wire enclosure Rusting gates were unlocked and pulled back on creaking hinges. Marines took up position around the perimeter, but were not allowed more than twenty yards back from the wire They were there as sentries, to stop intruders to discourage anyone who might linger out side.

The sergeant of the small Marine detail saw the car coming. He glanced up at the gates, the trucks straddling either side, and the darkened window was powered down no more than an inch, just sufficient to show the special pass. The sergeant could not see into the car through the glass. He briefly wondered how anyone could drive like that, but it was not his business. The glass was a special variety; the driver could see adequately.

The car swept on through, and went up the main causeway between the dilapidated studios. Soon it turned right and disappeared from the sight of those at the gate.

Marshall had been here several times before. He had examined many likely sites but this had seemed the best. And the president of the film company who had just bought the studios was a personal friend. It made life easier with no explanations to give, no questions asked, no bills to pay. Behind him was a bullet-proof glass partition and behind that sat Rafael Calvera, who would not discover he was locked in until he tried to get out.

Marshall drove to an isolated section on the north-east corner of the complex. It was a part that at some time during the affluent days of the studios had been added on because the land was available and the company did not know what to do with its profits. Commercially it had been a mistake, but it was there.

The other side of the wire was rising waste land—in security terms a weak link. But Marshall wanted nobody to see or hear what was to happen. It was a risk he had considered and was willing to take.

Strangely, it was not concern for his enemies that worried him—he believed he had adequately taken care of them—but of snooping from the F.B.I. They would not for one moment approve what he was doing unless they handled it, and there was no question of that. Had they known he had with him a killer, awaiting trial, there would have been an interdepartmental backlash which could develop into a national row. It was one of the reasons he had not used his own men for security duty. If it came to it, the presence of the Marines as sentries could be explained away; they did not know why they were there, and they had no knowledge of who had gone in.

These factors were going through Marshall's head as he searched for the right location. The C.I.A. and its manipulative powers had a lot of enemies *in* the States. There had been enough damage already. He was quite convinced that he personally would not survive the scandal if this operation got out. The President would deny any connection. Presidents always did. And Prime Ministers. He smothered a bitter smile as he thought of Higgs. They did it more smoothly over there. But then they'd had more practice.

He pulled up and climbed out, gazing up at the convincing façade of a building held up by supports from behind. For a moment he forgot Calvera until he heard the banging on the rear door. He let Calvera out.

"You locked me in, you bastard."

"For you own sake I didn't want you to be seen."

Marshall opened the trunk. "A nice day for shooting." It was important to get Calvera's mind back on the job. Marshall pulled the case forward, unlocked it, and took out the rifle. He screwed on the telescopic sight while Calvera watched.

"If the range is as short as you say I won't need those." Calvera's eyes were dancing. He smelled freedom.

"I'm not interested in seeing how good you are. I want a one-shot certainty. We can pretty well simulate the actual conditions here." Marshall gazed at a row of windows three floors up.

Close up, the peeling paint and some of the struts showing through holes where the façade had been vandalised, illustrated the sham. But at a distance the erection still looked convincingly like the real thing.

"I'll put a target across the street here. No. A bit further away." Marshall studied Calvera closely. "A head and shoulder target.

Almost certainly he'll be standing behind a car."

"No sweat."

"I don't want over-confidence. I want him dead."

"Like Kennedy?"

Marshall hesitated, watched the gum-chewing jaws and wondered if he had the right man. But Calvera's gaze was on the corner, eyes screwed. Marshall said, "No. Not like Kennedy. This man will be standing. But the aim will be oblique."

Calvera gazed up at the windows then back to the corner. "That angle's acute. I'll only have a second or two?"

"It's the best I can do. The security's tight. I've had to find out the arrangements and take whatever loophole there is. This is it. Can you do it?"

Calvera grinned, still weighing it up. "Sure I can do it. But maybe you're right about the 'scope. Just to make sure."

"Third floor up." Marshall pointed. "That window there. There's a platform behind the façade. You climb up the scaffolding. I'll put the target out, on its own at first, then I'll fix it to the car." Marshall loaded the rifle before handing it over.

"It won't get you anywhere except inside on another homicide rap," said Marshall coldly. "You need your new identity, and I'm the only one who can supply it. Now let's see if you're as good as you think you are."

# 15

THE Rovers shook with the force of the gale. They crouched in the vehicles, listening to the violence outside. There was no sign of abatement. Each massive gust hurled sand at the canopies which sounded as if they were being torn to shreds.

The canopies held, but sand was getting through gaps forced open by the sheer strength of the wind. Everything was slowly being coated. It crept over equipment, inside clothes, the grit even lining their mouths.

The wind had struck the previous day and had worsened as they went further north, close to the Afghanistan border. They were half way to the Russian border and had branched east to replenish water supplies at the fresh water lake, Hamun-e-Saberi, which was half in Iran and half in Afghanistan. Fed from the Helmund river in the Afghan Highlands, the lake was in the lowest part of the Seistan Basin. It was an almost uninhabited area. A few lived in the reedy marshes and others managed to raise grain and pasture a few cattle, but it was a harsh, often violent country, virtually deserted.

As they had progressed, mainly by road, but sometimes taking to the floors of the valleys where short cuts were available, sand dunes and shallow salt lakes had become more evident with the increasing winds. The advantages of leaving the road became fewer.

Houshang showed that his experience belied his years. He was quick to locate the *dasht*, the hard sand and gravel surfaces they could use. But increasingly they ran into *kavir*, the black muddy marshes covered by salt crusts. Deceptive and treacherous, the crusts covered liquid mud of considerable depth. A truck could easily sink into a black, suctioning mess.

The wind grew fiercer as they continued north. Although only Houshang had previously experienced it, Leila explained that in this barren, eastern border country, cursed by low rainfall, extreme temperature and violent winds, the gale was called "the wind of a hundred and twenty days", and started from early June. Its creation of dunes and its dust storms were well-known.

There were times when the Westerners doubted the value of going on. To the small group of Iranians, however, the whole project was different. They wanted sanity back in their country. And hope. They would do whatever was necessary to help in achieving this. If they could command Russian attention while the armies marched from the west then it was all worthwhile, even if what they did was no more than a splinter in the bear's foot; they had seen too closely what the Russians had done to their neighbours.

The present winds had caught them out. They had been approaching the road when the gusts had suddenly struck. They had piled up together in the lead Rover as if the extra company would give them strength. The noise was too deafening for talk, and they huddled together in discomfort, tasted the sand in their mouths, saw it gradually cake around the brows and lips of those sitting opposite and listened to, and felt, the frantic buffeting.

Ben Waffa was also caught by the winds. It had taken him a little time to raise a few reliable men to join him. It was made easier when he explained that the fugitives were American with pro-American Iranians. For some time now this ploy was a certain spark to kindle a hatred well indoctrinated into an unthinking populace. America had sheltered the Shah: it was enough.

Transport, too, he had managed, but he was unable to raise arms of quality in so short a time. Old-fashioned rifles were of no use to him. He radioed his contact in Esfahan, with no result. The relays worked well, though, and that same day he received his instrucions.

The Russians in Kabul received the coded message and did not waste time. Kalashnikov submachine-guns were loaded, with ample ammunition and grenades, on to a light transport plane which was flown down to Kandahar, the load transferred to helicopter and flown to Lake Hamun-e-Saberi via Dilaram for refuelling. On the last leg went four Russian-trained Afghan Marxists, should Ben Waffa need support.

The helicopter landed in an isolated spot over the Iranian border. The cargo was unloaded with the Afghans, and the helicopter went straight back. It had been an efficient and effective exercise: Ben Waffa had his arms and extra men the day after he had demanded them.

He had also asked for air surveillance to

help him, but his masters had baulked at that
With one plane lost they were not anxious to
supply another. What they did arrange
unknown to him, was the high-altitude
photography that General Rogov had already
ordered from Moscow.

If the Russian planes were at least as good
as the Americans their photo equipment was
not. The photographs would readily show
anything like installations or troop movements, but two vehicles would not be so easy
to identify. And even that presupposed they
knew the number of vehicles involved, and
the type. Ben Waffa had not had sight of
them and Riza and Naim—for whom he had
not shown the slightest remorse—had taken
their knowledge with them.

Meanwhile he had hired an old but service-
able American Jeep, its side already daubed
with the Iranian national colours so that there
could be no mistake, and two safari cars. The
Russians had not been mean with their
money and Waffa knew that he was paying
his recruits well over the odds. It did no
matter. He now commanded reasonable
speed and a dozen well-armed men.

At first there had been problems between
the four Afghans and the eight Iranians. The

Iranians strongly resented the intrusion of the Afghans, whom they knew were Russian ent. Two promises saved the day: the Afghans, who had also been selected because of a knowledge of Farsi, promised to return across the border once the enemy was dealt with, and they had provided the very sophisticated arms which they said they were willing to leave. They had also brought with them a message for Ben Waffa: eliminate the Iranians you are chasing, but capture the Westerners alive.

At the time Waffa's convoy ran into the worst of the winds it was on the road. It continued until visibility disappeared under the sand storm and the cars were swaying too much. The convoy was forced to stop, and the men closed the windows. The suffocating oppressiveness was something most of them were used to. They did not know it yet but they had made ground against their prey.

Leila's party had to dig the Rovers out. They were packed in with sand. As they worked away with spades even the Iranians, more used to these extremes, felt they would never rid themselves of the grit; hair, clothes and bodies were impregnated with it. Pores were closed and eyes bunged up. Yet they worked uncomplainingly. There was a general feeling that speed was essential, although they had no knowledge that Ben Waffa was closing in from behind. They had considered the destruction of the plane the end of that particular source of danger.

They were not overconfident. There were other dangers, always, and the ultimate one at the border was something about which they preferred not to think. But they might have exerted themselves just that much more had they known of the fire power just behind them.

Even during the tremendous task of extricating themselves, Wilson and the others noticed the laughter between Leila and Shearer as they worked side by side. Wilson began to see Shearer in a different light. He made no warning for Shearer not to get in too deep—what point was there? Let the American enjoy the crumbs of comfort he could get. The girl was vibrant and attractive; she had changed to denim shirt now they were completely away from habitation and her neat figure was eye-catching.

They lost almost two hours in digging, and had barely got moving when a tyre blew on the rear Rover, which overturned. Arms ammunition and stores crashed on to those in the back, but no one was really hurt. They were lucky. In the blazing heat and a wind still high they struggled with stores and arms.

One can of petrol was punctured and had emptied over bedding and food. They dragged the bedding out, the smell of petrol pervading everything. And then, sweat streaming and the wind trying to denude them, grouped together to get the Rover back on its wheels, they changed the blown tyre.

They agreed to stick to the road until they were within a few miles of Mashhad, known as the granary of Eastern Persia. A sizeable town, it was well-cultivated and a pilgrimage centre, at all costs to be avoided. It was only fifty miles from the Russian border, but before that their route would take them through a notorious earthquake belt.

Occasionally they had to refuel. In spite of their spare cans they needed both more petrol and more water. The type of country they had crossed had saved time up to the last hold-up, but the going had been hard, low gears prevalent, fuel consumption high. They used one Rover only, with just the driver and one companion for these replenishing expeditions, but it still left a trail. They fully realised that anyone curious enough could pin a route to them. It was unavoidable.

The nearer to the border the small convoy got, the bigger the dangers. Understandably they began to look in front of them for trouble instead of behind.

On the fourth day they drove on long after sundown to make up for lost time. The wind was still buffeting and lifting the sand but further north it began to drop, blocked somewhat by the Koppeh Dagh and Allah Dagh mountains.

They pulled off the road as they always did, having to use full beams to find a spot sheltered from both road and wind. There was little talk as they prepared for the night. The constant jarring had played up Mukhtar's wound but what had depressed the courageous little Arab most was his inability to help the others. That they understood was not enough; it was not in his nature to stand by. He did not tell them that his wound was seeping again and that he was sorely in need of a fresh dressing.

They were all exhausted and subdued as they shook out their bed rolls, which were now never free of sand. There had been little time for Wilson and Shearer to teach the others the use of explosives in relation to oil pipe lines. The explosive was not over-plentiful and had to be used efficiently.

Leila heated canned food for them over a primus. The mood was sombre and was due to extreme tiredness. When they were grouped in a hollow of rocks, hot food slowly raising morale, restoring a little of lost energy, Houshang apologised for the problems of the day.

The rest wouldn't hear of it. Houshang had been magnificent, his knowledge of their route and his instinct to do the right thing had been unfailing. He could not hold back the wind, his only failure a temporary forgetfulness of its caprices. But they had survived and were mobile again.

Houshang, elated by their warmth but unforgiving of himself, explained what lay ahead:

"There is a wide, drained valley, north-west below the border. It comes between the rivers Atrak to the west and Kashuf in the east." In the light of the lamp he looked even younger, no more than a boy. But there was nothing adolescent about what he was saying. "It is the old invasion and trade route from the Merv Steppes in Russia to Teheran and the Caspian. We can't use it. The Russians understand its vulnerability and it is well guarded." He offered a smile of apology. "So we have to squeeze in between the two mountain ranges, the Koppeh and the Allah. It means we can bypass west of Mashhad and save time."

"You know the route?" Shearer, sitting next to Leila, put down his plate.

"Oh yes. I've crossed into Russia. By night. Which is when we must go. We must go west of Ashkhabad. It is a big Russian town—about a hundred and fifty thousand people—and only about twenty miles from the border. We must stay well clear of it."

There was a general silence. Ashkhabad sounded big enough to have its activities far flung. There must be appreciable traffic to and fro.

Houshang had not overlooked the possibility.

"The Karakumskiy Kanal starts at Ashkhabad and works its way east along the border before moving to the lake south of Samarkand. The pipe line starts on the east side of the Caspian from Krasnovodsk and runs to Ashkhabad where the Kanal takes over. That is about three hundred and fifty miles of pipe line. The pumping stations are spaced at anything from fifty to a hundred miles. The pipe runs north of both the road and the railway."

"We have to cross the road and railtrack to reach it? That sounds dicey, mate."

"Once we're through the mountains we can shelter until the time is right. It can be done. The main bulk of Russian troops is on the west Caspian because the dangers are bigger there. The Turks face them, and they are afraid of an overspill of the Kurds from Iran and Turkey to join forces with their own Kurdish population along those frontiers.

"To the north-east there is no such risk. There is the natural defence of the mountains while the Iranian population is thin there, and the terrain not encouraging. We do not represent an invasion, we are too small. And because we are small they won't expect us anyway. Troops and tanks there are widespread. We can be in and out before they can muster."

The face of a boy, the thoughtful words of a man of considerable experience. Houshang hated Russia but it did not show; prejudice had been subjugated by common sense and a real will to succeed.

When Houshang had finished, Wilson said, "My back's itching."

They all stared at him but it took Shearer to interpret. "He means he thinks we're being followed."

It brought everyone back to earth. Danger. Now, not tomorrow.

"You've seen something?" asked Leila.

Wilson, who did not know of Ben Waffa, would have been surprised to learn that he shared something with him. "No. But I've had the feeling ever since the plane crashed. That wasn't the end of it."

Some of the others were sceptical. Shearer was not. "What's on your mind?"

"I dunno. Someone's breathing down my neck. I don't like the smell of his breath."

"If you're right they'll make sure they out-number us."

"And outgun. I'm not trying to alarm you. I don't think we've watched our backs enough."

Shearer did not argue. "We'd better post sentries." For the last two nights, well off the track, with the wind wiping out their trail, they had not troubled. Hands now reached for the nearby guns.

The impression Wilson and Shearer had made on the young group of revolutionaries had not come by trying to take over but by example and an uncomplaining work-rate during the last few days. Not once had either man mentioned their adventures in Oman or at sea. But Mukhtar had told the Iranians at odd moments in their own tongue, squatting and talking like a marketplace story-teller.

Now they were nearer to the border they were beginning to take critical stock of each other. They would be dependent on each other; they could not afford weak links. Wilson's words jolted them. Watch your backs. They sorted out a sentry roster, just one man at a time to act as listening post. It was not easy in a wind blowing in the wrong direction.

Nobody commented as Leila and Shearer left the tiny compound for the back of one of the Rovers. They had all seen that the feeling between them was genuine and almost instantaneous; there was no comment to make.

The canvas strained against the metal supports as the wind gusted viciously. The sound could have been unnerving but Leila and Shearer were immersed in each other. The constant violent flapping precluded serious talk. There was much to discuss but this was not the moment. As Leila lay curled up against the American, head on his chest as he stroked her long black hair, they both realised that the moment might never come. They had to take what they could while they could. Each knew that it could be terminated bloodily and far too quickly.

It was one of the Afghans who sighted the dark centre of the sand cloud. He was standing in the back of the jeep holding on to the support rail when his keen eyes detected the inner core of the sand stream. He thumped on the cab roof and Ben Waffa slowed, leaning towards the window to catch the shouted words of the Afghan.

They were still too far from Mashhad for there to be noticeable traffic. They were out in the wilds suffering the "hundred-and-twenty-day wind". Nothing had passed them. He switched on the hazard lights, a signal to those behind to slow. Then he pulled over, the two safari cars pulling in behind him. He climbed out and gave the others instructions to keep their distance once they sighted the dust cloud, and to continue, no matter for how long, until they found him parked at the roadside or until those they followed had stopped.

Waffa took over a safari car, the keen-eyed Afghan with him. The driver and passengers transferred to the jeep. Alone with the Afghan, their guns beside them, he pulled out and built up speed. He had the taste of action again.

He was careful. It was madness to go too fast in variable winds that could whip up the blinding sand. The long straight stretches of road were now behind them. He had one big advantage: the Afghan, born to the vast problems and periodic invasions of the Himalayas, could identify every sign, every changing sand pattern.

When the wind dropped for a while, way ahead the trailing dust streamers converged into one billowing cloud. Waffa smiled with satisfaction and carefully pressured the pedal. The Afghan glanced across unsmiling; but he too was satisfied.

It was impossible for Leila's group to locate Ben Waffa. Because of the conditions, there was a big gap between the Rovers to prevent those in the rear one from choking too much on the cloud thrown up by the first. Their rear view was cut off by their own dust trail.

Ben Waffa was able to approach comfortably. He pulled out when the dust began to obscure his vision and he passed the second Rover comfortably, remained in the middle of the road and overtook the first, cutting in front throwing up dust then slowly pulling away.

"Well?" He demanded of the Afghan.

"There are people in the back of each van. Two in front of each."

"How many altogether?"

The Afghan mentally counted. "Perhaps ten. One is a woman."

"*A woman*? You sure?"

This puzzled Ben Waffa yet he instinctively felt that these were the people he wanted. "Did you see the Americans?"

"No. I could only see shapes, sometimes only parts of shapes. The woman was at the back, easier to pick out."

"Arms?"

The Afghan hesitated. He was going over the whole scene again as they had passed. It had not been easy. The dust had not helped, the time in passing, short. "No. None visible."

"It's them," shouted Waffa, not influenced. "I am sure of it."

"I think you are right," said the Afghan helpfully. "They did not want to be seen. They drew back or turned their faces." His guttural observation came out tonelessly as though programmed. His sunken face was impassive, the dark eyes bright but expressionless.

Ben Waffa surveyed the empty road ahead, the uninviting desert to the west, the line of hills and mountains emerging to the north. He braked as another gust shook the car. "We'll have to go on. To drop back would be suspicious. If we knew where they were heading it would help."

"There do not appear to be many alternatives."

"It does not matter. Our comrades will follow them. We'll pull off the road after sundown when it will be too dark for them to see us, and we'll wait. If they pass, we'll follow. If they don't arrive after a while, we'll go slowly back to find our friends. Then we attack."

As Ben Waffa's car went past Leila shrank back from the tail board of the rear Land-Rover. "An Afghan," she shouted.

Wilson and Shearer, crouched back near

the cab, did not understand the significance of this but they could see Leila's obvious alarm. "So?" asked Shearer. "The border's near."

Leila wasn't sure of her own feeling. "The man with him, the driver, is not Iranian. He could be Palestinian."

"An Afghan and a Palestinian?" Shearer probed gently, not wanting to hurt Leila. "There were only two of them, weren't there?"

"Yes. But the Afghan was looking closely. There's something wrong. Where are the glasses?"

Shearer handed over the binoculars.

"Please hold me while I stand," Leila said.

The men crawled back. It was not easy in the bucking truck. They held her slim body, straddled on their knees to give stability while she raised the glasses. Viewing long distance through binoculars was almost hopeless when the field of view was both obscured and constantly moving, but she clung on.

Finally, Leila lowered the glasses and the men helped her to squat. She handed the binoculars back to Shearer. "There's something behind us."

"You can see through that lot?" Wilson asked.

Leila swallowed. "There was a sun reflection on glass. A windscreen."

"Okay. Do we flash Houshang?"

"Yes."

Wilson climbed forward over the equipment and yelled at the driver to slow and flash his lights. The Rovers stopped sharply, their trailing clouds suspended before the wind suddenly plucked them away.

Shearer now stood up. He held the glasses steady, taking his time. Then, "Okay. Move on."

Wilson bawled out again, the driver signalled Houshang in the lead Rover, and they moved off, gathering speed quickly. The halt had been brief but sufficient.

Shearer said, "Leila's right. There are two. A jeep in front, perhaps the same behind." And then, more significantly, "We caught them off-guard. They braked when they saw we had stopped."

Leila stayed by the tail board as Shearer climbed forward to join Wilson. "Do you think we were seen?" They looked to Leila.

"Perhaps seen. But he would need the eyes

of a falcon to identify you. What shall we do?" The appeal was to Shearer.

The American glanced at Wilson. "One car up front, two behind. I wonder how many of them there are?"

Nobody could answer. Shearer said to Leila, "Are they likely to ambush us on the road?"

"They might if they are Iranians. If they consider us the enemy they wouldn't care. If they are sent by the Russians they would try to do it more quietly. Kill us as we camp."

# 16

THEY flashed Houshang well before he expected to turn off. The sun was a red ball balancing on the edge of the salt desert to the west. The rays crept across the undulations like seeping blood, the crystals sparkling. Wilson jumped out and ran forward to inform Houshang of what had been happening.

Houshang was quick to respond. It was important to bivouac before it was dark. As Wilson raced back, Houshang found his spot and turned off the road. As the Rover slowed to cross the broken ground Khaled, in the front with him, opened the door and slipped out.

Khaled, aware of the importance to watch the road, moved fast to find cover in higher ground while the two Rovers bumped their way past. Houshang, knowing now that there were two following jeeps, kept his head. He found the highest outcrops, and squeezed his Rover into the tiny, rock-strewn valley beneath them.

At first it appeared that he had deliberately placed them in a trap. There was only one way out, and only one Rover at a time could use it. They were hemmed in by rock parched gorse sprouting from the crevices. As soon as the Rovers were settled Wilson and Shearer with S.M.G.s and spare magazines climbed the rocks to the north, separating in much the same way as they had done when they had shot down the plane. But there would be no single target now, and they did not know from which direction the enemy would come.

Leila stayed in the enclosure, convinced that someone should stay with the transport which itself should act as a magnet to the enemy.

Wilson and Shearer positioned themselves high enough to look out towards the road and into the narrow basin where the Rovers were so tightly packed that they would have to be reversed out. The sun was dipping as they took up position.

Well-hidden near the road, Khaled lay prone and watched the jeep stop some twenty yards from the turn-off point. Because of the constant wind he had removed his kaffiyeh, stuffing it in a pocket. He now saw that the second vehicle was a safari car. He squinted against the sun. He thought he could see five men in the car, five in the jeep: equal numbers to their own. But a car had passed them with two men. And Mukhtar was ailing. The little Omani was holding his side too often: they had all noticed. Mukhtar was a virile fighter, yet over the last two days he had fallen very silent and was clearly in pain. Ten of them, then, with twelve against?

Khaled lay there watching, thinking. He wasn't afraid. How could he show fear when their leader was a woman? It was a strange feeling for him because he was not a Kurd. She led well and fearlessly but showed herself as a woman by giving herself to the American. But the American was fighting alongside them. So it was all right.

Nothing was happening. The jeep and the car squatted there like dust-cloaked camels. The windows were down but the men still sat. He saw the nozzle of a submachine-gun above the window level, then two more in the jeep. If there had been doubt there was none now. Were they waiting for the other car to come back? He silently slipped away to warn Leila while there was still light. He scuttled over the rocks, instinctively finding cover, then gave a soft cough, the prearranged signal before climbing down to Leila.

Leila listened to Khaled then sent him back. She dispersed the rest of her group with the exception of Mukhtar. The Omani insisted on staying with her. There had to be a bait, he said; but she, like the others, knew the real reason. Even the desert-hardened Mukhtar could not flaunt a deep bullet-wound indefinitely. She understood and agreed.

Discarded and spare djellabas were carefully arranged to look like people inside the back of the Rovers. Close up they would fool nobody, but at a distance the mock-up would do. It was a simple ruse. She lit the primus and prepared food. Mukhtar was out in the open with her: just the two of them visible. Both had handguns hidden in their clothes. S.M.G.s would be too obvious. It was a crude and hasty plan, but with the light about to go there was no time for another. It was better than being killed while asleep.

The sun sank, and soft colours transformed the desolate salt desert into an undulating par of beauty. It gradually turned to a muddy grey, darkening as they watched. Nobody came.

304

The waiting Khaled saw the jeep and the car slowly shrouded by darkness until he could only sense their position. Nobody had joined them. The desert night closed down and the wind began to take the heat from the air. The wind was a curse to Khaled for it covered sound, and now he'd lost visual contact, he needed some other guidance. He crept from his cover and moved down nearer to the road.

In the Basin the darkness was complete except for the small fire Leila had made. She had expected her attackers before the light went completely; now she realised she was wrong. It changed everything. If the enemy came now her group would be unable to see who to fire at. Leila had to think quickly. She whispered up at the rocks, and the soft sound of her voice hung in the static air of the basin. "Come down"—once in Farsi and once in English.

She stood in the basin listening to them climbing down the rocks. When they were all present she doused the fire.

"It's not working the way I expected. They must be waiting for us to sleep or for the return of the other car. It would be better if we join Khaled by the road. If we spread

out, get cover, we can open fire as they leav
the cars."

Again a hasty plan was being forced o
them. There was not time to argue. At th
moment they were a perfectly grouped target
They left the shelter in single file, headin;
towards Khaled's position and stringing out
Silence was imperative. This time Mukhta
insisted on being with them.

It was a ghostly string of shadows tha
picked its way across an area not designed to
help them. Khaled had explained to Leila
exactly where he was, but when she reached
the place he was not there. She searched
noiselessly and when Houshang joined her
she whispered her fears.

Mukhtar literally stumbled across Khaled
He couldn't quite see in the dark but he could
feel the kaffiyeh that had been tied round the
mouth and he could feel the great tacky gap
where the throat had been slit. Mukhtar
wiped his fingers on the kaffiyeh and continued on to report to Leila.

She listened bravely, full of grief, and
blamed herself. She could not know that
Khaled had left his hiding place, that one of
the sharp-eyed Afghans had seen the faintest of
movements and, together with a companion,

had slipped from the jeep to circle and come up behind the young Iranian. They had tried to get information from him: had he been the only one to see them? Was his a standard stint of sentry duty or had he been dropped off because they had been seen?

It was to Khaled's eternal credit that he died telling a lie to protect the others. Leila was not the only one to be pushed into hasty plans. The Afghans knew they had little time. They were forced to kill too quickly. Before he died Khaled told them that a sentry was always dropped off near the road before they turned off. A little more time and perseverance might have brought the Afghans nearer to the truth. They finished their job as crudely as they'd begun it and dragged the body off the road to fling it into a rock cluster higher up.

What Khaled had also told them was that sentry duty lasted at least two hours. One of those hours had already gone, and the waiting party in the jeep and safari car were now impatient for the return of Ben Waffa.

Leila was sick at heart. She was confused, too, having no idea of what might have been extracted from Khaled. She felt her lack of years and experience. She needed Shearer to turn to, but the American had dispersed with the others to positions in odd pockets of rocks and crevices above the road.

There was one benefit Khaled had not enjoyed. An early moon had risen. It was less than half full and it was very low. Under its pale glow the desert took on a dark, forbidding form, its depressions and gulleys shadowed and exaggerated. But it penetrated the thick coating of dust on the bonnets of the two vehicles down the road. There was just enough reflection to pin-point them.

Leila could think of no other course than to wait. In view of Khaled she could not be sure that there was anyone in the cars. They, too, might be waiting in the rocks. She was glad there was nobody near enough to sense her dilemma and her fear. Again she yearned for Shearer.

Lights heading south caught their attention. All were positioned so that they had command of that section of road. The car was not travelling fast and it was on dipped headlamps. Suddenly the full beams shot up for a second or two, then were dipped again. There was no response from the two waiting cars and the beams of the approaching car were still too far away to pick them out.

The car drew nearer and there was a series of flashes. It was still not travelling fast. This time the jeep flashed once, its lights blazing out, startling those above them. Darkness again apart from the oncoming, now accelerating, car.

The jeep's parking lights came on so it could be picked up easily. The approaching car gave a quick flash of acknowledgement and coasted towards them. It came in slowly as if the driver wanted a minimum of noise, and pulled up almost opposite Leila. Someone in the jeep flashed a final signal, or perhaps to check the occupants of the car. In that short time those on the ridge had a clear view of Ben Waffa, and, to a lesser degree, of the Afghan sitting beside him. Perhaps five seconds went past before the car lights were extinguished. The parking lights of the jeep were switched off immediately after.

Total darkness once more. The click of a car door and the interior light came on as Ben Waffa and the Afghan climbed out each side of the car. With one protected by the car it would be possible only to shoot the nearest of them.

Leila hesitated. She had taken up the slack of the trigger; the rest of the group would be waiting for her first shot. But she had sight of only one man, and as the car doors were quietly closed even that single, vague image disappeared. There was no sound from the other two vehicles.

A set of footsteps crossed the road, measured, soft but distinct. Voices floated from the direction of the jeep. Silence, then a curt word or two followed by the sound of men jumping from the jeep and of the safari car doors opening.

Leila knew she could wait no longer. There was probably someone still by the car opposite but it was now or never. The sound of her gun cracked through the silence, the red flashes spitting out in the darkness as she sprayed the area of the two cars. The others fired immediately.

Nine submachine-guns blasted down, fanning the line where the moon still pinpointed the metalwork. There were screams of agony and cries of pain and alarm, the crash of glass and the prolonged rupturing of metal. Footsteps raced, and the gun fire followed them. A submachine-gun opened up opposite Leila and she ducked down as she felt the draught of bullets and the sharp sting as rock chips pierced her face. Crouching, she changed her position quickly and returned the fire coming from behind the car opposite. She didn't stop. There was more shattering of glass but her target seemed to be as concealed as she.

Shearer realised the jeep and the safari car would provide some protection for those below. Above the clatter of gun fire he listened for movement. Leila was on trial over this and he knew it. She had few options and he felt deeply for her. The ambush they had laid was wide open to faults. After the first burst of fire those still able to would scatter.

As yet there was no return fire except from the car which had just arrived, and that worried Shearer; it was opposite Leila. He didn't believe the rest were killed. He began to wonder about the vulnerability of his back.

So did Wilson. He had barely joined in the initial onslaught—there were enough without him—but had waited and listened and then fired a sweeping burst when he heard the faint sound of running footsteps. The scream was terrifying, the following, continuous whimpers nerve-racking.

Wilson fired at the direction of the dreadful whimpering and nearly had his own head blasted off as a prolonged burst hit the rock

just below him. He recoiled, blood streaming
from his face. The rock chips were like ice
picks piercing his skin. He hurriedly moved
position.

There was a stalemate where little appeared
to be happening. From both sides the firing
stopped, magazines were changed, nerves
became stretched. The feeling began to creep
through Leila's group that there had been a
change in initiative. Their general positions
were known. It was much more difficult to
know what was happening below.

Leila crept out and reached Houshang,
giving him quick whispered instructions.
Houshang and one of the others scrambled
back to form an outpost to watch the backs of
their colleagues. She continued on, using the
soft cough signal designed to carry only so
far, until she found Shearer. She made no
pretence.

"What shall we do?"

He'd been asking himself the same
question—they all had. Stick it out until
dawn? It wasn't long past sunset. Go back to
the Rovers? And if they did, then what?
"Let's give them another ravaging. Try to
scare the life out of them. Move slightly
further up where Ray is. Give 'em the lot."

As Shearer spoke Wilson's gun hammered away again and a terrible sigh floated up. A body crashed. "That guy's got radar eyes," said Shearer with reluctant admiration. "Come on, let's try the death or glory way."

They scrambled along, making sure the others knew who they were. They grouped, seven of them now that Khaled was dead and with two watching the rear. Two would concentrate on the far car, the other five on the two just below them. They each took a few rounds from the full magazines and loaded them into the emptied magazines as reserve. Leila gave the instruction and the silence was shattered again as they squeezed triggers. If they had set themselves up as a target they had also formed a formidable fire unit.

Bullets rained down, bringing back the screeching protest of torn metal. Most of the glass had already gone. Because of the clatter they missed the sound of an engine starting and the first they realised was as their firing tailed off and the isolated car was racing southward, a clang of metal as it went. They fired after it with no result.

When the firing stopped and the eerie silence returned only the lingering smell of cordite gave any indication of what had happened. Out of the acute silence it was noticeable that the whimpering had at last stopped.

There was an urgent whispered agreement and then, one by one, Leila's group stepped from cover and picked their way down to the road, fanning out, separating as much as possible. With guns at hip level they were ready.

Ben Waffa had been lucky not to be caught by the first frantic fire. He was standing to one side of the jeep listening to the report on Khaled and already thinking that he might have underestimated his enemy. He had even reached the point of self-excuse, of having to rely on a makeshift, assembled force when bullets started whining and red flashes stabbed out like accusing fingers.

Two men dropped before his eyes. The others all fled for cover behind the vehicles or into the rocks. The sound of crashing glass, punctured metal and screaming ricochets was frightening. They had believed they had everything under control and they cursed Ben Waffa for his lack of real planning.

During the uneasy gap between the two main bursts, some crept away to the far side of the road. They would wait until it was safe to emerge, whenever that might be. Apart from the Russian-trained Afghans, they had suddenly lost their taste for fighting. Let the Palestinian take care of the Americans.

Waffa was paying the price for his own ruthlessness. It didn't matter to him how many got killed provided he stopped his enemy. His reassurances were suddenly meaningless. There was nothing he could do to stop his men skulking off. He was even pleased when some sharp gunman in the rocks got two of them. He'd have shot them himself if he'd believed the others wouldn't shoot him in retaliation.

He knew the position was hopeless. He didn't know what damage had been done to the transport but he was sure that most of it was to the two vehicles they now crouched behind. His luck held when he slipped off his sandals and raced for his own car. The firing broke out again a second after he had moved. That second saved his life.

He found the Afghan half-dead, leaning over the bonnet. The car was now under constant fire and he kept low, pulling the Afghan down by the legs. The moans of pain did not disturb him. On his knees, he

315

managed to pull the door open, reach forward and turn the key. The still-warm engine fired at once and Waffa was swamped with relief; he had feared there would be too much danger to get the car going.

There was nothing more he could do but wait until there was a lull. The engine ticked over. The guns petered out one by one and he decided to wait no longer. He crept up on to the seat, feeling glass splinters and torn material. Keeping his head just high enough to see through the shattered windshield he engaged gear and pressed the pedal hard. The tyres burned as they skidded on the rough surface. He could barely see. The edges of the road were obscured and he was going too fast; but he dare not put on his lights. The car rocked dangerously as it passed over two prostrate bodies.

Waffa aimed at what he considered to be the middle of the road and stayed there hopefully. He could hear the thudding in the back of the car and several shots crashed into the dashboard only inches from him. But the car kept going, in spite of the terrible scraping of metal, as if something were partially ripped off. He kept his head down and believed Allah protected him, and i seemed that he did, if not the others for whom Waffa was responsible.

When Waffa considered the timing to be right he switched on the beams. Only one worked, and the front glass of that was shattered, the bulb somehow surviving. It was enough. He sat further up in his seat and drove on. The scraping on the road suddenly stopped as something dropped away clanging out behind him. By the sway of the tail he guessed that one rear tyre was deflated but he dare not stop.

What would he now do? There was the cost to face. The Russians: they wouldn't like it. To hell with them; they'd have to provide more cash. Ben Waffa, the fanatic protected by his God, began to plan again.

After earlier caution they used flashlights: the scene was ugly, The road was strewn with bodies, blood and glass. They found four dead and two dying, so near to death that it would be merciful to finish the job. Nobody wanted to, but it would have to be done.

They pulled the dead bodies into the rocks, hiding them as best they could so they would not be seen by passing cars. Leila, realising that the two wounded could not be ignored

any longer, shot them both. One was th
Afghan who had helped Waffa. The othe
had a stomach wound which he might hav
survived had Waffa not run straight over hin
with the car. Both had been far too injure
to talk. It did not help Leila face th
responsibility of finishing them.

Shearer saw this, felt the effect on her
offered no words of understanding. The
carried on, clearing up as best they could. A
unexpected bonus was to find grenades in th
jeep and the jeep itself, even with burst tyre
still mobile, its engine functioning. Th
safari car behind it was a wreck. They fitted
tow rope from the jeep to the car and, witl
the help of straining hands and the radiato
riddled jeep, they got both vehicles off th
road, finally giving them a push to toppl
them into a shallow gulley.

They tried to clear up the glass with dea
branches. The flashlights picked up the glas
reflection well but there were too man
fragments to cope completely. All they coul
hope for was to improve the scene sufficientl
for police or military not to be called in. The
could not wait for daylight to see hov
effective they had been. They did not knov
the number of men against them, how man

were still around. All the time they worked, three of them, in turn, squatted in the shadows as sentries. Mukhtar was the only one not to be relieved from this duty.

By the time they had finished most of night had gone. It was far too dangerous to bivouac where the Rovers were. Utterly weary, they drove back on to the road and headed north again. The victory had depleted them. None of them wanted sleep—not then. But they would pay the price for missing it.

Over the next forty-eight hours the wind dropped progressively as they neared the protection of the Allah Dagh, and were then climbing up into its harsh, protective folds. As agreed they kept well clear of Mashhad while enjoying the more fertile landscapes of its environs. But that was a temporary respite. Just as the night before, they knew, had been a temporary victory.

Now they climbed through the Iranian border mountains skirting the direct road that wound through to Ashkhabad. That had to be avoided at all costs, as did the road much further to the west. Houshang had done his research thoroughly. He was already established as a guide of remarkable talent, but to the Londoner and the New Yorker it was a continuing miracle that he led them through mountain passes, not all immediately evident and all of which the Rovers coped with, i sometimes with luck and manhandling.

On the seventh day they paused in a defile to eat a meal and to worry about the ailing Mukhtar. He needed rest and they could offer him none. They could not leave him behind for he would perish. Mukhtar himself did no complain and insisted on continuing. Bu how much more could he take? He was eating little and even his small frame seemed to be shrinking. Mukhtar was too experienced to listen to false reassurance. He knew and they knew, so nothing was said.

But as a result of his condition a most serious issue had to be faced before it was too late. Shearer broached it while they were cleaning the plates in sand pockets in the mountain crevices.

"You're not fit enough to go to the pipe line." Direct, a matter of fact.

Mukhtar was filled with the urgent wish to see the job done. It was vital to him. "I'm not fit as you say, but I'll see it through. I've come this far."

"Ray and I will do it."

"My instructions were that you two must stay this side of the border. There are reasons, I suspect, why the Russians must not get you. You are explosives advisors, and must carry the news of success back."

"It makes no odds. Ask Ray. We've lost Khaled. When we near the border you stay, we go. Don't waste energy arguing. You'll need it for getting back. We know what to do better than any of you."

Mukhtar hesitated, cross-legged, hand held to his side. Before he could reply, Wilson, who was listening, said quickly, "What's the name of these mountains?"

"Allah Dagh," replied Leila who was watching Shearer's efforts with Mukhtar.

"*No.*" Houshang rose, polishing his plate on a sleeve. "Kopeh Dagh."

Leila wheeled to face the youngster. "*Kopeh?*" She showed mixed feelings, one of them sudden apprehension.

"Kopeh," confirmed Houshang. He pointed north. "Between those low-lying peaks you see a haze, far down like a yellow shroud." They all strained to look. "That's the Karakumy desert." He grinned boyishly. "You think of Russia as cold Siberia. Down in that sand there you can fry an egg. That's where the pipe line is." He paused, adding almost as an aside, "We are already in Russia."

# 17

THE news had mixed effect. They were pleased to have come so far, but having reached a point of comparative tranquillity they were in the greatest danger.

On this northern Iranian border with Russia there were only three main roads, roughly equi-distant: to the west, central and to the east. All three, along with the Atrak river which skirted Iran to the west, were heavily guarded. For the rest there was the natural barrier of three mountain ranges interleaving and overlapping. Where an army could penetrate the safeguards were immense.

Even Russia could not closely guard *all* her lengthy frontiers. Satellites could pick out enemy troop movements and Russian military would adjust accordingly. But a small group of people crossing the formidable natural defenses of the mountains would be difficult to detect. Houshang had led the small party of saboteurs to the least guarded of the Iranian borders and had made good use of its considerable cover.

Ashkhabad had a sizeable garrison of troops, and patrols were frequent along the road that fringed the pipe line and the railway. There were plenty of tanks and other tracked vehicles readily available. A panic button could summon airborne troops in from Bukhara and Samarkand. That apart, no armoured force could get through the mountain barrier. Two small, four-wheel-drive vehicles could if the route was carefully enough planned. And this route had been tried and planned long before Ray Wilson and Doug Shearer had come to the minds of Sir Maurice Higgs and Joseph Marshall.

That, however, might achieve a penetration of the mountains. There was a vast difference between the comparatively simple act of entering Russia and effectively doing so. The Russians didn't tolerate opposition; they simply crushed it. Battling through a sparsely populated part of Iran was one thing. What the group now had to face was quite another.

The silence was in keeping with the mountains themselves. The wind had dropped now, the sky was blue, a bird, perhaps a falcon or a young eagle, glided with open wings on the eddies between the peaks reaching high above them, as if it had come to survey and to report back. It circled majestically, a sign of strong life in these unfriendly barriers, then floated out of sight.

It was strange how they all watched it, then, without a word, returned their gaze to the golden shroud of desert just discernible so far below. It was as if they all held the same thoughts and were afraid of expressing them. Quietly, they packed away the plates and discarded empty cans into a tiny gorge. They drove on in silence.

There was no easy way down to the Karakumy desert. It was still a considerable distance away, and the courses of mountain ranges are rarely simple to traverse. They had to climb again before they could descend. And when it looked as if the descent had started, up they would go again, with Houshang making the odd but still rare mistake, and they would carefully have to reverse—there was never a space to turn—and then start again.

Nobody complained. The hazardous journey could not be hurried. So they took it slowly, easing the wheels carefully over every negotiable obstruction, judging balance, holding breath, making sickly grins of relief. No one at any time suggested they should give up.

Shearer's thoughts were concentrated on Leila. The nearer they got to the real danger zone the more he worried for her.

It was crazy at his age, he told himself. But whatever happened he had to get her out. Even without the problem of Mukhtar he would go over the border with her. Beneath the tough, assured front she displayed to her compatriots, she was unsure of herself. In his arms at night she was another person, but even to him, he knew, she would not voice all her fears. His presence had perhaps confused her yet he was sure she needed him.

What surprised him was that Wilson had issued no warning, no criticism. The Londoner had shown considerable understanding, even a tenderness towards them. Wilson and he were fall guys, not liking each other and suspicious of each other. Yet being forced to work together had demanded a need to rely on one another. Like it or not their relationship had changed.

They covered raised valleys, old camel train routes, disused since the advent of roads, dry river beds that in another month would be gushing with water, huge escarpments, frightening climbs and descents.

They reached the stage where the desert was showing more frequently. When they gazed down at the vast emptiness, even from their elevated position, it was as far as the eye could see. The heat formed a haze that obscured the distance. But even with unrestricted view they would not have seen its end, nor the far-flung marshes and salt deserts to the north-west, nor the lava belts. All they saw was desert, endless and forbidding.

There were times now when they were vulnerable. As they descended they were more constantly in view from the Russian side. Not blatantly so, for there were far too many folds and crevices and peaks, but occasionally, to anyone using binoculars in their direction, they could have been seen.

They camped that night in a pebble-strewn gulley. Water had flowed there at some time but now it was dry and hidden and they could use the primus freely. It was cold at this height and, once dark, they lit a fire knowing that it could not be seen below them.

When they had eaten Houshang suggested that some of them would like to climb to the ridge of the gulley with him. They all went, with the exception of Mukhtar. The going was quite easy even in the dark. Though they slipped repeatedly on the shingle, the slope was not steep. They lined the ridge and looked down.

Houshang's pointing finger was not needed. Below, to the north-east, startlingly close, was the illuminated spread of Ashkhabad. A myriad of lights, the lines of streets distinct, the limited size of the height of buildings clear. The unrestricted view was breathtaking. They watched in silence, overawed by the sight. And they were all thinking the same; there were thousands of Russians down there.

It was dangerous to start too soon. They could have done with the darkness to cover their approach, but they needed light to avert calamity. Houshang, who was by now desperately tired, guided them down in a grey early dawn.

The sun favoured them. Its rise in the east smothered them in the shadows of the mountains. It was a good time to descend, to edge their way through the foothills, always heading north-west, away from Ashkhabad. Such a route, lengthened the distance from the

Iranian border; but they had known that at the outset.

They found shelter behind the last folds of hills with the mountains rising at their back, red in the sun, purple in the shadows.

The final decision had to be Leila's but they all had their say. It had taken until mid-morning to reach their present shelter. Ashkhabad lay out of sight, some twenty miles away. The best place to blow the pipe line was between a small place called Geok-Tepe and another, about thirty-five miles further on, called Bakharden. If they aimed for the centre between these two it would push them some forty miles west of Ashkhabad: the further from there the better.

They could either set out in darkness—the going was far less treacherous now—or they could wait for tomorrow's pre-dawn. Darkness was a good cover but made getting back more difficult. Daylight gave them speed but obviously made them open to detection.

None of them wanted to travel by day. Night travel was the lesser of two evils and darkness gave them time *and* cover. But it would be slow.

There was nothing to do but wait. The road was only a few miles from where they were hiding. Each one in turn, careful to avoid reflection, used the binoculars to watch the road. The amount of military movement was more than they expected. In the main, troop convoys were travelling west towards the Caspian, suggesting that something might be stirring there.

A long, low freight train trundled past, each open truck carrying a tank. There was no sign of air activity but they heard the drone of planes. They could pick up no vapour trails.

"There weren't this number of army trucks when I came before." Houshang was puzzled. As things stood there was no way they could have approached in daylight. There was an almost-constant dust cloud.

When Shearer used the glasses he focused beyond the road and the railway and picked up the hazy outline of the pipe line. From here it looked as if it was bedded into the sand but he guessed it would be raised above it. It seemed close to the rail track but the haze partially obscured it and the perspective was all wrong. It could be miles from the track. At times it was so indistinct that he thought he was imagining it. He wiped the lenses and handed them to Wilson.

There was no escape from the rising sun except under the Rovers. The extreme heat after the coldness of the mountain passes made them drowsy. They'd had little sleep but a healthy fear kept them awake. Even those not on sentry duty were reluctant to doze off.

The evening came all too slowly, the sun dipping early behind the Kopeh Dagh, its magical rays lancing the gaps between the peaks. But the group concentrated on the road. Convoys had been regular all day and were still moving.

Houshang used the binoculars more than anyone. He carefully sought higher ground in the foothills, wedged himself behind solid cover and studied, as far as the angle permitted, the ground between themselves and the road. With the Kopeh rising immediately behind them, the uninterrupted desert really lay beyond the road.

The area of pipe line they wanted was about twenty-five miles from the border but they were much nearer to it than that. Houshang estimated the road was about five miles away, if that. Dead ground was difficult to estimate. The pipe line was roughly four miles further on. It would be a mistake to

331

leave too early. Both road and rail were active, and he had sighted eight-wheeler armoured patrol cars covering the pipe line in the distance.

Meanwhile Wilson and Shearer were once more checking the plastic explosive, the adhesives, the timing devices, detonators and primers, as they had been doing on and off all day. Only one Rover would be used. Mukhtar and two Iranians would stay at base with the second Rover. That left Leila, Wilson, Shearer, Houshang and two other Iranians as the sabotage party. Magazines were loaded, spares stuck in belts, a grenade placed in each trouser pocket. Guns were cleaned, barrels cleared of oil, and loaded. They had too much time on their hands. Nerves were stretched as darkness neared. And still they had to wait.

It was not enough that the sun had gone. It was still far too early to start. Dipped headlights showed a stream of Red Army trucks continuing north-west. There were only two logical places the convoys could be heading, to Krasnovodsk on the eastern Caspian, south of which were the oil fields from which the pipe line came, and from which there was a train ferry straight across the Caspian to the main town of Baku, a major on- and off-shore source of oil. If the convoys branched off at Kyzl-Arvat then they were going to the south-east section of the Caspian along the Iranian border. Something had to be happening for this amount of military movement. There was far less coming the other way.

It was a few hours before the convoys eased. The group had watched fascinated at the constant line of lights and were relieved when they began to tail off. It was ten o'clock: they could really wait no longer. There was still traffic on the road but it had largely been reduced to intermittent, solitary vehicles.

They sorted themselves out, slung the S.M.G.s across their shoulders to prevent them from striking anything else. The lead Rover had been ready for some time and had been repeatedly checked. The indefatigable Houshang again took the wheel. To him it was an energy source, and once in the cab his weariness disappeared.

The temptation of those going was to shake hands with those who were not. One by one, without prompting each other, they came to the same conclusion. To shake hands was to suggest they might not meet again. Super-titiously, they decided against it. Away from the others for a moment, Shearer held Leila tightly and they clung together to kiss hard, before she climbed in beside Houshang. The others got in the back.

The noise of the engine ticking over seemed shattering after the enforced silence of the day. They moved off bumpily. The pace was agonisingly slow and low gears meant more noise. But the bucking that sent those in the back sprawling against each other was sufficient to show the problems. Houshang was driving blind, relying solely on his earlier restricted survey. And on his natural judgement.

Detonators and explosive had been made easily accessible and wedged in to prevent mishap against erratic movement. On the other hand, the arms clattered whatever they did. The lurching was so severe that the back riders spent their time clutching and cursing. During that very short ride Houshang was re-named many times, but the cursing was for relief.

The Rover braked suddenly and they were all flung forward. The engine ticked over like a massive metronome across the desert. Houshang came round to the tail board. "I'm sorry. I saw a depression just in time."

334

Wilson clambered up, knees sore, adjusted his S.M.G. and was the first to jump from the back. One look round and he was surprised that Houshang could see anything at all except the headlights along the road. The road seemed uncomfortably close. "What now, cocker?"

"Off-load. I'll get the truck out of sight in this depression, if I can. We walk from here."

It had already been agreed. None of them expected the Rover to cross the road and the railway track.

"How far?" asked Wilson.

"The road? Half a mile; but there will be another hour and a half's walk from there. Say two hours from here. At most."

The Rover had saved them only about four and a half miles' walking, but that meant a valuable hour or so. And the same coming back. They had about six clear hours before dawn, by which time they must be on the move through the mountains again.

While Shearer and the two Iranians, Rajai and Ahmed, sorted out the packs they would carry, Leila, Wilson and Houshang clambered down the depression to give it what scrutiny darkness would allow. It wasn't as deep as Houshang had suspected. They agreed that it

was too shallow to hide the Rover completely
A well-trained light would pick out part of
the canopy.

There was not time to search for better
They off-loaded what was needed. Houshang
climbed up into the cab alone and reversed
with blind insight, but they all helped ease
the Rover down into the depression. Once
down Houshang took her back further in the
event of needing a run at the slope on the
return. He switched off.

They were all ready. With the explosive
materials in haversacks carried between
Wilson and Shearer, they started out toward
the road. In the general flatness of the
country they had ample warning of approaching lights either way. There was no problem
of direction.

Underfoot was another matter. They found
that one of the reasons the Rover had lurched
so much was that the crusted surface could
suddenly give way. They trod with care.

The nearer they came to the road the
greater the danger of being picked out by the
beams of passing traffic. And then, just a few
yards from the road, they saw what they had
all dreaded, a trail of twin lights that seemed

endless. A military convoy. The lead truck on full beam.

They could risk running across or taking cover where they were. Wilson saw the answer first. "Come on. Bloody quick." He ran for the road where it was built up above the desert. He threw himself beside it, quickly slipping off the pack and the gun and trying to wedge himself under the road itself, thrusting the equipment ahead of him.

They all burrowed, faces down, bodies thrust against the raised hardcore. The front truck beams were stretching out, illuminating the faults in the road surface.

Crammed in, heads against the hard sand and rubble, they could hear the convoy approaching with deafening clarity. They could feel the vibrations. They couldn't see the lights any more, they dare not face them, but they had no need. They all had the same strong feelings that the heavy convoy of carriers was going to pass straight over them, crush and grind them to blood and bone. The convoy should have been the far side of the road but it seemed to be travelling along its centre.

The road shook as the first truck approached. The beams played well ahead, the stream of dipped ones well spaced behind, shrouded in dust like moons trying to penetrate cloud. The first truck tumbled past, a tuneless voice bawling out some Russian song. One by one they came, unhurried, heavily laden.

The convoy seemed endless. Once the lead truck was past the risks eased because of the dust. But the dust created another problem, and the effort to stifle coughs and spluttering was acute and sometimes impossible. Finally it was gone, now leaving a faint trail of filtered red lights.

They waited, raising heads carefully. Nothing more. They rose quickly, retrieved gear, mounted the road in a group like an untrained bunch of recruits. They were too relieved to worry. Hastening across the hard surface brought no further problems, and then they were on the other side.

Somehow the road had acted as a demarcation line. The Kopeh side of it represented reasonable safety, the side they were now on increased danger. They broke into a trot at the approach of a car and flattened before the beams were too near. But it was a precautionary measure; none of them felt real danger.

338

At this point the rail track was very close to the road running parallel to it. They crossed the tracks awkwardly, Houshang almost tripping over them. It was the first lack of concentration he had shown. He took a compass bearing.

They headed north-east across open desert, not sure how far they had to go but estimating about five miles. It was important to stay on a direct course with a small township either side and salt desert to the west. But at least they were alone, the only noise now the odd swish of traffic at their backs. There were no more convoys, as if the night had finally closed down military activity.

Above them, suddenly, was the thudding of helicopter blades, the blinking navigation light quite close. The chopper seemed to be heading for Ashkhabad. Again, they sank down until it was well out of range.

After the first mile the vast emptiness engulfed them. It would be so easy to get lost. Wilson was completely out of his depth. He kept moving; walking did not worry him; the total absence of streets and buildings did. Leila and Shearer walked side by side just behind Houshang.

The eerieness and emptiness communicated, warned, subjugated. They simply kept moving. If someone stumbled the nearest person would help and the other would wait. They were in a fairly loose pack. They were in need of each other; the desert made them feel isolated. And, intermittently, a low, strange whine reached them from ahead; Brown in London had told them to home on such a sound; a pumping station.

It took them well over an hour to reach the pipe line. It rose out of nothing, the effect suddenly slowing them. The sight was awe-inspiring in an empty desert. Through binoculars it had seemed like a narrow pipe that stretched to eternity. It was different now. Raised on concrete supports it was held up like a massive, metal artery sending a life flow from the Caspian to the vast interior. Its huge shape dominated the barrenness around it until its diminishing shadow gradually receded into the darkness in each direction.

"Where's the bloody pumping station?"

They were all thinking the same.

Shearer said, "For God's sake we heard it."

They listened but there was no sound. "Which way do we go? We could walk away from it." Wilson's desperate tone spoke for them all. They had been so sure of their position.

Leila made her decision. "We must settle for the pipe alone. We can still badly hurt them. There's no time to explore."

Wilson and Shearer wasted no time. They unslung their haversacks and got down to work. They stuck the explosive under the enormous belly of the pipe for two sound reasons. It was less likely to be seen by a casual inspection and the explosive would take the line of least resistance.

It would rupture the pipe all right, while the biggest blast would expand out against the ground which would trap a good deal of blast, sending shock waves back against the pipe to tear the metal again.

Working quickly they fixed three spaced charges and set the explosion for six a.m. There was a small risk of discovery in this but if it went off before they could head for the cover of the mountains they would never reach them. The Russians would make a massive search.

When Wilson and Shearer glanced at each other as they set the timing they were possibly thinking the same thing. Once the pipe was blown their chances were minimal anyway. They must all know it, yet they worked on, sentries placed at each end of their working area.

The moon was high now but they still had to make careful use of pencil flashlights, particularly when time setting. It was during one of these instances that they heard the whine again. It was steady, and a little distance away.

Shearer said, "It's the pumping station." He glanced at his watch. "There's time if we can find it. It's that way." He pointed, then finished what he was doing before they all followed the pipe south-east, the Ashkhabad direction. They could only go so far because of the time left. But it wouldn't take long to set charges.

The whine was so distinct now that they wondered why they hadn't heard it constantly. A wind change was probably responsible for the inconsistency of the sound. They broke into a run. Brown had explained the importance of pumping stations: they were difficult to replace in the West; it was unlikely that the Russians would find it any easier. Destruction of one could hold up the flow of oil for a considerable time. It would be a crippling blow if one could be put out of action.

It was less than half a mile away and it stood out of the desert like a gigantic pill box, the sound like a muted jet engine. They went round its square shape carefully. Twice their height, it had inspection doors but it was obviously unmanned as most stations were. It would be difficult to leave the charges un-sighted against the plain tempered walls and to be effective they needed a good deal of ex-plosive against the reinforced casing. They worked hard and fast fixing the plastic around the inspection points, the weakest parts. They fixed three blocks and decided they needed one more to be sure of total destruction.

They had no more. Wilson volunteered to go back to remove one from the pipe itself. He ran as fast as he could, the time factor drumming through his head. It took him a little while to dismantle one of the charges under the belly of the pipe; it was delicate work he could not rush. He knew the others would be worrying over the delay. By the time he arrived back at the pumping station he was sweating and breathless and they had lost valuable time.

Shearer fixed the last charge. As he was about to set the timing, they belatedly became aware of distant lights. They had been so excited by this unexpected bonus, something that would take a long time to repair, that they had been concentrating on fixing the charges.

There was little doubt that it was a routine patrol. One of the personnel carriers armed with a 16mm.-cannon; this apart from what the troops themselves carried. Shearer coolly continued to set the time, the narrow beam of the flashlight steady on the steel casing.

Whether the carrier speeded up because someone had seen them or because of the whim of the driver was unimportant. The group was suddenly faced with the need to escape and nowhere to hide. A spotlight flooded out ahead of the carrier. It didn't quite reach them. A second light came on and each powerful beam swept over the desert side of the pipe.

The group might have heard the approach earlier but for the whine of the pump. They quickly picked up their haversacks plus any tell tale bits and pieces and sheltered behind the station. It was a cover that could not last.

There was a few seconds' respite when the

344

spotlights went out and Shearer wondered about making a run for it. The lights came on again, swinging casually, and solved the problem for them. It would have been a mistake to run. And it would be a mistake to stay.

"There is only one thing to do," Leila whispered urgently.

"It's our only hope," she explained rapidly.

"For chrissake it's crazy. *No!*" Shearer exploded. But there was no time for argument. Shearer shook Leila.

"*No!*" he repeated fiercely.

The others did not intervene. It was too late anyway. The carrier would soon pick them up in its headlamps without the spotlights. The pumping station could not conceal the six of them even if they worked their way round it. Just as they would be seen, so too would the explosive charges. It had all been for nothing. A week of effort and attacks, all in vain.

Wilson had been squatting at the base of the station with uncomplaining resignation. Now he looked up at the pale shadows of Shearer and Leila and he felt sorry for them. There was no point in interfering. Leila suddenly broke away and ran out into the desert.

Shearer called out, then went to follow and
Wilson put a foot out. Shearer went crashing
to the ground. Wilson said laconically, "She's
the guts to do what she thinks is best. Now
you do what she wants."

"She'll get killed." Shearer wiped san
from his face. "For chrissake, I can't leave
her there."

"We'll all get killed. Leave her alone and
move. The bloody thing's almost here."

"You bastard."

"Ain't I always been?" Wilson rose, gun
cocked. He dropped his haversack and
scooped it under the pipe with his foot.

Shearer, suddenly realising that he was
only adding to Leila's problems, rolled under
the belly of the pipe. Houshang took up
position the other side of the pumping
station. The two others, Rajai and Ahmed
ran towards the carrier under cover of the
pipe.

The carrier was very near now. It was clear
that those in charge of the spotlights were so
bored with the daily routine that they varied
it. One of them was trying to make figures of
eight in the desert but an obvious rebuke
brought the beam back to regimental traversing.

The dispersed group waited. Wilson and Shearer were quite calm now that they had only one course. The three Iranians were different; they hated the Russians. But for Leila they'd have jumped up now and would have fired point-blank at the carrier. Leila was laying her life on the line—almost literally. They would obey her. But it was an effort.

The carrier was on full beams and those beams picked up the prostrate huddled figure of Leila. The actual time of sighting could be judged by the sudden braking of the carrier. It came to a stop, its lights focused on Leila who had her head averted, and then the spotlights swung round and pinpointed her more clearly in two rays of white light. From the reflection of these lights the barrel of the 16mm.-cannon was seen to come down slowly until it was pointing straight at the motionless body. Shearer, watching from the protective shadow of the pipe line, squirmed. Sound of the movement of arms was quite clear from the back of the carrier.

Nothing stirred for a moment as the Russians could not believe what they saw: a lone body of a woman, in the wilderness. Then one spotlight spread out to the north, the other to follow the line of the pipe.

Those under the pipe drew back until they were cast in the shadow of the pipe itself. The light picked its way along, then came back slowly, reached the pumping station, passed it, then shot back to it, staying there.

Wilson and Houshang were out of sight the powerful light cascading either side of them. Wilson guessed the charges had been seen.

One spotlight returned to Leila, the angle of it sharpening as the carrier started to roll forward again. The angle of the cannon sharpened too. Leila had not moved. Shearer watched in anguish, her body almost opposite him some thirty feet away. He was having trouble controlling his breathing. They must depend on hearing alone, with the spotlight fingering everything, rarely keeping still.

The near spotlight probed again, but provided the group kept still they were shadowed for the moment. The carrier stopped within feet of Leila. Shearer could just see the front of the carrier from where he lay. He heard men jump out. Footsteps, slow, wary.

The near spotlight had returned to the pumping station, holding it in its glare as if it were stage scenery. There was nothing Wilson and Houshang could do while the ight blazed all round them. But their guns were held ready.

Someone spoke in Russian. Two men came nto Shearer's vision as they approached Leila. One held a Kalaschnikov machine pistol, the other an automatic rifle. Both were pointing at Leila. As they stopped near her he 16mm.-cannon swivelled round to the general direction of the pump.

A jackboot kicked at Leila and Shearer bit his lip. She slumped back. Shearer saw the rank on the man's arm: a warrant officer. The boot was pushed forward again. More slowly but with more strength, Leila was hefted over on to her back, the guns still trained on her. One of her arms swung over limply and hit the ground. The warrant officer moved round, his back to Shearer. He spoke slowly in Russian, the second man nodded. The warrant officer placed his heel on Leila's out-stretched hand and ground down on it, intent on ensuring she was not shamming. Leila showed no sign.

Shearer could take no more. He could see the slight bulge of the grenade at the waist level under Leila's loose shirt; the Russians must surely see it too. He sighted carefully. The two Russians were full in the beams of the carrier, although the spotlight that had held Leila was now functioning elsewhere.

Shearer fired, angry. What the hell, it's got to happen anyway: there was no way back.

# 18

HOUSHANG sprang from behind the station and blew out the near spotlight with his first burst.

Rajai and Ahmed, unable to curb themselves any longer, helped each other to a standing position on top of the pipe and opened fire from there. They were firing down into the carrier which had pulled up beyond them.

Wilson rolled round the side of the pumping station and added his own fire power. Leila had the sense and the nerve to remain absolutely still. On full view, she would be the first to be shot if she moved. She had a moment of luck. Of the two Russians who died, the warrant officer fell partially across her. He fell so heavily over her legs that she thought he had broken them. Only then, cautiously, as she opened one eye, did she decide to move.

She reached out slowly for the Kalaschnikov, groping for it with stealthy fingers at the side of the dead Russian. When she was satisfied she had a firm grip she sat up and smashed the headlamps with a continuou burst. She rolled quickly, then heaved the body away, and scrambled as fast as she could towards the cover of the carrier.

She drew a grenade, pulled the pin, tossed it over the front and ducked. Before her head went down she saw the young Russian radio operator sitting in the front. He was petrified. The white blob of his face showed through the armoured glass, his eyes staring straight ahead. It was clear to Leila that the whole blazing eruption had taken him by surprise and that his nerves had not yet unlocked.

On the back of the carrier his surviving colleagues, stunned by the sudden, well-spread gun fire, gathered their wits and fired from behind their armour. When the grenade landed with a warning, metallic clunk several tried to climb over the side.

Some were slain as they jumped, some shredded by the grenade. After its red, searing burst, Leila tossed her second one ducked again and edged round to the driver's side. An armed Russian was staggering from side to side, blood gushing down his face. Shearer, still under the pipe, had been about to shoot him, saw Leila rush round, held his fire and left it to her. The youth collapsed at her feet.

It was a miracle the radio operator had not been hit. He was just emerging from shock when Leila yanked open the door. She shot him as he was about to relay and she was never to forget the look of surprise and of innocence on the young Mongolian face. A boy. Like Khaled had been.

The Russians had been taken completely by surprise, fooled by a simple trick, but really routed by the conviction of their own invincibility. They had been slow to move, and by the time they had they had lost valuable men. Before they could remuster, form some sort of organised fire power, Leila's first grenade had reduced them to a disorganised rabble.

But there were still some alive, and there were also casualties in Leila's group. Rajai and Ahmed were killed because fervour had made them reckless and they received a fusillade of shots while still standing on the pipe. But they had taken many with them in their first cold-blooded bursts of fire. They had departed to Allah now, their stained and ruptured shells unmoving on the hard sand at the base of the pipe.

There were four Russians alive. They backed against the side of the huge carrier with its impotent 16mm.-cannon still directed pointlessly at the pumping station, and they stood with hands raised as Wilson, Shearer and a wounded Houshang came slowly forward. The single spotlight on the far side of the carrier shone out aimlessly to provide an overspill of bad light. It was enough.

It was a dreadful moment for the victors. They had four prisoners, but there was no possibility of coping with them. And they could not take the slightest risk of them getting back to base. As far as they could see the Russians weren't dying or wounded. They had simply surrendered. News must not get back. Even in this light Wilson and Shearer were clearly not Arabs or Iranians.

In something like a croak, Shearer said, "We'd better do it together. *Now*."

The four Russians did not understand the words and were dead before there was any possibility that they might.

Wilson vomited on the spot, leaning against the carrier. It was Leila who showed no sign of emotion. Like Rajai and Ahmed she hated the Russians with every fibre. Pity for the Russian boy-soldier was to strike her later but now she had consideration only for their own position, which had worsened considerably.

They split up to search the carrier, climbing up warily. Shearer, who was on the far side where the remaining spotlight still operated, swung the beam round to shine into the interior.

Carnage. The two men felt their nausea return. Bodies were everywhere, twisted and sightless, dead uniformed chunks. The grenades had accounted for most of them.

Some lay across others, legs and arms in eerie unnatural positions. There was no movement. The three watching saboteurs showed no inclination to poke around the bodies to be sure there were no wounded. With the wounds some of them carried it would have been impossible for them to have survived.

There was, however, one man forward, hunched over a portable radio, that made their blood go cold. His short dark hair was cupped by a headpiece. The radio was on the floor on its side, its aerial twisted by the fall.

The same question was in all their minds. Had a distress call gone out? Or had it all been too quick? Almost as one the three looked back towards Ashkhabad and then the other way. There was no sign of anything.

"He's been shot and blasted. If he was killed at the outset we might be lucky." Shearer stopped to retrieve the radio. "The front is smashed. But that still doesn't mean a signal didn't go out first."

"What shall we do?" Reaction was slowly settling on Leila. After brilliantly instigating such a devastating coup, with the immediate danger past, she was appealing to Shearer again.

"We keep our cool and hope for the best. Tidy up. Even if a radio call didn't go out, we'll still be in trouble when they fail to report in later. There'll be another patrol and the balloon will go up. They'll find the charges and they'll find us."

From below Houshang called out to remind them that time was running out. His face was bleeding where a bullet had passed straight through the flesh of his cheek. Incredibly, it had entered through his open mouth.

They couldn't leave the evidence of an ambush. They must try to slow down a search.

Wilson said brusquely, "Load the dead on the carrier. Quick as you can."

Wilson and Shearer worked as a team. grabbing the feet and arms of each body and swinging it over. Even with the tail down it was hard, tedious work. Leila used the spotlight to locate the bodies.

There could be no compassion, no segregation, for the dead. Rajai and Ahmed went in with the rest.

As fast as they worked it still took time. They offloaded two Kalaschnikovs and two automatic rifles to take back with them. Finally they had the last body on board. At a rough estimate they reckoned there were about fifteen dead Russians.

Wilson worked fast in the back of the carrier removing braces and belts as he found them. He made a crude but tough rope from them, pulling and testing its strength. He climbed into the driver's seat and with the aid of a torch ran through the gears by following the diagram on the panel of the gear lever casing. He started up and swung the carrier round to face north. He lined it up straight then climbed out leaving the engine running.

He tied his unlikely rope one side of the steering wheel, above its crossbar so that it would not slip down, passed the end under the clutch pedal, tied a rough knot above it, pulled up the free end to tie it the other side of the steering wheel.

He climbed over the back and threw down the broken radio, jumped down, wedged the radio over the accelerator, adjusting it until he was satisfied, then climbed behind the wheel again. He depressed the clutch, put her in gear, released the clutch pedal and the carrier moved forward. He moved up a gear and she continued to move.

He took his hands from the steering wheel. Immediately the wheel tried to turn. They were crossing open desert, the ground uneven. The makeshift rope held. There was play but not enough to change direction drastically, and the play came from both sides so that there was almost self-adjusting compensation. It would have to do.

He opened the door, careful to avoid the radio on the floor. After taking a last look he jumped out, slamming the heavy door as he went. He hit the ground awkwardly, rolled and cursed.

His knees and shoulder were sore. He rose slowly. The carrier lumbered on, no lights, a tenuous steering device, but it kept moving at a speed approaching thirty miles an hour. If the rope held, if there was enough fuel, if there were no treacherous gulleys or depressions in its path, no rocks, no sudden surface subsidence, it could be a hundred miles north by daylight. With luck. And with its silent, gruesome cargo. Wilson loped back to the pipe line.

The others had not been idle in his absence. They had scraped away at the sand, wet it from a water bottle taken from one of the Russians and plastered the areas where they'd placed the charges on the pumping station.

It was a crude, very rudimentary form of camouflage and not all of it stuck. But it broke up the general appearance. They smeared surface sand over wide areas of the casing to give a general impression of sand blast and wind shift.

The camouflage would not stand up to daylight inspection and might even attract attention. But in darkness, even under artificial light, it might work. The important thing was not to show that this had been an area of battle and sabotage.

The bodies and the carrier had gone. Everything had been collected. There was nothing that could be done about the blood, scattered in wide patches, but that wouldn't be seen at night and by dawn it would be well dried in. What had happened to the patrol should become a time-consuming mystery for the Russians.

The group started back for the railway and the road. Only four of them now, but their losses were nothing in proportion to the routed Russians. Twice, to Leila's credit, they had succeeded in squeezing an element of surprise from an adverse situation. Such luck was unlikely to continue for ever.

They alternately ran and walked on the return to try to make up for lost time. The running stretches became shorter and fewer. Wilson and Shearer, who were older than the others, felt it most, panting and heaving and complaining they were beyond it. They began to lag and the others slowed for them.

They made the best speed they could, stopping now and then for Houshang to take a compass bearing. He had only to be fractionally out in his direction for them to lose their transport. He was in pain, but the blood on his face had congealed.

They crossed the rail track, then the road. The cold had set in with the night but they were all sweating profusely by the time they reached the Rover. The relief of finding it broke their silence. It was a refuge.

Houshang again took a bearing before moving off, and then passed the compass to Wilson who climbed in beside him to leave Shearer and Leila alone in the back. Wilson sat and watched the illuminated dial, warning Houshang of any variance of course. If they stuck to the same route there should be no trouble, but they were still driving without lights, resisting the temptation to speed.

The few miles seemed like infinity. The desert remained dark. Nothing yet had happened by the pipe line. No sign of an alert. A faint light flicked on to their right. It was so quick Houshang thought it was an optical illusion but Wilson had seen it too. It appeared again.

"It's a covered flashlight," said Wilson. "That will be Mukhtar; he must have heard us."

Houshang steered to his right, annoyed that he had erred. The others ran out to greet them as they approached, guiding the Rover into its position of cover, and facing it towards the hills with the other one. All they needed now was the first sign of light.

There was still work to do. Magazines to refill, ammunition to check. They had two reserve blocks of plastic explosive in the second Rover, and the remainder of the grenades they'd taken from Ben Waffa's jeep. Petrol, oil and water were just about adequate, food was low. But Leila had planned well; provided there were no problems going back.

They were still working when the darkness began to turn grey. Houshang said it was time to move, and they started off. Wilson could see in the bad light so he travelled in front with the driver of the second Rover. Mukhtar, because it was easier for him to hold his side, was in front with Houshang. Precaution was now less important than to reach the border as soon as possible.

For them the true dawn came all too quickly. They were climbing the lowest of the foothills by the time the sun cast shadows from the east.

And then a different light appeared, a red explosion some miles behind them. The driver of the second Rover saw it first, in his rear-view mirror. He told Wilson, who turned. Shearer and Leila saw it from the back of the first Rover. Shearer shouted out,

362

but Houshang too had picked it up in his mirror.

They could not stop. It was time for all the speed they could manage. There was a long and difficult way to go before they left Russian soil. But they saw enough.

What they did not know was that the two explosions had coincided with the frantic search for the long-overdue personnel carrier.

In the early dawn one of the many armoured vehicles despatched to locate the carrier along the pipe line had stopped at the pumping station when a discerning officer had disliked what he saw. He had disembarked with a sergeant when it blew up, killing them instantly, wounding some of those showing their faces above the armour plating, and rocking the carrier to an extent that it had almost overturned.

As it was the driver was lucky his engine was still running. He moved off, swinging away from a massive blaze that would bake them if they stayed. There was nothing to be done for the officer and the sergeant. They had been torn to bits by the blast. As the oil gushed out a gory balloon of fire and smoke shot up, and expanded into the lightening sky.

Further on the blasted pipe line told the same story. The explosions were separated, as were the racing ground fires, but above, as they mushroomed, flame and smoke converged and locked to form a single canopy for the spreading inferno.

In the carrier, still pulling away as fast as it could, the radio operator was sending out frantic calls, his trained procedure faltering as emotion and fright confused his action. But the essential messages went out.

Within minutes, instructions were being relayed from Ashkhabad, and army and air force units were put into immediate operation. The area was so remote that advice to other areas such as Chardzhou or Samarkand was withheld, as they were considered too far away, which they were from the point of view of the search. Ashkhabad was bigger than either and had a much larger garrison.

When the news reached the K.G.B. headquarters in Ashkhabad no local restriction would be recognised. A signal advising that the pipe line had been sabotaged was sent immediately to Moscow. By this time Leila's party had been mobile for well over an hour.

They were working their way up the narrow passes of the Kopeh Dagh. Sight of the oil fire improved with height as Houshang picked his way carefully, remembering, refusing to panic. Those in the back of the Rovers had the best view of the awesome sight. Even at such a distance they could see the two towering red and black pillars, twisting like circular staircases and joining in an enormous tumbling, thickening, ever-moving cloud above them.

Shearer gripped Leila's hand fiercely, pleased by the spectacle, satisfied that the risks had been worth it, but knowing that new dangers were about to begin.

Ten minutes later they saw the first of them. Aircraft approaching the flames at a fairly high altitude then turning towards the border.

There were three planes at first, passing the ground at different altitudes, screaming overhead, leaving pale vapour trails to drift above the black oil smoke. In their anxiety the pilots were travelling too fast for thorough survey, but it was a pattern that changed.

As good as Houshang was he could not make the two Rovers invisible. He had reached the mountains proper but not the highest passes. They were still climbing. Inevitably, they were seen.

The Russians had sent up MiGs for speed, and one of them spotted the two vehicles. It could not close in because of the mountains but it was there. It soared above the peaks almost like an eagle, and circled there in the tightest circle the pilot could achieve.

It was much too high for it to be fired upon. But neither could it fire at them. It was impossible for it to dive because it would never pull out. Nor could it get near enough on either flank. The route was such that first one flank of the Rovers was exposed and then the other. There was far too much danger in the irregularities of the mountain barrier itself for the jet to do any more than it was doing—reporting their position.

Meanwhile the Rovers struggled on, their passengers knowing they had been seen and accepting that the jet was acting as a constant observer. It wouldn't end there. The Russians would be in a frenzy over the blown pipe line.

All Houshang could do was to plod on, making it as difficult as he could for the plane but trying to reach the Iranian border just as soon as he could and before some form of attack was devised.

In Moscow the frenzy was real. This was not

news General Rogov could keep to himself even if it had been relayed by one of his chiefs from a place of which he had seldom heard. This was for the Politburo; he knew it as he listened on the scrambler, his face white with rage. "Get them!" he growled. "Get them. I don't give a damn about the Iranian border. If they cross it, we cross it. You make sure we get them or you report to me, here in person." The rest did not need explaining.

At last Rogov knew why the small, unlikely group that Ben Waffa had failed to stop had been heading north. He sat down slowly. He couldn't believe it. It was impossible for vehicles to get through the mountain ranges without sticking to the roads; that was why they were not so heavily guarded. Yet it had been done. Patrols would have to be increased to prevent further sabotage. In the back of his mind Rogov knew that he had slipped up; he had anticipated nothing so audacious as this, believing that the small group of saboteurs would finish over the Afghanistan border where they would easily find more supporters to stir trouble. He was glad now that he had never voiced this belief to Panovich. He stared at the scrambler, snarled silently at it, then reached for it again with the speed of a snake's strike.

They weren't sure when they first heard the monotonous thudding of the chopper but they all saw it clearly enough. Unlike the jet it was able to descend much lower. Its door was open and they could see the muzzle of the machine-gun it was so close. And then, descending behind it, they saw another helicopter coming towards them.

# 19

IN the jagged, compact peaks of the Kopeh
Dagh even choppers had their limitations.
The pilot had to be constantly alert to
steer the great rotor blades clear of the rugged
formations around them. It was not enough
to be told to go lower and home in on one
side; he had to watch all sides if he was to stay
up.

Although clearly in pain, Houshang
seemed to be inspired in making it difficult
for the nearest helicopter. Only one of the
helicopters could operate effectively against
them at a time if a mid-air accident was to be
avoided.

The machine-gun opened up but the gunner wasn't well placed and the shots spattered
the rock. The ugly rattle of it, together with
the engine thump, echoed round the
mountains.

Houshang squeezed through a narrow
defile knowing the helicopter could not
follow. He stopped there, under an overhang
that almost formed a tunnel. The shadow of

the chopper passed across the narrow sun strip of the defile's base like a thunder cloud.

They climbed down from the Rovers and had a quick conference. The chopper had only to wait for them to continue on to get in some accurate fire. Their submachine-guns had nothing like the range of a machine-gun, so given time and opportunity the choppers could outgun them from a distance.

Unless the group stayed where it was. But to do that was to wait for ground forces to overtake them. It would have come as no surprise to them to learn that a convoy of machine-gun-mounted Russian jeeps was already heading towards them, directed by the second helicopter. They accepted that this would be so. They were still in Russia: but none of them believed anyway that a geographical border would stop the Russians.

With little time to spare they talked it over quickly. They had enough explosive to block the pass behind them. That would leave them to the mercy of the helicopters unless the Russian ground forces could find another way through. Aided by the helicopters they might.

In the end it seemed that their fate might hinge on opportunism from either side. At the moment the Russian choppers had done what they had set out to do: slow them down.

Houshang explained that beyond the defile was the course of a dry river bed with fairly open ground most of the way. In this very shallow valley they would be open targets.

Wilson put forward a suggestion. They listened. It seemed suicidal, but possibly no more than anything else. They agreed. They would have to fight their way out of the trap one way or another. It was better than waiting.

Wilson and Shearer off-loaded the remaining explosive. They needed Houshang's guidance now. They climbed up the side of the defile well above the pass they had just left. More exposed here, there was at least ample cover to use if the choppers veered round. Both machines were hovering over the defile like huge moving eyes.

The theory was to find convenient boulders to block the pass. But boulders were not there when wanted. The mountains here were sheer in parts, almost unclimbable. There was also the matter of blasting. It wasn't simply destruction they wanted—they were well versed in that—but a calculated reaction that would block the pass. *At precisely the right time.*

They rested on a ledge. The drop below them was formidable. Both men were panting. They had insisted that the others stay behind and had left their own arms with them. The two choppers were out of sight, but the shattering thud of the rotors was constant.

A beetle-like shadow crept over the rock face as the still-rising sun found a gap in the mass. After a breather Wilson began to climb the blind side of the bluff that right-angled out above the pass and the huge drop below it.

"Jesus Christ," ejected Shearer. "You're not a goddamn fly."

Wilson came down, then looked up at the rock face, trying to work it out. He was panting a little.

Shearer ran his gaze over the rock. "If one of us has to commit suicide we'll draw for it."

They had to take sudden cover as a chopper came round the bluff but it was merely re-positioning and soon moved back out of sight again. Shearer pulled some dry grass from a crevice. Taking two strands he held them in a clenched fist. "You draw. The shortest takes the climb. Don't argue or it'll never get done."

Wilson grinned. "I really believe you care." He took a strand of grass. Shearer opened his hand; he held the shortest piece. "How much instantaneous fuse have we got?"

Wilson pulled a roll from his pocket, unwound the red fuse wire. "Maybe sixty feet."

"It's barely enough. Can you fix a detonator one end?"

Wilson did what nobody should do. He inserted the wire into the detonator which he crimped with his teeth, holding his breath to prevent hot air covering it.

Shearer took off his djellaba. Now in slacks and shirt, he pulled the detonator and wire through his belt so that it was held firm with the detonator overhanging, away from his body. He checked the explosive in his pocket. "I'd better take yours as well. One detonator should do it."

Wilson handed over his plastic and Shearer rammed it into his other pocket.

"I did a lot of rock climbing in the commandos," said Wilson, trying to talk Shearer out of it.

Shearer shrugged. "I've done my share. The draw was fair."

"Well, I hope this cures whatever's bugging you. Good luck, Doug."

They shook hands silently, both hiding their feelings.

Shearer said, "Our lot will chop us anyway. The stakes are too high to let us loose. We both know." He found hand grips, raised a foot and smiled at Wilson, warm and sincere. "Watch me go." He pulled himself up.

Wilson watched Shearer climb. Instinctively the New Yorker knew where to obtain toe and finger grips, and his experience at using them was clear. If he fell he would be lucky to be uninjured landing on the ledge; luckier still to stay on it unless Wilson could grab him. But what worried Wilson was what Shearer had in mind.

Shearer intended to climb out to the massive overhang, below which was nothing but the pass they had used to reach the defile where Leila and the rest now waited.

The pass was a narrow passage, uneven and at first sight unnavigable, strewn with shale and rocks and a trap to anyone less enlightened than Houshang. But the helicopter crews had seen it done and would ensure that follow-up troops did no less.

Shearer seemed to have reached an impasse. He was poised high above Wilson, arms and legs stretched, literally holding on by toes and fingertips, body close to the rock, the fuse wire trailing. Wilson's stomach suddenly heaved with apprehension. Shearer didn't move. Wilson wanted to call out to him, to give some sort of friendly reassurance, but fortunately his throat seized up.

Then the chopper came in view again and Wilson dived for cover. If he was seen they would find Shearer too; and he was a stationary target.

For the moment Shearer was safe from view because of the nature of the bluff, its bulge hiding him. Wilson waited until the chopper disappeared again, left his recess and noticed that, incredibly, Shearer had moved to his right and had reached the beginning of the overhang. Wilson felt he could not watch any more. Conversely, he could not take his eyes away. He was rooted.

Shearer did not think of what was below him. Whether it was fifty feet or five thousand, it made no difference if he fell. Fifty feet was enough to kill him here. There was no soft ground. His concentration was complete. He'd heard the chopper but instantly put it from his mind. If he was seen, there was nothing he could do but drop. He'd rather be shot in the back first.

His approach was totally professional, his main misgiving the strength of his arms, legs and fingers. They had not been used in this way for a long time. He was out of trim, as his aching muscles reminded him every second.

Sweat was pouring out of him and his breathing was irregular and uncontrolled. He tried to think out what should be his next step. His position was misleading. He was leaning forward from the waist, his legs, at that moment, taking minimum strain. And then, as he stayed suspended, he picked out a noise that was different from the two restless helicopters. Somewhere below was the grind of engines.

Before he could move two helicopters thundered round from behind him and he knew that they could not be the original two.

If they'd seen him they'd be back. When two whirled past the other way, he guessed they were the originals who had been relieved, probably to refuel.

It made no difference, except perhaps to

give him a slight edge over fresh pilots not yet tuned to the perils around them. Until they were they might be less adventurous.

He continued to work his way across. Without looking down he knew he had passed the ledge Wilson was on. The drop was now academic. As if to compensate there was more to hang on to, the surface in places deeply pitted.

Shearer wanted to get as near to the underside of the overhang as he could. It was impossible to reach the crotch of it, but that was where he needed to be. The growl of motor engines was clearer now, climbing in low gear. He found a pitted section that might at one time have harboured a bird colony.

Getting himself into a reasonably safe position he crammed one pack of plastic into the crude hole, pushing hard until it held, then applied adhesive. One-handed, he groped for the detonator, pulled the wire up through his belt, then primed the plastic, using more adhesive. He groped for the second pack of plastic. It would not wedge into the same hole.

He paused. Shifting position to maintain balance was pulling at his muscles. His using one hand meant having only one to hold

on with. He found another niche just with
in reach further out on the overhang. H
rammed the plastic in, not sure how i
would react where he had put it.

He now started to crab-crawl back toward
the main rock face. As he went he pulled th
wire through his belt, giving it a good stretc
each time but not too much to foul it. It was
difficult operation, with risk of the detonato
being pulled from the pack as he moved.

Before he left the overhang he looke
down. Heights had never worried him an
this was no exception. The mountain
stretched below in folds and masses o
infinitely varying heights. He couldn't see th
Russian convoy, there was too much in th
way, but it was noticeably louder. There wer
a good many vehicles down there windin
their way up towards the pass.

One helicopter seemed to have positione
itself just round the bluff, and no doubt ha
the convoy fully in view, directing it to wher
the Rovers were trapped. Shearer continue
across and then down, paying out the fus
wire as he went.

Shearer was almost down and then stoppe
as if stuck. Yet he could have jumped from

there. His feet were at most fifteen feet from base.

Without moving Shearer called out, "You here, Ray?"

"Of course I'm here!"

"The goddamn fuse isn't going to reach."

"Shit. How short?"

"It'll reach below my feet. Just about. I daren't pull it."

"You can't stay there. You got some plasticine?" It wasn't actually plasticine, but an adhesive that felt and looked like plasticine. He'd used it on both the pipe line and on the overhang.

"I've used it all."

"Hang on. I'm coming up." Wilson started to climb; if Shearer let the wire go it would float out of reach above the pass.

He stopped just below and to one side of Shearer. "Grab."

Shearer reached for Wilson's outstretched hand. "Got it."

Shearer pressed the wad over the wire and thumbed it well in. They had now used all their explosive wire and adhesive. He came down slowly after Wilson.

"I heard their trucks. Listen."

The sound wasn't quite as clear as it had

been above the pass, but they could still pick up the rumble.

"I'll have to stand on your shoulders," said Shearer. He pointed. "To reach the fuse." The fuse wire angled down from the overhang, a thin shadow against the rock.

They dived into cover as a helicopter came round the bluff again. This time it stayed, hovering almost at eye level with them.

They lay crouched in a tiny crevice. "It's an M.R.25," observed Shearer.

"What the hell does that mean?"

"A gun ship. The latest. Came into service in eighty-three. A five-barrelled heavy machine-gun in its nose."

"He's guiding the convoy in. The bastard's right in the way."

The chopper hung suspended, moving in eddies of wind. The grind of the convoy was noticeably clearer.

Wilson said, "We'll have to risk it. And be careful where you put your big feet."

They laughed. Suddenly high in the Kopeh Dagh, alone and once more in danger, perhaps for the first time all barriers between them were down. They felt now as if they'd known each other all their lives, understood each other's moods, read each other's minds

Shearer pulled off his shirt, because its colour would have stood out, and handed it to Wilson who screwed it up and stuffed it in a pocket. Shearer crawled forward, flat on his face. His brown body toned with the dun-coloured background. He pulled himself to the edge and looked down. The chopper seemed only feet away, the noise deafening. At this point it completely covered the sound of the convoy.

As he looked across the Gulf he could see someone behind the perspex wearing a helmet with ear pads. Fortunately the crew were preoccupied with what was below them. Shearer could see nothing on the approaches to the pass but it was a very limited view. The convoy would reach the pass itself before he would see it. He simply had to wait and hope that the chopper would drop a few feet.

But it didn't. It hung suspended, swaying and thunderous, and joined by a hundred echoes. Shearer stayed where he was, flat, part of his head over the edge. He doubted that he would be seen as he was. Behind him, thinking ahead, Wilson was carefully wriggling out of his djellaba.

Shearer kept his face down so that his dark hair was towards the chopper. He thought he

heard something. He tried to shut out th
clatter of the blades. Nothing. He waited
keyed up and nervous. If he failed the Rover
would never get out of the defile.

The first snub nose of a jeep radiator ease
its way into view. For a moment Shearer wa
paralysed. The jeep eased its way forward
He could see the driver, an officer next t
him, and four soldiers on each side of th
open back, facing inwards. Another jee
appeared behind. And another.

The first jeep was half-way along the pas
and now there were four in sight and a fift
edging forward. Shearer felt there were mor
to come, but he couldn't wait any longer.

Each jeep had a tripod-mounted machine
gun fixed behind the cab. A soldier in th
first jeep rose to take position behind the gun
The officer, wearing earphones, had presum
ably instructed him on advice from the heli
copter pilot. His last impression was of a re
star, distinct on the cap of the officer as h
turned his head.

Shearer backed away, still facing front. H
called to Wilson as he moved. Nobody bu
the Cockney would hear him above th
racket. By the time he rose, still watching th
chopper, Wilson had positioned himsel

gainst the rock face. He bent down to make
t easier for Shearer.

Shearer stepped on to Wilson's back and
hen on to his shoulders, steadying himself
gainst the rock. He pulled out his matches,
eached up to the loose end of the fuse, and
truck one. It blew out at once.

Shearer swore. "They should've been fuse
natches."

Wilson did not answer. Shearer's feet were
rinding into his shoulders, and he was also
rying to keep an eye on the chopper. He
elled suddenly, "He's seen us."

Shearer needed no prompting but he had to
eep his nerve. He struck a match in cupped
ands, balancing awkwardly, raising the shel-
ered flame towards the fuse.

The helicopter pilot had indeed seen
hearer. He gyrated his machine so that his
unner could use the machine-gun effec-
ively. The gunner got sight of the two men
n the ledge and tried to take aim, but the
hopper was still swinging. It was not easy in
he confines of the cabin and the chopper
ever kept really still. The gunner fired.

The first heavy burst went behind
hearer's back and he almost dropped the
natch. It had nearly burned out when he put

it to the fuse and for a terrible, heart
sickening moment he thought the powde
would not ignite. Then the fuse let out a sud
den whoosh!

There wasn't time to shout. He jumpe
back from Wilson's shoulders. A mass of roc
chips flew out from around the fuse where h
had just been. As his feet hit the ground h
grabbed at Wilson and they clung desperatel
as the surface beneath them trembled witl
shock waves as a great roar swept over th
valley and air rushed down at them like
storm force wind.

It seemed an eternity before they coul
separate to flatten themselves, aware of th
tremendous vibration above them; the instan
taneous fuse had done its job in the breathles
speed it was designed for. The whole side o
the bluff blew out, at first seemingly in on
enormous solid piece. Sight of it was lost t
the two men, but its magnitude was conveye
by the incredible roar of the two explosions
one detonating the other.

The overhang split from the bluff flev
straight at first like a meteor racing throug
space, and then suddenly slowed as if b
some massive gravitational pull. It appeare
to halt, poised in air, before it fragmented

384

blowing out before falling in a gigantic cloud of rock and rubble.

The pilot was too busy fighting his controls, the shock waves hitting him one after the other, to see what was happening. He was lucky to be preoccupied. The gunner saw it all to the last, to the moment when a great portion of the air-born avalanche hit the helicopter and buried it before its tangled mess landed in the valley beyond the pass.

As the helicopter struck the ground the fuel ignited and flame escaped through a dozen fissures in the rubble, puncturing the huge dust cloud, changing its colour and helping it rise on a heat haze.

Wilson and Shearer clutched at the ledge, at times believing it would collapse on them. The tremor eased, leaving just odd rumbles as parts of the rock fall changed position. Wilson hurried to the edge. A huge cloud of particles swirled over the pass. There were screams floating through it, men crying out in agony. It was impossible to see what damage was done but it was considerable. Beyond the pass the drifting dust spread over the valley. The flames, partially hidden, tinged the rolling underside of the cloud with pink.

"There must have been a fissure, a weakness," said Wilson hoarsely. He was stunned. "Let's get back quick. Some jeeps may have got through."

The same possibility had occurred to Shearer, who was already on his way. They scrambled along the ledge and over the hump that led the way down to the defile. Their legs were shaky, minds confused, ears still ringing from the roars, but instinct demanded that they hurried. The sound of machine-gun fire gave them added impetus.

# 20

AS they clambered down into the defile they realised that the gunfire was from the higher ground. Leila shouted and they saw her crouched behind cover, firing down. Taking spare guns she had placed her small squad of Houshang, the ailing Mukhtar and two youngsters called Arat and Ibrahim as high up the defile as she could, facing the gap through which the Russians must come.

They had not escaped the reverberations of the blast. To her tiny group it meant that Wilson and Shearer had set it off but also that the enemy was approaching.

The first jeep was in the defile when the explosion came and escaped serious damage. The soldiers on the back had jumped off with fright, a number falling over as the jeep literally shook. Some of them had sight of the massive rock fall behind them and the huge cloud that filtered into the defile, rising through the gap above which one helicopter still hovered.

The second jeep had partially escaped. A mass of rock fell on it but a few men had the presence of mind to jump clear and run. Three succeeded; the remainder were killed. The rear of the jeep was crushed, its bonnet, now angled and twisted, protruding from the fall.

All this happened in seconds. The Russians were sitting ducks as Leila's small force opened fire on them; they had no cover, they were dazed and shocked and not sure what had happened. Some fired back but they weren't sure at what. They received no mercy.

Others recovered their senses more quickly and hid under the first jeep. The mounted machine-gun on the back remained un-manned and pointing at the sky. It was a classic mountain ambush.

It was at this stage, with a few Russians holding out but pinned down, that Wilson and Shearer arrived. They crawled to where Leila was. She had their guns waiting. They told her briefly what had happened but most of it she was already able to guess. The defile was blocked. Unless there was another way through they had effectively cut off the main danger. Leila made no secret of her joy at seeing Shearer.

"We've got to get out quick. Before more choppers turn up." Shearer was gazing down at the jeep. "How many men there?"

"Two, maybe three."

"They could keep us here for hours."

Leila shook her head. "No. We have grenades. We will blow them out. We heard you coming, we waited."

"Where are the others?"

Leila pointed: Houshang tucked away to her left, the other three across the defile. The intact jeep lay to their front, just inside the rock fall, a few feet from the partially buried jeep.

Wilson said softly, "We want them alive."

Leila was more surprised. "We agreed. We can't handle prisoners."

"Things have changed, love. We're on the home run."

"We still can't cope, and there are only seven of us now, one badly injured."

"There's no time to explain. We have to get out. We need their heavy machine-gun and we need them. Believe me. Tell her, Doug."

"Do as he says, Leila."

"All right. But you make a mystery."

"It's too involved to explain now. Doug knows. Anyway, if you use grenades you could well damage both jeep and gun."

"But if they don't surrender we'll *have* to blow them out."

"They'll have grenades, too," Shearer broke in. "All they have to do is hold us here until more choppers are thrown in." Shearer, like Wilson, wanted to get out fast.

Leila, raising her voice, called out to Mukhtar. "Tell them to surrender, Mukhtar. We need them."

Mukhtar called out quite distinctly in Russian. It must have been an effort. Then again.

Nobody moved. Mukhtar called a further time. The Russians refused to respond.

"Give me a grenade," said Shearer. Leila handed one over. "Give me covering fire." He rose as the others opened up, firing along the nearest flank of the jeep. Then he drew the pin, taking his time, and carefully lobbing the grenade overarm.

It exploded, well in front of the jeep but fragments tore into its side. Because a grenade is apt to explode upwards and out, those beneath the jeep were reasonably safe from the lack of flat trajectory. But it must have shaken them. If the grenade had been nearer and another lobbed behind they could not have escaped the blast.

"Tell them," bawled Leila. "We won't kill them. We could have done it then had we wanted."

Mukhtar shouted the message in Russian, adding that the next time there would be a whole batch of grenades back and front.

Someone stirred under the jeep but it was another second or so before a handkerchief appeared on the end of a gun muzzle.

"Come out," shouted Mukhtar. "Stand up with hands in the air."

They stood up one by one on the far side of the jeep.

"They're going to try something," snarled Shearer. "Keep down."

But Mukhtar had seen it all. He was too wise to be deceived by crude tricks. "Put your hands up or we'll shoot you as you are."

Three pairs of arms were reluctantly raised. The sound of guns being dropped was clear.

"Step to your right. One at a time. We have a dozen guns pointing at you."

One by one they came into the open and

they must have been shattered by the clearer sight of their dead colleagues strewn around the defile. For the first time, too, they had full sight of what was left of the second jeep and the blockage to the gap. At that stage all thought of fight left them.

On Leila's orders, Arat alone went down to the jeep to be sure that no one else was hiding in or around it. He raised his gun as a signal that all was clear, and they left their cover to approach the three Russians.

As the squad came into view one by one, the Russians' pride was further dented by the small numbers. Seven people had taken out a complete Russian convoy, and of those who had entered the pass most were dead.

They bound the Russians' hands behind their backs, and, when they were re-embarked on to the back of their own jeep, tied their feet together. Two metal seats ran the short length of each side of the jeep. There were protrusions at the side for fixing a canopy, at the moment not in use, and they fastened the bound wrists to these.

Wilson sorted out the machine-gun. He had no idea of the make but it was clearly air-cooled and magazine-loaded. He quickly found the bolt and the safety catch which combined the single-shot lever with the rapid fire. He fired the briefest of bursts into the air. Spare, loaded magazines, together with ammo for the automatic rifles, were in a locker behind the cab, used also as a seat.

He looked down at the Russians. Mukhtar had identified the ranks. A major, scowling, angry at being caught by so few and by such a strange mixture. He assumed the two whites were American. A sergeant, short, tough and pudding-faced, showing no emotion at all; probably glad to be out of it. And a private soldier, tall and gangly with the high cheek-bones of Mongolia. His eyes were darting and scared. He'd been taught from enlistment that the Russian Army was invincible. And now he had been captured by a small group, the leader of whom seemed to be the woman. He just hoped that they would not kill him. There was no dissent from Shearer when Wilson stayed with the gun. They would always be balancing the books between them.

The American drove one of the Rovers with Ibrahim beside him. Houshang took over the Russian jeep with Mukhtar. He would lead in it, the theory being that Wilson on the back would want no dust trail cloaking his aim. And it was important that the three prisoners on the back should be clearly seen.

Arat drove the second Rover with Leila in the passenger seat. They moved off, still aware of the helicopter—aware too, that others would be on their way. It was doubtful if any could get near enough in to rope-lift survivors in the pass, or even drop medical supplies.

Houshang, cool all along, did not panic now. They could not avoid showing themselves across the valley floor until they reached the comparative safety of the protective folds the other side.

There was sparse growth in the valley but no sign of animal life. They were high up, peaks all around the basin. Once out in the open there was nothing to do but keep going and hope.

The Russian prisoners had the worst of the ride. Every lurch of the jeep strained at their wrists, the cord biting and chafing the flesh. They couldn't balance themselves against the movement, nor even spread their feet with bound ankles. Wilson was having almost as rough a ride but he was too busy watching the sky to let it worry him.

He supposed they were halfway across when the helicopter came scudding round, low over the defile. It had obviously been round by the bluff, relaying back the tremendous damage to the convoy of jeeps and suggesting the form of rescue operation needed.

The way the chopper came round the bluff carried the suggestion that the pilot had been ordered to get the enemy; the wounded must look after themselves.

The pilot picked up the small convoy almost at once. After a couple of passes over the defile he pivoted like a top, increased altitude and flew after it. He had every reason to be cautious. More than anyone he had seen what these people had done to his comrades. His gunner could hardly wait to get his first shots in; he had friends among the tangled and buried wreckage in the pass. He did not know whether they were dead or injured, but when the pilot had drifted in as near as he dared he had seen waving hands and fists, tortured, twisted bodies, white faces, lips drawn back in pain. And he had seen two men fall over the edge, legs and arms flying. Oh, yes, he couldn't wait to get at those bastards below.

The pilot was less primitive in his thoughts. He considered that perhaps he had the edge. There would be more bumping on the ground than in the air. The last two vehicles would be more difficult, because they were partially covered by the sand trail of a jeep which he recognised as one of their own. He saw the gun, Wilson behind it, its barrel following his own movements.

And he recognised the uniforms of the prisoners. Three white blobs stared back apprehensively. He took the helicopter up, radioed as soon as the mountains stopped interfering with his transmission. By this time the three vehicles were toys, detail lost. He received instructions and his eyes became opaque.

As they climbed, the gunner had been watching him, wondering. The gunner had become confused on seeing some of his colleagues in the jeep. Suddenly it wasn't so easy.

The pilot turned, gaze bleak. "I'll get as close as I can. You'll have to put out the gun first."

"I'm to fire? Our own men are down there."

"You're arguing with me?"

"No, sir. I'll try to miss them." There was

o way to miss them if he was to stop the ep.

"If it helps, I don't like it either." The pilot rought the chopper down carefully. "But lose, comrade, are our orders." He paused. Would it be easier with flanking fire?" He vas wishing he had one of the new M.R.25s o that he could come in straight from the ear, the machine-gun operating through the ose.

It made little difference to the gunner. Ieight would help to pick out the man ehind the gun on the jeep, but height made is own firing much more difficult. He hrugged, avoiding the pilot's glance.

Wilson waited below. They were going to ome for him. They'd have to take him out rst to silence the machine-gun. The pilot vould know that he had only to keep out of ange of the S.M.G.s and leave his gunner to ope with the others. The pilot would know, oo, that if the rear vehicles possessed heavy lachine-guns they would have used them by ow.

The three prisoners knew what was going o happen too. They stared, horrified by the pproaching helicopter, unable to believe heir eyes. The private started to shout.

For the first time Wilson felt compassio
He took a quick look to the front. They we
some way from safety, the pilot could take h
time. Wilson lowered his shoulders behir
the gun, rammed the butt hard in, and too
hold of the pistol grip, fingers on the trigge
It was a question of where to aim. The jee
was lurching. To try to take out the gunn
was too ambitious. Anyway he was obscure
in the bubble behind his gun. The pilot w
on the blind side, swinging away to give h
gunner a better chance.

The helicopter pilot had to come fairly lo
for the gunner's sake, but he had instal
mobility on his side. He could rise like :
elevator or side skip. The earth-bound jee
was confined to the narrow course dictated b
the many restrictions of the valley.

The first burst took Wilson by surprise. F
didn't think the gunner was well-sighted ar
he realised immediately afterwards that th
shots had been exploratory, high above h
head as if the gunner didn't like the idea
shooting his own colleagues.

Wilson lined up. Fired. No reaction. A
three prisoners now showed open concer
The major's face was purple with rage. F
was bawling at the helicopter in a tirade

Russian. The other two joined in, all shouting, moving their heads, the only real motion they could manage.

The next burst started low, kicking up the sand behind and to one side of the jeep. Wilson lost his aim and flung himself flat as a spray of bullets thudded into the jeep which swerved and straightened as if it had skidded. Houshang must have felt the impact to have swerved like that.

Wilson scrambled up, swearing, but above his voice was another. Blood was streaming down the sergeant's arm and he was bellowing in pain and fury. Three faces turned to Wilson, mutely pleading for him to release them.

He raised the gun again, annoyed with himself. The helicopter had roared over and was performing a fast turn to come back. Wilson was cold-blooded now. He had the range, while the gunner was not yet placed to fire. He aimed at the bubble and kept his fingers on the trigger. It was too risky and too elusive a target to go for the blades. He strafed her at the slowest moment of her turn.

The helicopter swung away and up and he knew that his firing had had some effect. The Colt clicked, he whipped off the magazine and dived for another. By the time he had the new magazine on, the chopper was at to tantalising a distance. Then it started to com back.

Wilson thumped on the cab, roaring dow at Houshang. The jeep stopped, swallowe by its own dust trail. A hail of fire spat fron the helicopter, but the gunner had bee misled by the stop. And he had bee reluctant to the last to fire on his own mer He had briefly seen the sergeant yell i agony, had watched each time as the thre Russian heads went down.

Meanwhile Wilson fired point-blank an hoped for the best. Suddenly the helicopter engine faltered, the blades slowed, and th helicopter fell straight down. It plummete on its belly, hard but still in one piece. The it cracked open, the sides falling out, befor the tanks burst and a ball of fire engulfed i There was no sign of anyone getting out.

Wilson let the gun go and thumped the cal He remained leaning on it, unable to fac what was behind him. The two Rover strung out to make it easier for Wilson an more difficult for the pilot, followed, bot flashing lights. Wilson wondered if the othe were as sickened as he. There seemed no en

400

to it. And by God, if they were ever caught they would pay a terrible price.

When he eventually turned round he was drained. The Russian prisoners were staring back at the fire ball but stealing the odd uncomfortable glance at Wilson. Their gazes were a mixture of relief and horror. They would never know whether to thank or curse him. Wilson stumbled forward to see what he could do for the sergeant's arm.

They were well beyond the valley and into the encompassing arms of the higher peaks again by the time the MiGs appeared. The presence of the jets was an act of desperation. There was little they could do in the cramped confines of the Kopeh Dagh. They peeled off and fired their cannons, perhaps hoping to do what Wilson and Shearer had done—blast the side of a mountain on to the convoy. But their performance was merely token, something to report back to irate commanders who in turn must advise Moscow. The convoy was never in real danger.

More helicopters came later but their crews already knew that two of their machines had already been lost and they were careful. Also, in the knowledge that the ground forces had been cut off, Houshang could hole up whenever he felt too vulnerable. He would choose his spot and they would wait until the need to refuel lessened the opposition.

It was dusk when they stopped once more. MiGs were still overhead, helicopters zoning in and out, all following the route of the convoy. Before darkness fell Arat kindled a fire and they ate and drank in discomfort but in some relief. They hand-fed the Russians, refusing to untie them, but they did take them into the rocks one at a time when wrists only were untied.

The navigation lights of the MiGs flickered high above. The pilots wouldn't take too many risks at night but they intended to show that they were there.

Houshang sprang his surprise after a welcome coffee. His wounded cheek had made speech awkward. "We're in Iran," he said.

Nobody asked him how he knew. It was difficult to believe, with the shriek of jet engines above. "We're not going back the same way. And we'll travel at night."

Wilson rubbed knees still sore from his fall from the Russian personnel carrier. Leila made no comment. Shearer showed no surprise, while incredibly for him—Mukhtar was asleep from exhaustion.

Leila suddenly put a hand out and touched Houshang's undamaged cheek. "I'm sorry. We all are. We should not take you so much for granted. We are impressed and so grateful, Houshang. Now tell us."

"We don't need the Russian jeep any more."

Wilson immediately took interest. "We need its licence and engine number."

Shearer looked up sharply, understood, but said nothing. Leila, aware of an undercurrent that only affected the two Westerners, held her counsel. Something was going on they had not told her about. She watched Shearer with yearning and a new fear: he was in danger from something he kept to himself.

The one piece of equipment they appeared short of was a pen and some paper. Eventually they found both amongst Mukhtar's gear. Houshang helped Wilson to find the engine number. They used a flashlight freely. Wilson jotted down the number. "You sure we're in Iran?"

"Of course." Who could argue with Houshang?

They returned to the others. Houshang

stood near the fire, the flickering light showing the strain on his young face. He explained, "We have a choice here. We can cut through and join the route we came by—or we can go towards the Caspian. It is further and will keep us nearer the border for much longer. But it is more sheltered and eventually leads us to the Elburz mountains, much higher than these."

Leila, arms round her knees, glanced up as Houshang continued.

"I think it's more likely to fool the Russians. They will expect us to get back as soon as we can. The nearer we get to the southern Caspian, the nearer we'll be to Teheran, and that will make it impossible for the Russian planes to cross the border unless they make an open invasion."

"But we don't want to go anywhere near Teheran. Ray and Doug will be picked out too easily. And we have the prisoners."

"We won't go to Teheran. We'll come in behind the Elburz and take the coast road. Then down to the Gulf."

Leila nodded her assent. Houshang added, "We will have to use one truck only." He spread his hands in apology. "It's a risk, but we won't have the fuel otherwise. We suction off from the other two jeeps, fill the cans. We have water. It will be cramped, but our best chance."

He could see they didn't like the idea but accepted it.

Houshang climbed into the Russian jeep and somehow, even in such a confined space, repositioned it. He did the same with the second Rover.

They transferred the barest essentials to the first Rover and made a rough bed for Mukhtar behind the cab. As gently as they could they carried him to it. He barely stirred. They made sure they were not short of arms and ammunition and left the surplus behind.

The Russians complained forcibly when they were made to embark, the sergeant making great play of his bandaged wound. Their protests met deaf ears and they were tied to the stanchions as before.

Leila got into the front passenger seat. Shearer and Wilson, Arat and Ibrahim climbed into the back, careful not to disturb Mukhtar who was now ailing rapidly. They could not see the three Russians opposite but they could feel their animosity. The episode of the helicopter seemed to have been forgotten already.

Houshang built up the fire, switched on the dipped headlights of the Russian jeep and o the Rover they were leaving. In the blackness of the mountains, the effect was startling. Houshang had already explained that, from above, the fire and the headlamps could not be missed, even at high altitude. They would also subdue the effect of the sidelights Houshang now switched on in the remaining Rover.

He had chosen this particular area because he believed it to be a little easier for what he had in mind. Even for him, driving on sidelights was extremely difficult; but he believed that if he drove carefully he could get a great many miles between themselves and the discarded jeeps during the darkness.

Houshang drove thoughout the night, refusing to let anyone relieve him. This type of driving was quite different from anything else. There was also the question of the homing instinct. As an African native instinctively takes the correct route in virgin bush so too did Houshang in the mountains. For this mission it made the difference between success and failure. When his eyes could not keep open any longer he would stop, switch off engine and lights, and sleep for perhaps ten minutes. He would awaken, head clear, hand reaching for the ignition even as his eyes opened.

Periodically they heard the drone of planes and could not be sure whether or not their faint lights had been seen. All they knew was that the greater distraction was behind them. The lights and the fire should puzzle the Russians, hold their attention long enough.

At dawn, reconnaissance planes were out searching. By now the ruse would have been discovered, but the solitary Rover was out of sight, with everyone sleeping the sleep of exhaustion.

Later they stretched limbs, ate, attended to the needs of the Russians. There was no comfort, a whole day to wait before they could set off again by night.

It was late morning before they discovered that Mukhtar had died in his sleep. The indefatigable little Omani had been uncomplaining to the end. A sadness filled the group, for Mukhtar had stamped his mark on them. He had lived long enough to face the temptations and the fortunes of betrayal but he had died with honour, a man of considerable integrity in the codes under which he had lived.

The Russians sensed the considerable grief and were silent, unknowing that it was a much earlier bullet than one of theirs that had caused Mukhtar's death.

There was difficulty in finding a sufficiently sheltered place away from the presence of still prowling helicopters and MiGs in which to bury Mukhtar. There was a good deal of time left to search, and they ensured that he faced Mecca as they laid Mukhtar's body down. The best they could do for him was to cover him with rubble and stone. None of them stinted in their efforts while the Russians looked on, puzzled and perhaps moved by what they saw. They would not have received such reverence; hadn't their own men fired on them?

That night they found stretches between two mountain ranges where faster progress could be made. They felt the absence of Mukhtar and were largely silent, tolerating the bumps and bruises as if they had long been a part of life.

The following morning Houshang considered it safe to travel by day. They were now well inside Iran and there was no evidence of any Russian search. There was also the fact that they were so close to the Iranian Caspian and the coast road that Russian planes could hardly be missed from below and would have no mountains to blanket radar.

The risk now was small. They had had only three hours' sleep before setting off again about mid-morning. The rear flaps were tied, turning the back of the Rover into a furnace; but there was no question of removing the canopy. With five obvious foreigners in the back there was nothing else to be done.

They were able to refuel before reaching the main coastal road which they continued along towards Rasht. It was the next day, well north of Teheran, when they saw a blockage across the road. A truck had overturned on the crown of the road and fruit and vegetables were scattered about. There was no sign of anyone as though the driver had simply walked away from the scene. As there was no room to get past Houshang was forced to stop. He called back to the others to stay where they were while he inspected the prob-lem. He surveyed the truck, wondering whether there were enough of them with the three Russians to manhandle it out of the way.

The next moment a horde of armed men sprang from either side of the road, grabbed Houshang while others rushed to surround the Land-Rover, ripping back its flaps.

As the flaps were torn back those inside the Land-Rover were faced with a mass of pointing guns and gabbling voices. It was pointless to try to fight them back; they let their guns slide to the floor. The three Russians were as alarmed as the others.

# 21

AS they were manhandled from the Rover, pushed and kicked and jeered at, Leila cried out as she was separated from Shearer. The American struggled and was hit in the back with a rifle butt. He yelled in agony and fell to his knees. Wilson fought to help him and received the same treatment. They were bundled onto a truck, their rough-clad and heavily armed escort constantly reviling them. Behind them the road block remained untouched.

A great howl went up as the three Russians were pushed forward. Now they were all prisoners; there was no distinction between them. Once the truck moved off it seemed at times as though none of the prisoners would survive the journey as their guards frequently aimed guns at them and often fired over their heads. The direction, too, dismayed them as it was south, towards Teheran, which could be little more than sixty miles away; once in the main city where anti-West feeling had nurtured for so long, Wilson and Shearer would be shot out of hand.

But they did not go to Teheran. After only a short journey they pulled into a small township which Houshang recognised as Amol as they were bundled off the truck. Shearer was in agony with his back but he received no pity and Leila was not allowed to attend to him as much as she shouted at their captors. It was clear that there had been fighting in the town. Debris was everywhere and walls were pitted with gun shots.

Yet there was jubilation on the streets, arms waved high, activity ceaseless and there was the sound of distant guns and aircraft shrieking overhead. They were imprisoned in a room that smelled of goats. It hadn't been cleared out and the solitary window was boarded up. Guards were chatting outside, sometimes laughing. At one time several volleys of rifle fire sounded very near.

Inside the room the two groups were separated, the Russians huddled in one corner, Leila's group in another. Now that Mukhtar had gone there could be no verbal communication between the two groups. They squatted, dismayed and silent and wondering how they had fallen into such a trap.

It was Leila who eased their despair. To have done so much and to have come so far only to be caught on the final stage, was demoralising. But there was a strange jubilation about her. She made Shearer lean forward while she examined his back. She said, 'These aren't government troops. They're insurgents.''

"You sure? You think we'll be okay?''

Leila gently rubbed Shearer's back. "We need to find someone of authority to be believed. I tried talking to them on the truck. They didn't understand why the Russians are here. They saw that they were our prisoners but they're suspicious. And they're overflowing with the taste of victory. It's a dangerous mood for them.''

A person of authority did not arrive until late afternoon. During this time the prisoners had been given only brackish water. A tall man entered, surrounded by guards. He wore camouflage battledress and carried a sub-machine-gun.

He stood in the doorway, unshaven face drawn with fatigue, but eyes bright with triumph. Total silence spread through the

413

room. Deep brown eyes swept the prisoner.
A smile began to break beneath the heavy
moustache. Recognition came more slowly t
Wilson and Shearer. Then they too smiled
Arms were stretched out, words of greeting
flung out and the three men embraced, laugh
ing and joking. The tall man had been one of
the leaders apportioned a massive amount of
arms in the house in Oman, following which
Mukhtar had been shot.

The group were allocated a small villa, while
the three Russians remained prisoners. It was
good to feel clean again and to have a change
of clothing. For Leila and Shearer it was a
heady time and Wilson kept out of their way
to dream of Jennie in London. But his dreams
were spoiled by the hovering nightmare of
the future.

Wilson, alone a good deal during the two
days following their release, had more time to
view matters soberly. A carefully worded
signal had been sent to Higgs in London and
they were waiting for a reply. Meanwhile
they had been told that Iran had virtually col
lapsed against the insurgents. Moslem fough
Moslem, with the fanatical hard core still
fighting on but losing ground daily. Tehran

nd Esfahan were in insurgent hands and heir armies were moving east. The Government had collapsed.

No news had been released by the Russians hat one of their most important oil pipe nes, and, more seriously, a pumping station, ad been put out of action. But while they ept their silence satellite pictures showed a trange confusion of troop and armour move- nent to and from the Caspian. The President f the United States issued a strong warning the Russians to keep out of Iran and not to nterfere in an internal conflict.

On the second day of their freedom, the roup were shown newspapers from Italy, Germany and France which carried a story imilar to the one Wilson read in the airmail dition of the London *Daily Telegraph*. Russian Moslem dissidents had blown up a najor oil pipe line from the Caspian, which ad created serious fuel supply problems which might last some time. To Wilson it macked of the cunning of Higgs and Marshall. But it created more dangers for imself and Shearer.

He sought out Leila and Shearer and as oon as the American saw the newspaper nder Wilson's arm he said, "I know; talk

time. You didn't begrudge us a couple of day
of heaven?"

"You know I didn't. Have you told Lei
anything?"

"No. She knows something is wrong bu
I've held out."

Leila was standing by an open window (
the villa as they talked. She was looking out
the rubble of bomb damage. "You are bot
talking as though I am not here." She turned
"Isn't it time you confided in me? Do you no
know me well enough by now?"

Shearer looked at Wilson; with his ow
emotional involvement with Leila it wa
really up to the Cockney to decide.

"Let's sit down." Wilson pulled a chair ou
for Leila at the small table. The three of ther
sat and Leila knew she was about to hear ba
news.

Wilson laid the newspapers on the table
"We all know the truth behind the lie of tha
story. And that alone makes us expendable. I
the Russians could prove the lie, prove tha
Western Intelligence was behind the whol
thing great chunks of the Arab world woul
revolt against what's happened here. And th
Russians would seize the opportunity t
move in. But that's only a part of it."

Shearer held up a hand as Wilson was about to continue; he turned to Leila. "Although this puts you on the block too, honey, it's Ray and me they're really after. We know who briefed us, that could set the world alight, and it's best that you don't know them. This can't be explained away as any department stepping out of line, of Presidents and Prime Ministers having no knowledge of what's happened. But it's worse than that; Ray and I saw Colonel Rachid assassinated and we've more than a fair idea of how it was done. The Russians would give anything for that information, not as a calculated guess which they'll have made already anyway, but as a matter of fact provided by two eye witnesses." He paused, lowered his gaze. "There's only one certain way the Russians can be stopped from grabbing us."

"Your own people would kill you? Such an act of treachery after all that you've done?"

"Look at it this way, honey; they're trying to grab some oil back and to avoid a world war while they're doing it. Ray and I are like a couple of touchy detonators wedged into the explosive politics of it."

Leila breathed in slowly. "Are you saying you can't escape? Wherever you go?"

Wilson and Shearer exchanged glances and Wilson said, "It's like this, love. Doug and I haven't actually discussed a solution but at times we can read each other's minds. We know a possible answer. It's no guarantee in a situation like this but it's all we've got." Wilson glanced at Shearer again and smiled briefly. "He's leaving this part to me because we need your help and that places you even more on the line."

"Did you think I *wouldn't* help?"

"Not for a moment. But you've got to know what you're up against. Can you duck out of sight where nobody will find you? For months maybe? And take that Russian colonel with you?"

Leila put out a hand to cover one of Shearer's. "Will it mean we will be separated for so long?"

Shearer nodded slowly. "Could be. It's the only way. The only chance we stand of re-uniting later. That's worth waiting for from where I sit."

"And I've got a girl friend in London who I want to marry if we get out of this lot. If she doesn't die of heart failure when I ask her."

Beneath the banter Leila was aware that this literally was a game of life and death and

418

that she was the key. "What do you want me to do?"

Wilson and Shearer were flown from Teheran to the Salalah air base in Oman on the third day after being captured. They weren't allowed to leave the plane until an old unmarked D.C.7 drew close. They transferred to the D.C.7 to find, that, apart from the crew, they had the plane to themselves, with the one other person who had flown with them from Iran. The Russian sergeant now carried his arm in a sling. And he wore rough, civilian clothes that fitted him badly.

Wilson and Shearer expected their destination to be London: they were wrong. They did land at Northolt R.A.F. Station near London, but only to refuel and to take off again. It was dark.

For the next seven hours, the three passengers slept, and drank, and fed, changing seats now and then just to show each other that they could. Although there was no cabin service, a substantial cold buffet had been provided and more than adequate drink. The Russian, totally confused by all this, but encouraged by the other two, joined in; he had never eaten so well or had so much choice of liquor. Soon he was laughing; if he was to die then they had at least treated him well.

They landed at Kennedy Airport, New York, at two a.m. as though a deliberately quiet time had been pre-selected. At no point during either flight had a member of the crew made contact. The plane did not taxi into the disembarkation bays, but remained isolated, on a taxiing lane, its navigation lights still blinking, while a crew member opened a forward door and went straight back to the crew's cabin.

A car approached across the tarmac. It stopped under the door where Wilson and Shearer stood looking down into the darkness. The airport buildings weren't visible, the angle of the plane well chosen.

The headlamps were turned off and two men climbed out of the car. The taller man went to the trunk, removed something, then with the help of the other man started to erect a telescopic, light alloy ladder.

"Christ," shouted Shearer in disgust. "Don't we rate mobile passenger steps?"

"You rate a carpet of gold, dear fellow. And that would be only a token."

Sir Maurice Higgs, in the middle of the night? In New York?

"We're still trying to be quiet about this," Joe Marshall called up. "Dammit, Doug, we came personally."

"And don't we know why. Don't take us for fools, for chrissake."

"Oh, come now. Don't spoil things. There, it's up. Is Wilson there?"

"I'm here," Wilson called. He glanced at Shearer. "We'd better let Ruski go first with that arm." They helped the sergeant down. Finally, with the three of them in the back of the huge Cadillac, a glass partition separating them from Higgs and Marshall in front, they drove off, the beams cutting across the taxiing lanes.

Shearer whispered, "It's ominous, all right. Not to Langley or Washington for us."

"More like the nearest abattoir, mate. I hope those smug bastards in front are listening. If they top us they're in trouble." Wilson had deliberately spoken loudly.

Driven by Marshall they were taken to Brooklyn and across the Verrazano Narrows Bridge to Staten Island. As a matter of routine Shearer tried the door near him. It was locked. The Russian sitting opposite did not know what was going on. The effect of liquor was wearing off and he was worried again. He was not alone.

They were taken to an old and isolated house which was in darkness when they pulled up outside it. The bewildered Russian went ahead of the others and Marshall came up from behind to unlock the door. Lights were switched on inside. Marshall took the Russian upstairs; Wilson and Shearer never saw him again.

There was a lounge with a bar, which Higgs went behind with easy familiarity. "It's an atrocious hour to drink but I take it you'd both like one?" He poured Scotch on the rocks and handed them round. "It's up to you whether you'd prefer to talk now, or go to bed and talk later. We have a good room waiting for you."

"We slept on the plane. I think Ray and I would prefer to talk now."

Marshall came back. "His wound serious?" he pointed up the stairs.

"Bullet went straight through. From one of his own men. He'll remember that." Shearer sat down. So did Wilson across the room, so that whatever happened in the room would be seen by one of them.

"You did a great job," said Marshall, going to the bar and pouring himself a Bourbon. "A great job. Iran's well on the way to being taken and the Russians will be chasing their tails over the bust pipe line." He raised his glass, "Your health, gentlemen. Congratulations on beating the odds."

When they'd sipped their drinks Higgs sat down and observed mildly, "You were not supposed to cross the border. It could have been catastrophic had the Russians caught you."

"Mukhtar couldn't make it. The poor guy worked wonders as it was. The others were fighters but they weren't strong on explosive techniques. We gave them the help they needed."

Marshall slipped out of a light-weight topcoat, and draped it over a chair. He went back behind the bar.

Wilson said, "Now we've brought you back a real live Russian sergeant who'll say whatever you want him to say once you've finished with him, I take it you'll have no more need to top Doug and me?"

"Top you?"

"You know damn fine what Ray means," interjected Shearer.

423

"But why on earth should we want to? You've been magnificent, the pair of you."

"For the old-fashioned reason. We know too much. Not only what's gone on, the parts we've played ourselves, but that you two, and only you two, have instigated the whole thing from the beginning. No subordinate can be blamed. You've done it yourselves, through us. We're the dynamite that can blow the world to bits. We've brought you back a counter-balance, a dog to bark when you say."

"You're safe as long as the Russians don't get you."

Marshall hadn't touched his drink; he held it on the bar top.

"Don't you think they'll try?"

"Do they know about you?"

Denial would be a mistake. Wilson was watching Higgs closely. "Someone did. I think you know we were attacked twice on the way. And a plane being whipped up so quickly meant a big backing. It went wrong when Rachid was knocked off in our presence. You must've considered then, if not before, that there was no way back for us. We saw it. We know what happened."

"You've little trust in us."

"None, Sir Maurice. Not over this. So we brought back a bargaining factor." Shearer glanced over at Wilson.

"A very good one, too, wouldn't you say, Joe?"

"Well, I guess a well-trained parrot will say what you teach him. He'll pay the usual visit to Saks."

"There's a Russian jeep high in the mountains on the Iranian side of the border. We can tell you exactly where it is. It proves Russian military presence in Iran."

Marshall inclined his head. "You boys have thought it through."

"We had to. We'd need wing mirrors to walk in front of you two blokes."

Marshall sighed sadly. "You give us no credit."

"We give you the credit for finishing the job as you think best. You don't want loose ends that can cause repercussions. This isn't a routine situation. We understand. That's why we brought the insurance back."

"Then let's drink to your continued health," Higgs raised his glass. "Cheers."

The toast echoed round the room.

Marshall took his first sip and said cautiously, "We'll have to put a loose lead on you. For your own sakes." He saw their looks of disgust. "Nothing sinister. When the wind dies down it won't be necessary. We have one last job for you. Here, in New York. After what you've been through this one will be simple. A case of observation."

Immediately they were suspicious, eyes focused on Marshall, when perhaps just in that time, the owlish blinking of eyelids behind the glasses of Sir Maurice Higgs might have told them more.

"Go on" said Shearer.

"Sheik Marroum, the Saudi Oil Minister, is over here. Usual energy discussions with his American opposite number. He's been a good friend to us. To the West as a whole. If the oil prices are crazy they'd be crazier still without his influence."

"So?"

"We don't want anything to happen to him. The French have tipped us off that the guy who led the attacks on you is Ben Waffa, a well-known Russian-trained terrorist. Both the French and the Germans have picked up the word that he's been lined up to get Marroum while he's here. To cause the maximum embarrassment for us and to split the Saudis from us."

"You'll have Marroum well protected."

"No amount of protection can stop an assassination, Doug, you know that. And if it was pulled off you can bet your last dollar that the Russian propaganda machine would provide a well-versed case that we're behind it."

As Shearer started to argue Marshall waved him down. "Hear me out. It's a natural for them. To make it easier for the secret service boys we try to confine these expeditions, so far as we can, to the least busy days and the least busy time of day. Monday mid-morning, for instance.

"Now we can hole you up. It's an office we took over years ago; we continue to rent and keep a front as a toy importer. It's handy. Round the corner from Saks. Just stand there and watch. When Marroum returns to his car the job's over."

"Why us? You have men for the job."

"You've seen Ben Waffa, for God's sake. Both of you. You're the most likely to spot him. It could be a damp squib. Most tip-offs are. But you'll see him if he's there. Right now it's more important than ever to keep an eye on Marroum. It's not asking much. A couple of hours' work at the most."

Wilson observed quietly, "Well now, you've just told us quite a lot. We haven't mentioned Ben Waffa. We don't know the name of the bloke who attacked us. You say the French told you. But who told you we saw him, I wonder?"

"It's not important, old chap," Higgs replied for Marshall.

"It is to us, cocker. It would not be Leila. Houshang?"

"Does it matter? If it was, there would be nothing disloyal to you in him reporting that would there? Nothing sinister or detrimental to you?"

"No. Houshang wouldn't know how to be disloyal. Without him we'd be dead already. Did he report that we only saw this character, Ben Waffa, at night?"

"Even so, I understand it was a good sighting. More than anyone else has managed. You're all we've got."

Shearer had been listening carefully to this exchange between Wilson and Higgs. He asked, "And then that's it?"

"That's it. Honourable retirement. And our eternal gratitude," Higgs replied.

Marshall now said, "It sounds trivial. It is, of course, a very long shot; these things usually are. But with you both here, trained bodyguards, being able to recognise the man, t would be stupid not to call on your help." He turned to Wilson. "It's not just for America. The whole Western world could be affected."

"Are you ordering us?" asked Shearer mildly.

Marshall shook his head. His hand was still round the glass, the drink barely touched. "I don't see how we can order you. You've already done more than your bit. A favour, Doug. Nobody's coming the heavy hand."

"We'd like to discuss it together."

"Sure. You want to go to your room?"

"We'll go for a walk."

Marshall smiled. "You think your room's bugged?"

Shearer stood up. "If you're doing your job. Don't let the tail get too close. Ray and I have developed sensitive reactions over the last few weeks."

Outside it was dark, with an early morning chill. They walked side by side, their hands in their pockets.

"They haven't swallowed the sergeant bit," said Wilson uneasily. "They want to sleep nights. With us gone their worries are over."

"You think it's a set-up?"

"There's only one way to find out."

Shearer stopped. They had reached the fringe of what was obviously a residential area. One or two doorbell lights shone faintly in the dark. He looked back, saw a shadow slip out of sight.

"I heard 'em," said Wilson without looking back. "They wouldn't try it here?"

"Not on their own doorstep. We could be wrong. We may have sufficiently strong a card."

"It's a gut feeling, Doug. I've been here before. If we don't try it they'll know why, and they'll get us when we're least prepared. Will you take your cue from me?"

"You've done okay so far."

"Both of us."

As they turned to go back the skyscraper lights of Manhattan started to spread across the Hudson, as if a wand had brushed over them. Cleaners were moving into the offices block by block. The two men stood for a while watching.

"Not a bit like the Kopeh Dagh," said

Shearer with feeling. He was thinking of Leila and the pain of their parting.

"I've never seen anything like it," said Wilson. They walked back slowly, thinking it out, adding nothing more.

Once inside, Wilson rubbed his hands and picked up his drink. "It's fair enough," he said. "We'll help you out. But we'd like sight of the place first. It might be useless from our point of view."

"No problem," said Marshall. He hadn't moved from his position behind the bar. Higgs was now standing with his back to the empty fireplace. "Get some rest." Marshall glanced at his watch. "Soon be dawn. Say three this afternoon? We'll drop by."

They were shown their room. Apart from two comfortable beds it was Spartan but adequate, with a bathroom leading off. Pyjamas lay on the beds. There were newspapers and magazines on bedside tables. Neither man spoke as they undressed. Shearer set the alarm of a clock on a bed chest. He then went to the door to try it. It opened. Somehow it took them both by surprise. They slept with their guns under their pillows.

They were shown the office in the afternoon. Both had slept well, at first finding the beds too soft after Iran. They'd had a breakfast-cum-lunch which they cooked themselves in an old-fashioned kitchen. They wondered what had happened to the sergeant: they had searched the house, finding some doors locked, some open.

As promised, Joe Marshall called at three precisely. He was alone and took them on the ferry to Manhattan Island. The Hudson was sluggish below them and busy.

The office was well placed; there was a good view of Saks on the corner across Fifth Avenue. It was on what Wilson called the second floor and what Shearer called the third. There was nothing exceptional about it. The furniture was modern veneer and chrome, the room airy and comfortable and characterless. All three men stood looking down obliquely at the mid-Manhattan traffic. Shearer talked to Marshall while Wilson scanned the office, not missing a detail.

"You'll have two-way radios," Marshall said.

When they left, Marshall locked up. The neatly polished brass plaque on the door had

432

the engraved inscription: "Quality Toy Imports Inc. New York and Paris."

"Who's on either side?" asked Wilson.

Marshall looked surprised. "The board downstairs will tell you. I'm doing it all myself. Okay? Be reasonable."

"Still not delegating?" asked Shearer amicably as they ignored the elevators and took the stairs down. "Apart from us, I mean."

Marshall showed annoyance. "How can I? You know the form. Don't needle me, Doug." Suddenly he flapped his hands in apology. "We've been under strain, too, y'know. We still are."

When they reached the street Wilson and Shearer decided to stay on, to see in daylight a little of the fairyland they'd seen flickering at night.

It was quite in order but Marshall issued a warning, "Don't give your tail a rough time. Just let them string along and get in some practice. I just want to make sure nobody else is on to you."

When Marshall had gone they found a coffee bar. It was strange sitting in a crowd, seeing and hearing the constant movement of people and traffic, overshadowed by the immense buildings around them. After the privation of the desert and mountains, they found the noise deafening.

They had located their tail. Two men behind, possibly one in front. Over coffee Wilson said, "I want to slip back to that office block. Will you take care of these jokers for me?"

"They'll have instructions for a split."

"I can handle that. Give me an hour. I'll meet you back here."

"It'll get back to Marshall, Ray."

"What difference can it make? If we're set up it will go ahead. If not, what the hell?"

"Okay. We'll tell him we were trying them out. Limey style."

Wilson grinned. "I like that."

Wilson simply disappeared in a crowd in Times Square while Shearer stood looking around as if he had just missed him.

They met an hour later as arranged and ordered some more coffee. By now it was near to closing time.

"I looked over the place," said Wilson easily. He stirred sugar into his coffee.

"You caused a commotion. They'll be glad to see you back."

"One thing worries me, Doug."

"Only one?"

"Our guns were issued in England. We've held on to the same ones."

"So?"

"Don't you need a gun licence here? Nobody's remarked on it. Nobody's suggested we hand them in. It's as if they don't care whether we have them or not."

Shearer felt a chill. "Or perhaps they prefer us to have unlicenced guns."

Higgs said, "Do you think they've swallowed it?"

"Not all of it. There's nothing they can do. Once there, the rest is a matter of timing. We must wait for the shot. It's been worked out."

"No trouble with Calvera?"

"He's a psycho, Maurice. He'll be in the next office. He won't miss."

Higgs was thoughtful. "We'd better make damned certain that Wilson and Shearer's coffee is well drugged the night before."

"Those two have formed a perfect team."

"Yes. It's rather sad. And wholly ungrateful. Do you think we're going too far?"

"Do you?"

Higgs shook his head slowly. "No. It's unfortunate. The Russians will not stand by and let us get away with it so easily. They've already lost considerable face. They're aware we're behind it but we're too high up the tree for them to tackle us personally. Wilson and Shearer can tie us into every move and they can give first-hand accounts. Rogov will go flat out to pick the pieces from their heads. He needs them badly, and he's got to get them before we do. He's already tried. No, Joe, I'm merely echoing your own thoughts. Both of them have got to go."

Rafael Calvera waited dispassionately. His gun was already assembled. He looked down to the corner of Saks, satisfied with the angle and range and that one shot would be sufficient, provided the guy showed his head.

He heard a faint movement next door. It did not worry him. There should be two guys there, who, once they'd witnessed he'd done the job on the Arab sheik, would collect him and get him out to a place of safety. He already had documents, car licence and so on, in his new name. He was a Cuban, and didn't much fancy the name of Murillo, but what did it matter? There was considerable cash in his pockets, too, but the rest was to come after the job.

The car hadn't arrived yet. Suddenly his mind drifted and he smiled with satisfaction. Only the previous day he had read that the Warden of Tombs prison had been killed in a car accident. He hoped the bastard had died slowly.

In the next office they complained that only one pair of binoculars had been supplied between them but they each had a two-way radio on a pre-fixed band. When they first checked in over the air the voice on the other end was monosyllabic, like a record.

Shearer had remarked how deeply they had slept. Both had been keen to get to bed early, yawning and drowsy. It had not surprised them. They had been deprived of sleep for many days. The slight headaches they woke with soon went and they did not oversleep.

Now they awaited the car they had been told would arrive and stop in their sight. The rush hour had eased but traffic was still thick. In another hour the lunch-time snarl-up would start. They scanned in turn the mass of people that hovered around and went past the corner of Saks on view to them.

The car was due between ten and eleven a.m. Marshall had been unable to be more specific. Traffic varied, and the time also depended on the whims of the Sheik himself

"This is a waste of time," said Shearer, glasses to his eyes.

Wilson wasn't listening. He was wandering the room like an animal, with a scent scattered too far. He placed an ear to each wall, listened, heard nothing.

"Marroum's here," said Shearer.

Wilson went to him, peered down, saw the long black car pull up. And the one behind it. Wilson opened an end window, looked down. Shearer still had the glasses to his eyes.

Secret service men climbed out, heads turning, hands ready, taking up position. One opened the rear door of the first car and the well-known, handsome figure of Sheik Marroum appeared. He was smiling, a face that must have appeared on every television screen throughout the world.

He stepped on to the sidewalk, men in front and on either side of him. An usher from Saks was waiting on the fringe. Only the Sheik's head and shoulders appeared above the car. He stepped forward and it was the last step he ever took.

There was no crash of gun fire, but Wilson, head out of the window, heard the muffling effect of a silencer. He saw Marroum fall and the crowd of bodyguards closing in. He was trained as they were and knew what would happen next.

Shearer knew too. For a split second neither could believe his eyes. Shearer, white-faced, raised his radio.

Wilson, stunned, suddenly had the feeling that this had happened before. He shouted, "Run, for chrissake. Run!"

Shearer didn't question him. He dropped the radio and drawing his gun, rushed to the door. They had just reached it when it crashed open and two men hurtled in, guns in hand. Wilson was thrown back behind the door.

Expecting to find their prey near the window both men stopped halfway across the room. Shearer pulled the trigger as they spun round but his gun only clicked. In a moment of frightening enlightenment he realised that the failure of the gun was no coincidence and in a reflex action he threw it at the nearest man's face just as he was about to fire. The shot screamed over Shearer's head as the man staggered back and stumbled in front of his colleague. Wilson hurtled from behind the door and pushed Shearer's victim hard at the second man who was trying to step clear. They both fell back towards the window, blood gushing from the face of the man struck by Shearer's gun.

Wilson and Shearer raced from the room. The door of the next office away from them was open and they heard gun fire. They reached the end of the corridor and turned the corner, ran through the swing doors and Wilson headed straight for the stairs. They went up them two at a time.

After two floors they slowed. After eight they had to stop, panting on the landing, leaning against the wall unable to speak. They started off again up and up, stopping now and then, breath rasping. They finally reached the roof, stepping over pipes and around protrusions. Police sirens were wailing in the streets below, the sound being squeezed up the concrete canyons.

They raced to the edge furthest from Fifth Avenue. Wilson gasped. "There's a rain pipe to a lower roof."

He climbed over the parapet as if it wasn't there. He grasped the pipe, managing to grin. "Get your leg over, you Yankee sod." He slipped down the pipe with ease, gripping with knees and hands, Shearer just above him.

When they reached the lower roof they ran for the stairs canopy. Shearer had to break the lock but they were in. They sat on the first landing to get their breath back.

Shearer wiped his face. "They'll be after us."

Wilson let out a lungful of air. "They'll think we went down, not up. By the time they reckon they were wrong, they'll not know which floor we went to. They'll try them all and they've played this so close to the chest they won't have the men. It'll take too long."

"They'll try the roof."

"Come on. Let's go down and out by the front door."

Wilson leaned over to grip Shearer's arm. "You saved us, cocker. I don't know what fraction of a second it took you to find out your gun didn't work but if you hadn't let him have it in the face just then we'd be dead, accomplices to an assassination."

They rose together slowly.

"Plan B," said Shearer.

"It's your patch. Where do we hole up?"

Shearer put a hand on Wilson's shoulder. "As if I hadn't thought about it. Follow me."

The following morning the newspaper banners were virtually identical. Television news had already covered the brutal assassination within minutes of its happening. A last-minute tip-off had been just too late to stop the killing but the assassin had been shot dead when he turned his rifle on the security police who had rushed to the spot. Two other men were sought. It was known that these men had Middle East connections.

A day after that the F.B.I. released the information that the assassin had been a Cuban working for the Palestinian Liberation Organisation. His apartment had been traced and documents firmly established a connection with the P.L.O. together with payments in cash in several currencies and a bank draft notice from Beirut.

The pattern was established. The riots in Saudi Arabia, still continuing, were now tied to the assassination of Sheik Marroum. One brief note in the assassin's apartment was from one of the main terrorist ringleaders in Saudi Arabia.

The Saudi Government, seeing itself being

attacked and undermined on more than one front, its royal family in imminent danger, invited the United States to help. The Seventh Fleet was diverted to the Gulf. United States Army personnel were flown out in droves.

There were many in the Arab world who seethed at this manoeuvre. There was none who immediately would voice protest. The whole world was deeply shocked by the slaying of Marroum, who had been popular in the West. By the time the protests came it was too late. The collusion was complete.

The insurgents were now in control of Iran, temporary Government set up clearly favourable to the West, which had clandestinely supplied its arms. Libya was now in more moderate hands and Saudi Arabia had taken in American forces in large numbers. They had gone to stay for some considerable time.

Russia, in the shape of General Rogov, sought to break down the lies he knew to be there and continued the search for Wilson and Shearer. But the idea that the Americans had killed Marroum was preposterous. In years to come the world might listen to such an idea. For once Russia had been beaten at her own much-practised game.

"It should be safe enough to send it now," said Shearer.

They were sitting in a shabby apartment in Greenwich Village and both were practically unrecognisable. As Marshall and Higgs could not suddenly supply the F.B.I. with photographs of the men they could not confess to knowing, only descriptions had been issued to the press, but Wilson and Shearer had taken no chances. They had bought bottles of hair dye from a drugstore and over the last ten days Wilson had grown a moustache and Shearer a beard. They had worked on each other's hair the day they had fled. And they had changed apartments the following day and again two days later. They were still very near the scene of the crime but there might be a certain safety in that. And they had chosen an area where their appearance, whatever it might be, would cause no comment.

The treachery of Marshall and Higgs rankled deeply in them. Anticipating it had not diminished their feeling. But they were glad that they had taken out a double insurance against the betrayal.

They had been thrown together once more but all strain had long since left them. It would be difficult to find firmer friends any where and the trust they had developed for each other must have been near to being unique.

Shearer read out the note he had been writing. It was addressed to Joseph Marshall at his office in Langley.

"You will receive a tape cassette five days from now. Unless you want other ears to listen to it make sure that you, and you alone, open the envelope. To identify it, on the outside will be the initials W.S.—Wilson and Shearer. If you are away, whoever reads this had better make damn sure you come back to pick up the tape. You'd better get the postal department on their toes to prevent a slip-up."

"How's that?" asked Shearer.

"Bit melodramatic? I suppose it's got to be. Send it off and let the bastard squirm."

"I'll post it in Brooklyn. I don't want your London accent around the place yet."

Wilson shrugged. "It's a better prison than the one in Libya, matey. And the nosh is much better. Even so, I'll be glad when it's over. I miss Jennie."

Shearer folded the note and placed it in an envelope. "I miss Leila too. If we play it right we'll see them. A little luck and a little fear

445

instilled into those two bastards Marshall and Higgs." He licked the gum, stretched out his legs and leaned back in the chair. "Let's go over what we've got once more. Leila will keep her promise to remain holed up until she hears from us. And she'll keep the Russian colonel on ice for us as long as necessary. If we get hit she'll produce him to give the truth of what happened to the pipe line. She has the engine number of the Russian jeep and knows its position to substantiate what happened."

Wilson was listening attentively, ticking off the points on his fingers as Shearer mentioned them. They could not afford to miss anything. Everything that they considered a safety measure had to be seen through the eyes of Marshall and Higgs. "Maybe we should have landed them with the threat of the colonel in the first place."

"You know I didn't want Leila involved if it could be prevented. I still don't like bringing her into it. It puts her life on the line."

Wilson shook his head sadly. "Her life was on the line the moment we gave her the sealed envelope with our statement of all we know. You know that, cocker."

Shearer sat forward. "Yeah. Except at the moment only you and I know she's got it. The tape doesn't name who has it, but Marshall and Higgs are no fools."

Wilson stood up, placed a hand on Shearer's shoulder. "I know how you feel. But Leila's no fool either. She'd kill to protect you. And there's no way that statement won't reach the Russians if someone knocks you off."

He suddenly smiled. "It should be worth three months' intensive protection in a comfortable doss house somewhere on your west coast. Shouldn't it? After that nobody will care. It'll be too late."

Shearer was still worried for Leila. He too rose. "I'll post this." Then he suddenly brightened. "We've done all we can. It should work." He smiled back at Wilson. "I'd give a lot to see Marshall's face when he plays the tape. Maybe the bastard will have heart failure."

Wilson grinned. "Sure, then all we need worry about is the Russians."

# GUIDE
## TO THE COLOUR CODING
## OF
## ULVERSCROFT BOOKS

Many of our readers have written to us expressing their appreciation for the way in which our colour coding has assisted them in selecting the Ulverscroft books of their choice.

To remind everyone of our colour coding—this is as follows:

## BLACK COVERS
### Mysteries

★

## BLUE COVERS
### Romances

★

## RED COVERS
### Adventure Suspense and General Fiction

★

## ORANGE COVERS
### Westerns

★

## GREEN COVERS
### Non-Fiction

# FICTION TITLES
## *in the*
## Ulverscroft Large Print Series

The Onedin Line: The High Seas
*Cyril Abraham*
The Onedin Line: The Iron Ships
*Cyril Abraham*
The Onedin Line: The Shipmaster
*Cyril Abraham*
The Onedin Line: The Trade Winds
*Cyril Abraham*

| | |
|---|---|
| The Enemy | *Desmond Bagley* |
| Flyaway | *Desmond Bagley* |
| The Master Idol | *Anthony Burton* |
| The Navigators | *Anthony Burton* |
| A Place to Stand | *Anthony Burton* |
| The Doomsday Carrier | *Victor Canning* |
| The Cinder Path | *Catherine Cookson* |
| The Girl | *Catherine Cookson* |
| The Invisible Cord | *Catherine Cookson* |
| Life and Mary Ann | *Catherine Cookson* |
| Maggie Rowan | *Catherine Cookson* |
| Marriage and Mary Ann | *Catherine Cookson* |
| Mary Ann's Angels | *Catherine Cookson* |
| All Over the Town | *R. F. Delderfield* |
| Jamaica Inn | *Daphne du Maurier* |
| My Cousin Rachel | *Daphne du Maurier* |

| | |
|---|---|
| Enquiry | *Dick Francis* |
| Flying Finish | *Dick Francis* |
| Forfeit | *Dick Francis* |
| High Stakes | *Dick Francis* |
| In The Frame | *Dick Francis* |
| Knock Down | *Dick Francis* |
| Risk | *Dick Francis* |
| Band of Brothers | *Ernest K. Gann* |
| Twilight For The Gods | *Ernest K. Gann* |
| Army of Shadows | *John Harris* |
| The Claws of Mercy | *John Harris* |
| Getaway | *John Harris* |
| Winter Quarry | *Paul Henissart* |
| East of Desolation | *Jack Higgins* |
| In the Hour Before Midnight | *Jack Higgins* |
| Night Judgement at Sinos | *Jack Higgins* |
| Wrath of the Lion | *Jack Higgins* |
| Air Bridge | *Hammond Innes* |
| A Cleft of Stars | *Geoffrey Jenkins* |
| A Grue of Ice | *Geoffrey Jenkins* |
| Beloved Exiles | *Agnes Newton Keith* |
| Passport to Peril | *James Leasor* |
| Goodbye California | *Alistair MacLean* |
| South By Java Head | *Alistair MacLean* |
| All Other Perils | *Robert MacLeod* |
| Dragonship | *Robert MacLeod* |
| A Killing in Malta | *Robert MacLeod* |
| A Property in Cyprus | *Robert MacLeod* |

# NON-FICTION TITLES
## *in the*
## Ulverscroft Large Print Series

# THE SHADOWS
## OF THE CROWN TITLES
*in the*
## Ulverscroft Large Print Series

**LARGE TYPE EDITION**